DEADLY DECEIT

A TOM GRANT NOVEL

SAMANTHA ADAIR

Editing and Publishing Assistance provided by:

Michelle Morrow www.chellreads.com

CONTENT WARNING:

This book contains mature themes that might make some readers uncomfortable. Foul language, criminal activity, drug use, and self-harm are included in this book. Please proceed with caution.

For My Spicy Girls

1

TOM

Tom's eyes sweep the immaculate office. It's been six months, and yet it feels like six minutes since he last sat in this chair, waiting for Martha to give him orders. His irritation at being here prickles down his body and he shifts in the chair.

The desk in the room has nothing more than a pen and telephone sitting on it. He looks up to the walls where photographs of politicians and world leaders smile down at him while shaking hands with the same tiny woman.

A sofa sits in the corner with potted plants either side. A tree stump fashioned into a coffee table is in front. Tom remembers the sofa being lumpy when he'd slept on it, waking up hungover. He flicks his head side to side, cracking his neck at the memory of a stiff back and knotted muscles after using it as a bed for almost a week.

A door opening and footfalls behind him interrupt his reverie. He sits forward and adjusts his posture.

"So," Martha plonks a glass of sparkling water in front of Tom and sits behind her desk. "How are you?"

Tom leans back in the chair and peers at the glass. He keeps his arms folded firmly over his chest. "Great."

"Excellent. And now the truth?"

Tom stares into Martha's intense face. She folds her hands on the desk in front of her and waits.

He says nothing, swipes the glass up and gulps. He swallows the bitter water and grimaces. "How do you drink that?"

Martha's eyes singe holes in his face. "I don't."

Tom nods, staring at his thumbs as he twiddles them in his lap. The silence lingers. "Oh, Jesus, Martha. I'm fine." Tom rolls his eyes to the ceiling and huffs.

"In my years of experience Tom, I've often found those who claim to be fine… are not."

Tom sighs and scrubs both hands through his hair. "What do you want me to say?" He peers at her from across the desk. "I've been doing *nothing* for six months. No socialising, no working, no… women. *Nothing.* It's been a blast."

"No drinking?"

Tom flicks his eyes down to the desk and says nothing.

"Have you been going to the meetings?"

"I told you… I went to a couple. It's not my thing."

Martha leans forward over her folded hands and purses her lips. Tom looks straight back at her without flinching. Martha reaches into a desk drawer and pulls out an envelope. She slides it across to Tom. "This came for you last week."

Tom looks at it. "What is it?"

"No idea." She pauses. "But it's from Belgium."

Tom's chest tightens. "Right," he squeezes out. He slides it off the desk and shoves it into the pocket of his motorcycle jacket hanging over the back of his chair.

Martha continues to stare. "Have you *heard* from—"

"Nope." Tom holds his breath a moment. He exhales slowly, and his curiosity gets the better of him. "Have you?"

"No. But, it's safer this way. For now."

For now.

Tom bounces his leg and nods. Martha's eyes slide to his knee and back to his face. "I think another meeting wouldn't hurt." Martha taps a finger on the desk.

Tom rolls his eyes and slaps his hand over his knee to curb the jitter. "Aren't I here for some kind of meet and greet?"

Martha nods. "Yes. He's late."

"And you put up with that? Since when?"

Martha purses her lips before opening her mouth to answer. Her phone rings and she snatches it up. "Yes?"

Tom folds his arms again.

"Send him in." She drops the receiver back into its cradle as the office door swings open.

Tom twists in his chair. A male of about twenty-eight strides into the room. He's wearing designer jeans and a slim fit black t-shirt. The Vans on his feet would be more fitting on a sixteen-year-old. His blonde hair is in a man bun, an earring hangs on his left earlobe and a dragon sleeve is tattooed on his left arm.

A man bun? Really?

Tom turns to Martha and quirks a brow, dropping his mouth open.

"What time do you call this, James?" Martha clips.

James makes a show of checking his watch. "It's precisely eight thirty-seven." He grins at Martha. "A.m."

Tom bites the inside of his cheek and watches Martha. She slides her eyes to him. *You have got to be kidding me.*

"Tom Grant," Martha gestures to the loudmouth. "James Moore."

"Get the *fuck* out!" James grabs Tom's hand and shakes. "Tom Grant?" James shakes his head, "Heard a lot about you."

Tom pulls his hand back in an effort to stop it being completely torn off his arm. "Is that right?"

"Hell yeah! I'm dying to hear about how on earth the senator got shot… I mean, how does that even happen?"

Tom eyes him for a moment, "Clearly, I fucked up," he growls. *I was drunk.*

James slaps Tom on the back and laughs. "Clearly. And what about Paris? That was your last assignment wasn't it?" James inhales and appears to hold his breath a moment. "I mean…"

Tom's throat constricts and he swallows a mouthful of the bitter water to clear it. Narrowing his eyes at Martha, he stands up. "A word?" He grabs his jacket from the back of the chair and stalks out the door of the office.

He waits for Martha to catch up. She waves her hands in a calm down motion before Tom can open his mouth.

"What the *hell,* Martha?"

"I know, I know. But as I said… it's James *Moore.*" She raises her eyebrows and waits.

"You say that like I'm supposed to know what it means?"

"Moore?"

"Again, drawing a blank."

"He's Admiral Peter Moore's nephew." Martha presses her lips together and breathes in through her nose.

Tom grimaces at the mention of the First Sea Lord and Chief of Naval Staff's name. "Well, this keeps getting better and better," Tom grunts.

Why can't I outrun the Royal Navy?

"Despite the fact he's a complete git," Martha starts, "I believe he actually has potential."

"Have you gone senile?" Tom hisses at her, tapping both index fingers to his temples. "Have I missed something in the last six months?"

"He bombed out of the Royal Navy in spectacular fashion, has been floundering about for eighteen months while suspended on full pay. And… to avoid embarrassment, he has been *referred* to me."

So, he's being investigated. Excellent.

"Referred?" Tom raises an eyebrow. "Is this like the senator job all over again? You know it's a fucking bad idea but they're making you do it?"

"Ordered to do it. I have no choice but to give him a job." She holds one hand up as Tom goes to argue. "Until he mucks up."

"Until he…?" Tom runs both hands through his hair. "How is it, whenever you need some shitty job *handled,* I end up in the middle of it?"

"Because I trust you."

Tom stares at Martha and blows air out of his mouth slowly. "You can't keep hitting me with that."

"And you trust me." Martha smirks.

Tom shrugs his leather jacket on. "Okay, you know what? I agreed to an *easy-ish* job, of following around some pop star. And now I'm expected to drag this halfwit around with me?" Tom jerks his thumb over his shoulder at the door.

"Well, yes. I wanted to ease you back into it." Martha bites her cheek.

"I don't need to be eased…" Tom stares at the ceiling, taking another breath in.

"Be at The Savoy, tomorrow morning. Max Morgan's staying there to acclimatise after flying in from Sydney three days ago." Martha waits until Tom looks at her. "In the meantime, maybe you go to a meeting, tonight? Yes?" She turns and walks back into her office before Tom can say anything.

Tom's pulse heats up and he barges into the office behind Martha. He overtakes her and stands in front of James, who is still sitting in the chair flicking his thumb along his phone screen.

"James," Tom barks.

"Tom," James grins and tosses the phone onto Martha's desk.

Tom stares into the smarmy, grinning face and instantly hates him. "Are you going to be a pain in my arse?"

"Absolutely."

Tom nods, "I see."

James stands and laughs. "Tom, calm down chap, it's gonna be great. I mean, think about it." He slips an arm along Tom's shoulders and sweeps a hand in front of him. "Pop stars have *women,* women who will do anything for a glimpse of them. And he's Australian to boot! The ladies love their accent." He raises an eyebrow at Tom, "You feelin' me?"

Tom plucks James' hand up off his shoulder, as though picking up a dead fish and drops it.

Tom's eyes slide to Martha before he spins and stalks to the door.

"Oh eight hundred tomorrow Tom, The Savoy." Martha's voice chases him out the door.

Tom sits on his Harley and slams his helmet on. He starts the engine and takes off. *God, why does it have to be The Savoy?*

"Tom, all you need to do is take her out of The Savoy and get her to the Hotel Sophia, room eighteen. Easy."

Tom raised an eyebrow as he tied his bow tie. "The Sophia? Wow, you're going all out for this one." He pat his trouser pocket, checking for the signal jammer.

He turned to walk out of Martha's office, and she grabbed his wrist. "She's been told to try and seduce you... so don't be a dick."

"Never."

"Oh, and Tom?" Martha waited for Tom to turn around and look at her. "No drinking."

He stared back at Martha before sniffing in a sharp breath and walking out.

TOM PULLS UP OUTSIDE HIS BLOCK OF FLATS AND FLICKS HIS kickstand down. He stares up at the window to his flat a moment and squeezes his jacket pocket, the envelope still where he shoved it.

Fuck it.

He flicks the kickstand up and takes off.

AS TOM APPROACHES MARLBOROUGH HIS SHOULDERS UNTENSE AND his body relaxes. The further away from the city he gets, the more his body lets go and calm settles his angst.

Only seven miles to go.

He rolls into Avebury. The familiar warmth that floods his heart every time he sees the village brings him back to earth. His mother still roams these streets, he feels it. He looks across High Street to the small 'Henge Shop' and smiles, remembering his mother taking him there. She showed him all the shiny crystals and made him smell little bottles of oils.

"THOMAS, COME LOOK AT THIS," HEATHER HELD UP A SHINY BLACK rock. "This is for you, my sunshine." She placed the rock in his hand and folded his fingers over it.

"What is it?"

"It will protect you."

"From what?" Tom *scrunched his nose up and stared at his mother's serene face.*

"Everything." She took his hand and led him out into the sunshine.

TOM HEADS TO THE STONE CIRCLE. *THE SANCTUARY. EXACTLY WHAT IT is.* He walks around the outer edge of the circle, away from anyone else hovering about. *They don't know this place like I do.*

He is calm and free; the way he always felt when he came here with his mother. He sits on the grass and the light breeze and warm rays of sunshine sweep over him. Laying back he looks up at the clouds, knowing that tomorrow he's going to be in the thick of screaming females and arrogant *showbiz* types. *Ugh.*

He slides his hand into the pocket of his jacket and pulls out the envelope from Belgium. *From Isabella. A goodbye letter. Has to be.*

Sitting up, he stares at the handwritten address. He turns it over and toys with the tape holding it together. His heart twitches in his chest and he remembers her warm breath on his neck, her nails clawing down his back. He squeezes his eyes shut and shoves it back into his pocket.

Not today.

2

JAMES

James scurries down the busy London street. *Too hard, too early. I shouldn't have asked about Paris... Yet.*

James sticks his spare hand into his jacket pocket and crosses the road, slipping into a pub. He slides into a booth at the back after surveying the half empty room and puts his phone to his ear.

"Yes?" A gruff voice barks.

James rolls his eyes. *Calm down, Uncle Pete.* "It's me."

"And?"

"And... she paired me with Grant, like you said she would."

"Excellent. You know what your instructions are. I expect compliance."

"Yeah, about that... I'm predicting we won't speak much."

"If you want to avoid jail time, you'll speak. Am I making myself clear?"

James swallows and peers at the dark wood panelled wall surrounding the booth he's hiding in. "Yeah... clear."

"If Tom isn't going to play ball, get it out of Martha."

"Will she know?"

"She'll know. Those two are thick as thieves."

"Fuck," James mumbles into his phone.

"Get some booze and go to his place."

"Booze?"

"Yeah... he's fond of a drink or two. Might make him chatty. Or punchy. Either way, it'll be a satisfying result."

"But I don't know where he lives."

"Fucking hell, James! Are you twenty-five or five? Work it out."

James rubs his eyes and sighs. "Okay."

"I look forward to an update." Uncle Pete hangs up. James throws the phone onto the table.

He drops his face into his hands and rubs, scrunching his face into a mush before looking up. "How did I get myself into this," James whispers, scratching at the table with his thumb. *I guess Tom and I need to become mates.*

James walks out of the pub five minutes later to find an off-license.

3

TOM

Tom climbs off his bike and stares at the church hall in front of him.

Why am I here?

He checks his watch. *Nearly eighteen hundred.* He has time to get back on the bike and leave, like he was never there. He huffs an irritated sigh, thinking of Martha's disapproving glare. *Fine.*

He walks into the hall and sits in a folding chair. Not a folding chair forming part of the circle near the front of the room, but right at the back next to the coffee urn and plate of sad looking biscuits.

The host looks up from her white board where she is writing inspirational quotes and spies Tom. She smiles and walks towards him.

Tom's jaw clenches. *Please don't.*

"Hi there," she sits beside him. "Third time lucky?"

"I haven't been counting."

"Maybe you'll join the circle today?" She gestures towards the chairs, about half of which are occupied.

"Maybe," Tom nods, but stays firmly planted in his chair.

The woman smiles and gives his shoulder a quick squeeze, standing. "Well, I'm Amanda, if you need anything." She walks towards the front of the room again.

"I'm only here because…" Tom bites his tongue.

Amanda turns around and raises a brow, "You're only here because?" She lifts her chin.

Tom drops his eyes to the floor and shakes his head.

Amanda's feet disappear from his field of vision.

God, I need a drink.

Amanda clears her throat. "Welcome, everyone. I'm Amanda, and I'm an alcoholic." She shoots a glance over at Tom and back to the group. "How about we read through our steps, and then we can talk about them?"

Tom leans forward in his chair and massages his head. *Why am I here?* He tunes out Amanda's voice and focuses inwardly on the last time he had a drink. Two nights ago, on his sofa watching the football. Didn't make it to bed. *God, I'm pathetic.* His mind drifts to a hotel room. In Paris. Not a drink; a one-and-a-half-bottles-of whisky bender. *I had a good reason.*

Movement at the window to his left catches his eye. He glances up but there's nothing there. He sighs, shifts in the chair and looks to the circle again to see a female nodding and smiling as the other members give her a little clap.

"Yes, thank you. I'm Myra. And I'm on step eight." She stops and takes a breath. "Love…" she chokes out.

Tom flicks his eyes to the ceiling. *Give me strength.*

Amanda holds a box of tissues out and Myra takes one, dabbing at her eyes.

"When I was drinking, I would lash out at everyone."

Tom rolls his eyes. *Yes, but did you cause an international incident?*

"No one was safe from my outbursts." She looks up at the group and smiles. "Needless to say, I haven't gotten around to everyone to apologise yet."

The group chuckles and nods.

Yep. I'm done.

Tom stands and slides his jacket on. Amanda raises her eyes up to him; he looks back for a second before skulking out the door. *Avebury does more for me than this place.*

He sits on his bike and starts the engine. He puts his helmet on and takes another look back at the church hall. Warm light from the windows floats out into the dark of the evening.

A prickle runs down the back of Tom's neck and he lifts his gaze to the shadows beyond the hall. Movement catches his eye, and he leans forward, squinting into the darkness. He kills the engine, climbs off the bike and removes his helmet. He pauses to listen to the silence around him. He takes a couple of steps, his eyes adjust to the darkness, before the shadows move again.

I knew I didn't imagine it.

"Hello?"

The frosty grass crunches somewhere behind the building. His heart jolts and he runs to the back of the church hall. He looks at the empty space between the hall and the church. Shadows hit the grass from the spotlights around the spires. *No one here.* He peers into the darkness a moment longer before turning back towards his bike.

He walks past the light filled windows and glances in at the chair he had been sitting on. He places a hand on the windowsill and something spiky jabs his palm. Looking down he sees a stemless rose, laying on the sill. His gut contracts and he picks it up. *What the hell?* He looks back at the shadows and down at the rose in his hand.

No. Can't be.

Tom takes a step backwards, scrunching the flower in his hand. Gritting his teeth, he hurls it into the darkness. He draws in a breath and lets it out slowly. He shakes his head and climbs back on the bike. Sitting on the bike but not starting it, he waits a moment longer before wrapping his hands around the handlebars and taking off.

The chill of the night bites Tom's neck as he cuts through the streets to his block of flats. The rumble of the engine shields him from the rest of the world and it's a secluded place to be with his thoughts. Though, the envelope in his pocket weighs him down. *A lot.*

Tom climbs the stairs to his third floor flat. A grey and white tabby cat wanders the hall. Tom scoops her up, "Evening, Pebbles. Got out again, did you?" He taps on the door across from his. "Lorna?" Moments later the door opens a crack and Lorna peeps out.

Her blue eyes travel up to Tom's face and she opens the door. "Oh, dear," she crackles.

Tom plops the cat into Lorna's wrinkly hands.

"Thank you, Tom. I had no idea she was out again."

Tom smiles, not bothering to remind her that it happens every night. "Have a nice evening, Lorna." He wanders over to his own door, knowing Lorna will wait until he goes inside before letting the cat wander the halls again.

Inside the sanctuary of his own flat, he drops his keys on the coffee table and falls onto the couch. He pulls the crumpled envelope out of his pocket and stares at it.

Opening this envelope would be ripping open a wound that isn't healed. He reads the handwritten address again before closing his eyes. He pictures the half full bottle of whisky, tucked in the cupboard above the fridge and claws a hand on his knee.

A loud knock at the door interrupts his silent struggle. He drops the envelope on the coffee table and looks through the peephole. He scowls.

Do you have a radar?

"I'm not home," he mutters through the door.

"Open the door." Martha's voice is blunt.

Tom opens the door and peers out. "Surely it's past your bedtime?"

Martha furrows her brow, "It's seven p.m., Tom."

"I know." He walks away from the door.

"I'm here to brief you on your job. You stormed out earlier before I could finish." Martha's eyes survey the room and Tom is grateful he didn't pull the whisky bottle out as soon as he walked in the door. Martha sits on the sofa and pulls papers out of her Mary

Poppins bag. Her eyes rest on the envelope a moment before finding Tom's face.

"I didn't storm out," Tom drops into the armchair. "Shouldn't James be part of this *briefing*?" He raises an eyebrow. "Not that I want him in my flat."

"Yes. But… I've lost him."

"You have a habit of losing people, you know that?" Tom stares at Martha a moment. "I've been back on the clock with you for a day." He holds a finger up. "One fucking day, and already the shit's hit the fan." Another knock at the door and Tom grunts. "Peace and quiet isn't allowed, is it?" He stalks to the door, yanking it open.

James stands on the other side. Tom grimaces. "Found him." Tom peers at James. "How do you know where I live? No one knows where I live." *Except Martha.*

"I followed the boss lady." James pushes past Tom; he's carrying a six pack of beer. "Thought we could, you know, shoot the breeze." He flops onto the couch and looks at Martha.

"You followed the…" Tom swings around and smirks at Martha.

Martha purses her mouth into a tight ball and grabs James' shirt at the collar, pulling him towards her.

Tom grins and sits in the armchair resting his elbows on his knees and cupping his jaw in his hands. *Here we go.*

"Whoa, whoa," James slaps at Martha's hand. "Calm down, Boss. Are you angry I followed you or angry you didn't notice?"

She lets go but doesn't move from where she stands over him. He winks and pulls a bottle from the six pack. He holds it out to Tom as he stares back at Martha.

Tom folds his arms across his chest. "Get out."

"One moment, Tom." She leans closer, into James' face. "You listen to me lad, and you listen well."

Tom has heard this speech a million times. He waits and watches James' face as it slowly fades from an insolent grin to confusion.

"You don't cross me. Because those who cross me end up dead. Do you understand?"

James gives a hesitant grin, "Dead?" He looks to Tom and back at Martha. "What? You shoot them in the head?" He laughs as Martha keeps her face stony.

"More or less," she deadpans. She lets go of James' shirt and steals a glance at Tom. "However, the fact you followed me here without me noticing… my hunch that you have potential is correct."

Tom exhales and presses his mouth together. *Potential to be a pain in my arse.*

She picks up a folder and hands it to Tom, keeping her eyes stuck on James. "Supreme Order have taken exception to Max Morgan and threatened to disrupt his tour and use violence against him and his fans. They're an extremist right-wing group with very militant members."

"What did he say?" Tom opens the folder and reads.

"Many things. You should also be aware that by all accounts he is difficult to work with and very demanding." Martha smirks and looks at Tom. "You'll get along famously, no doubt."

Tom grimaces and reads the mission of the group in question. "To bring the human race back to order." He glances up at Martha. "We're out of order? They sound charming." Tom slaps the folder onto the table and pulls across more papers. He frowns as the threats he reads filter through his brain. "Cut his toes off one by one? While he hangs from a meat hook? Jesus."

"They sound like psychopaths." James cracks open a beer and takes a swig.

Tom watches him a moment and swallows the saliva pooling on his tongue. "Well done Einstein, yes. We don't deal with Nanna Sue picking flowers on a Sunday morning here. Just a heads up."

"Has anyone ever told you—"

"So!" Martha stands and barks at the pair of them.

Tom sits back in his chair and folds his arms.

"They are an extreme, *extreme* right group who love to make their point and make it in spectacular fashion. Do you understand?" She looks between both of them and taps her foot. When neither of them says anything, Martha takes a deep breath and nods. "And then there's his fans. They aren't out of the firing line either." Martha shakes her head.

"So why doesn't he cancel the tour?" James asks, taking another swig.

Tom stalks across the room and grabs the beer out of his hand. "Do you usually carry on like a hoodlum during intelligence briefings?" Tom squeezes the neck of the bottle to stop himself raising it to his own lips.

James stands and eyeballs Tom, making Tom's blood pressure ratchet. "We're in *your* flat, it's hardly a secure room now, is it?"

"*My* flat, that you weren't invited to."

James grins, "Don't pretend you're a rule follower, Tom. I've heard *all* about you." James pauses. "You don't fool me," he whispers, before yanking the bottle out of Tom's hand and taking another swig. "Again, how *was* Paris?" James eyes Tom, and it makes the skin on the back of Tom's neck prickle.

What's your deal?

Tom's hand shoots out and he grabs James by the shirtfront.

"Tom!" Martha stands. "Sit. Both of you. You're carrying on like two ten-year-olds in a school yard."

Tom twists James' shirt in his fist before letting go, pushing James away from him. He lowers himself into the armchair, glaring at James the whole time.

James also sits, plonking his beer onto the coffee table. He picks up the envelope from Belgium and peers at it. "What's this? Looks like female handwriting. Got a secret girlfriend, Grant?" He grins but his eyes hold something more sinister.

Tom leaps out of his chair again and snatches it out of James' hand. "What the *fuck* is wrong with you?" *Don't fucking touch it.*

"Okay, okay." James flaps his hands. "Calm down, chap."

Tom takes a breath and bites down on his tongue. "My name is Tom."

"You know what," Martha slaps the paperwork into Tom's stomach. "You read this, and brief James tomorrow morning before you meet with Max. Tonight's pointless."

Right. And I'm thirsty.

James huffs and grabs his six pack of beer. He eyes Tom before walking out without looking back.

Tom glares at Martha. "Are you serious with this guy?"

Martha pinches the bridge of her nose and sighs deeply. "Tom, humour me. I've got the Secretary of State breathing down my neck." She drops her hand from her face and looks up at Tom. "Do this for me?"

And there it is. Martha doing what she does best and giving Tom no choice.

You know I will.

Tom rolls his eyes and nods. "Yeah… right."

"Just… get him through this one job."

Tom squints at Martha as she picks up her bag.

There's more to this. There always is.

Tom looks at Martha for a moment and bites his lip. "Hey, earlier…"

Martha looks at Tom and raises her eyebrows. "Earlier?"

Tom holds his breath a moment. *Anyone could have left that rose there.* "Nothing."

"Except...something?"

"Do we have a track on Kat?"

Martha's eyebrows wiggle together, and she tilts her head to the side. "Kat? No… she's gone to ground the last few months. Why?"

Tom shakes his head. "No reason. Just… asking."

"If I get a track on her you'll be the first to know." She pauses a moment. "Are you sure you're up to this?"

Tom rolls his eyes to the ceiling. "Yes."

Martha walks to the door and turns to Tom. She puts her hand on his arm. "I wouldn't be asking you to do this if I had another choice."

Flattered. "I'm fine."

Martha penetrates his eyes with her own.

Stop. Tom blinks and looks at the ceiling.

"You can keep lying to me, Tom. But know that I'm not buying it." She steps into the hallway and glances back at him. "Never have, never will."

Tom closes the door behind her and leans his forehead against it.

She never has.

"*Hello?*" *An abrupt voice cut through the fog of sleep and Tom opened his eyes. A small woman leaned down from the step, peering at him.*

Tom jumped and rubbed his eyes, wincing as he remembers one of them was bruised. "Ouch," he mumbled.

The woman reached over and tilted his chin up. "What happened to you?" Her tone was neither friendly or unfriendly, but it was direct.

"Nothing."

"Nothing?" The woman raised her eyebrows. "Forgive me, but you're hiding in the shrub alongside my front door with a black eye." She looked towards the other end of the street. "You only look about thirteen. Do your parents know you're here?"

"They aren't my parents," Tom snapped, his heart beating so loud, the sound filled his ears.

"They what?"

"Nothing."

"Well, you can't stay here. Apart from the fact you'll ruin my father's roses, it's going to rain soon."

"You still live with your Dad?" Tom looked the woman up and down.

She smiled a tight smile and stood upright, holding her hand out to help Tom from the shrub. "He lived with me until he died." She winked. "When your parents are old, you'll probably have to look after them too." She jutted her head towards the end of the street.

"I told you, they aren't my parents," Tom stood up and brushed the dirt from his trousers. "Anyway, sorry I squashed your Dad's roses."

For the first time, Tom looked at the woman properly. She was wearing some kind of uniform with epaulets.

"Are you in the army or something?"

"Royal Navy," she said proudly. "I've just returned home from deployment for some leave."

"Right." Tom kicked a foot into the pavement. "Well, see ya."

"Where are you going?"

Tom shrugged and walked up the road.

TOM SITS ON THE SOFA AND TAPS THE ENVELOPE FROM ISABELLA ON his knee. *I don't want to read that I'll never see you again.* He stands and walks to the desk in the corner. He slaps Martha's folder down and pulls open a small drawer. He sticks the envelope inside, next to a shiny black rock, and closes it.

Not tonight.

4

MAX

Max peers around the sheer curtains hanging from the hotel room window. At first, a couple of fans spot him and squeal before the rest join in. He leans back and grunts. "Pathetic." He flops on the plush couch and swigs his vodka. He throws the last of it back and holds the glass in the air. "More."

The glass is plucked from his grasp. "You should do a walkabout, Max," Ally, his manager, sits next to him. "Those fans have been camped out for three days and you haven't made one appearance."

Max looks Ally in the eyes. "They aren't going anywhere." He clicks his fingers and Ally hands him the new drink. "Now, tell me what I have to do today before I get to do what I want." *Cocaine, for example.* He takes a mouthful of his vodka and swishes it around. He stares at the room service waiter as he fiddles with the drinks cart.

Ally taps her fingers on her clipboard and blows her hair out of her eyes. "Well, you have a briefing regarding the threats."

Max rolls his eyes. "The threats," he scoffs.

"Yes," Ally snaps. "The threats." She grabs the fresh glass of vodka from his hand and slaps it on the table, a small amount splashing over the rim. "This is serious, Max. You've really pissed them off and it's not just you that'll get hurt."

Anger bubbles in Max's veins and he leans forward, glaring into her soft face. "I'm the only one anyone will care about if I get hurt, mind you." He snatches the glass up and swigs. "So, if I don't care, neither should you." The screaming and squealing outside carries on, piercing a hole through Max's skull. "Can someone shut those idiots up?" He shouts across the room. The room service waiter stares at him. "Well?" Max's eyes are wide, and he scans the room, glaring at Ally and the waiter individually. He points to the waiter. "You! Go out there and tell them to shut the fuck up." *This wouldn't be an issue if I was in the Royal Suite. Where I belong.*

Ally lets out an exaggerated sigh, and Max smirks at her irritation.

"Max, stop." She looks over at the waiter and waves him out of the room with an apologetic smile.

Max peers at Ally as he gulps the last of his drink. "You're such an apologist," he slurs.

"Max, just…" Ally slaps her hand to her forehead and huffs out a breath. "Go have a lie down, will you? It's only nine a.m. You have a meeting at eleven with the special protection people and you need to sober up. For god's sake, we were meant to have the meeting at eight, but I couldn't get you out of bed. I've already had to move it once. I'm not doing it again. Can you for once in your life help me out here? You're completely plastered, and I need you sober in two hours. Go!"

Max glares at her as he slowly stands, and the room swirls around him. He walks to the bedroom and climbs into the king size bed, "Right, fuck off then." He buries his head under the covers. "I said *fuck off!*"

He hears the door shut and peers out from under the covers, grimacing. He takes in the empty room; it's walls wobble and the rest of the room swirls. *How good is my fucking life?* He drifts off to sleep as the screaming outside fades and he sinks into the black.

Seconds after passing out he is shaken awake.

"Max," Ally hisses in his ear. "They're here. I've been trying to wake you for half an hour! Go have a shower and for God's sake, use mouthwash." She slaps aspirin and codeine on the table next to him. Max eyes the pills and reaches across, sliding them off the table. He sits up and pops more tablets than he should. He swallows them with a gulp of whatever was left in the glass on the table next to him. The liquid burns and fizzes on its way down as it interacts with the pills. *Vodka.*

He sighs a rough, loud breath out and stumbles to the door, peeking out. Two men in suits are there. *Hmmm, don't mind a suit.*

Max's eyes fall to the taller of the pair: dark hair, strong jaw. *And that suit fits like a glove. Saville Row cut. Has to be.* Dropping his eyes to his backside he gasps in a little breath. *That's fine by me.*

The second one isn't quite Max's cup of tea. *Pink shirt? Man bun? Oh sweetheart, you need some queer eye intervention.* The ill-fitting pinstripe suit says it all. *You aren't in charge.* Max smiles to himself, knowing he's found the one he can manipulate.

"Max! Get ready." Ally points towards the bathroom. "You are the most frustrating human on the planet. You know that?"

He sighs a loud breath and slumps forward. "Fine," he huffs, sweeping to the bathroom.

5

TOM

Tom wanders around the decadent hotel room, having been ushered in by a woman introducing herself as Ally, before she ran off to the bedroom.

Interesting he's not in the Royal Suite. Tom flicks his eyes to James, who stands near the door, dressed in an off -the-rack suit with his hair pulled back into a knot at the nape of his neck. *That hair has to go. And what's that suit about?* He swallows the distaste he has for James and slides his eyes to the drinks bar on the other side of the room. It's stacked with bottles of vodka, whisky and rum. *Fuck.* Tom's mouth waters and he clears his throat.

James glances at him. "Thirsty?" He smirks.

"No."

James wanders across the room, grinning at Tom. "Why don't I believe you?"

"Because you're an arrogant twerp?"

"You're stuck with me, and I'm stuck with you. We may as well make the best of it."

Tom grunts as Ally walks in. She doesn't appear anything like a professional in a pair of baggy tracks and an oversized t-shirt. *Classy.*

She blows her blonde shoulder length hair out of her face as she approaches Tom, extending her hand. "G'day again, so sorry for the mix up. Ally Morgan. I manage Max." She looks at Tom and her eyes widen.

Tom smiles smoothly. *Time to pretend.* "Tom Grant, and this is James Moore." He nods towards James, pretending he holds him in high esteem.

James grins at Ally. "Pleasure," he holds his hand out and Ally shakes it.

"Morgan? Are you related to Max?" Tom asks, staring into her eyes.

"Ahhh…" She stares back appearing to forget what he asked her. "Max is my…" She shakes her head. "My brother. My annoying little brother." She smiles.

"I see." Tom smiles. *C'mon. Take the bait.*

"Yes, well Max shouldn't be a moment, he um…" Ally blows her hair off her face again and stares at Tom. She blinks a couple of times as her voice trails away then she clears her throat, giving her shoulders a shake.

"He's hung over and doesn't want to get out of bed," Tom elaborates for her. Tom grins as Ally's eyebrows climb to the top of her head. "This isn't my first rodeo," Tom whispers, leaning forward.

Ally laughs, "Thank god," she gestures to the couches for the pair of them to sit. "I thought I was going to get stuffy bastards."

"Well, I'm not stuffy anyway." Tom remarks staring at Ally without blinking as he sits.

Ally gazes back, chewing on her lip.

And... she's hooked. Tom twitches his mouth and watches her throat as she swallows.

"Um..." Ally trails off looking between Tom and James. "Can I get you a drink? Anything you want?"

Wouldn't that be nice.

"Ah, water is fine." Tom checks his watch.

"Grand!" James enthuses, "I'll have a—"

"Water," Tom grunts. "He'll have water." Tom eyes James, who glares back.

Ally scurries off to get the water and James leans towards Tom. "Loosen up, yeah?"

"Act professional. Yeah?" Tom snipes back.

"Says he, who just melted the knickers off a woman after three minutes," James scoffs.

Tom leans towards him. "Lesson one. Play to your strengths, James."

"You're kidding me." James grumbles under his breath.

"Jealousy's a curse."

"I'm not jealous." James spits.

Tom snorts as Ally reappears with bottles of spring water. She places them on the table and wipes her hands along her tracksuit clad thighs. "I'll go and see—"

The door behind her swings open.

Tom takes in the red-eyed, scruffy figure standing in the door-frame. He wears a gold threaded kimono and fluffy purple slippers. His blue-tipped, black dyed hair has obviously been towel dried, sticking up all over his head.

"Well," he flounces into the room and perches on a wingback chair. "Aren't you two a pair of suits." He clicks his fingers at a point behind Tom's head and Tom hears Ally sigh and start clinking glasses.

"I'm Tom Grant, this is—"

"James Moore," James interrupts, sticking his hand out. "Bloody great to meet you."

"Hmmm," Max manages, his eyes slide back up to Tom. "My, my. Aren't you pretty?"

"Thanks," Tom doesn't miss a beat. "It's a new suit."

Ally scurries in front of them and hands Max his drink. Max sips from his glass, not taking his eyes off Tom.

Tom stares back. *When you're ready?*

"Behave," Ally hisses at Max as she pulls a chair over and sits next to him.

Max shrugs and swirls his drink in the glass.

Tom clears his throat. "As of tomorrow morning, when you leave London, we'll be with you twenty-four seven," Max's eyes light up and Tom goes on, "Well, close by, anyway."

Max pouts and sips his drink.

This is bizarre. Tom shoots a glance at James who is staring at

Max with his mouth half open. *There are five million females down-stairs screaming for… this guy?*

"Um, I have the threats if you'd like to see them?" Ally offers, sliding a large envelope across the table.

Tom gladly takes it and starts pulling papers out. "Jesus," he utters under his breath.

"Right?" Max squeals a little too enthusiastically.

Tom looks up, "This excites you?" He holds up one of the photographs, it depicts a dead rabbit in a box with a knife still through its chest.

Max waggles his finger in the air, "No, that one was particularly gruesome. I didn't like that. But, you know what they say about publicity." He shrugs.

Tom's head snaps up from the papers. "What?"

"Just that, you know. No publicity is bad publicity?" Max rolls his eyes and sips from his glass.

Tom gazes at Max's drink and nods. "Yes, of course. That's exactly what they say about publicity. Isn't it?"

Max frowns before giggling. "Yeah… that's what I said."

Tom watches Max for a moment and fights the urge to pick him up by his gold kimono and hang him on the coat hook beside the door. *You arrogant dickhead.* He glances back down at the papers. He reads dates and hotel rooms typed in sequential order. He looks up at Ally. "I think you got your itinerary mixed up in—"

"No," she shakes her head. "Keep reading."

Tom's eyes slide down the page. "They know where you're staying and when?" Tom looks up. "How?"

Max points his finger at Tom, "You're the expert, aren't you?"

"Lovely of you to notice," Tom holds up the fist full of paper. "They had to get the information from *somewhere*." Tom looks between Max and Ally. "Someone who knows your movements inside out?"

Max rolls his eyes around the room. "No doubt."

So... one of the two of you.

Tom narrows his eyes but decides against saying anything more. *For now.* "Well, you're going to have to change every single hotel you're booked into. And all public appearances need to be vetted *and* approved."

"By who?" Ally squeaks.

Tom's eyes snap to her face and she bites her lip and frowns.

"By me." Tom slaps the papers onto the table and looks between Ally and Max.

What's going on here?

"Okay," Max stands and waltzes around the room, sipping his drink. "First of all, I'm not changing my hotels. All bar one, I've got the penthouse or grand suites. That's non-negotiable. Second—"

"I'm gonna stop you right there." Tom stands. "You have pages and pages of threats against you. Every single country you plan to visit, these people, this…" He picks up a piece of paper and reads, "Supreme Order has people willing to shoot you through the head or plant some sort of device to cause injury to others. This isn't a game, and it isn't some kind of publicity building exercise."

Tom waits for Max to stop wandering the room and look at him.

"Ignoring this won't make it go away." Tom tracks Max, waiting for a reply. "I'm not standing here watching you prance about in a robe for my own enjoyment."

Max marches across the room and eyes Tom. "Isn't that a pity," he murmurs. "I'm quite enjoying watching you get flustered in your new suit. Feel free to take it off." Max raises an eyebrow. "If it's getting too hot."

Tom stares straight back at him, heat rising up the back of his neck. "You don't fluster me. In fact, I don't particularly like you. But I'm paid to make sure you don't get knocked. So, here I am."

Max's eyes shift slightly, and it makes Tom's gut clench. *I don't trust you.*

"Hmmm," Max swirls his drink again, "You've got skeletons in your own closet, haven't you, Tom Grant?" Max leans towards him. "I can tell."

Tom lets a smile creep across his lips. "You're telling me *I* have skeletons?" Tom points towards the window. "Do the ladies down there know that you enjoy a man in a suit?"

Max smirks. "I pretend every single time I walk out of these rooms and into that hyena pit down there." He jabs a thumb towards the windows. "The Max they see isn't the Max I am. But it's the Max they want. So, I give it to them. I laugh, I smile, I pretend I'm actually interested in the blonde hair and perky boobs being shoved in my face." Tom doesn't flinch and waits for Max to go on. "When it's actually their boyfriends I'm more interested in seeing... in my face..." Max runs his eyes up and down Tom, "fancy suit or no fancy suit."

"Flattered," Tom quips. "But the real issue here is your noncommittal attitude to protecting the people around you." *And yourself.*

"I'm committed." He wanders again and glances out the window. The screams follow. He turns to Tom and grins. "I was thinking of doing a walkabout this morning. Care to see me in action?" He winks and flounces off to the bedroom, slamming the door behind him.

Tom stares at the bedroom door. *What planet have I landed on?*

"Melting jocks off cocks too, then," James' voice is behind him.

Tom turns and glares at him. "Watch it James, the green eyed monster lurks."

James curls his lip and glares at Tom.

"Ah, sorry to interrupt," Ally stands behind them, her hands clasped together. "But would you like to see where he'll do the walkabout?"

"Yes, please," Tom answers.

James huffs and spins, stalking out the door. Tom folds his arms over his chest and watches him go.

"Um…" Ally starts.

Tom holds a finger up and waits.

Moments later James comes storming back into the room. "I have no idea where we're going."

"No." Tom stalks to the door. "You don't."

Tom stands back and gestures Ally into the hall. "After you."

Her cheeks deepen in colour and she scurries ahead of them. Tom walks with James, watching Ally and noting the nerves clearly visible in every jerky movement she makes. "Now James, lesson two. Don't jump the gun." Tom points at him. "Should you be writing these down?" He grins as James scowls before he saunters off after Ally, leaving James behind him.

"Listen, um… sorry about Max." Ally stares at the lift doors, chewing on her lip.

"Why?"

"Oh, he's… difficult."

"He's nothing."

Ally pushes her hand to her chest and laughs, "God, don't let him hear you say that. As far as Max is concerned, he's *everything.*" The tone in Ally's voice piques Tom's interest, but James appears next to him and he lets it drop.

Later.

The lift opens and the three of them get in. James stands at the front, facing the doors as they close. Tom squints at the back of his head. *Sulking won't get you anywhere with me.*

The lift descends and Tom feels Ally's gaze on him. He glances down to her and she drops her eyes to the floor.

He looks up again and smirks to himself.

Hooked.

6

MAX

Max taps the white powder on the bathroom vanity with his credit card, separating it neatly into two even lines. *That's the shit.* Max bends down with his gold-plated straw and sniffs. He throws his head back and sighs loudly. He shakes his head as his nose tingles and warms. *Whatever gets me through the next half hour.*

Walking into the bedroom he drops his gold robe and taps a finger to his bottom lip. He stares at himself in the mirror, proud of the sculpted muscles he maintains beautifully. He peers closer at his chest in the mirror. *Due for a wax, though.* He runs his fingers over the long, skinny scars striping his side. The freshest is still bright pink. He digs his nails into the scar and sucks in a breath as pain shoots into his ribs. The urge to pick up his razor and add to the scars makes his fingers itch. *Better than the hyena pit.*

Screams erupt from the street below and Max's head snaps to the window. He creeps over and peeks down. The screams die away as they realise it isn't Max.

He looks through the glass roof below him and sees Tom and James following Ally. She points at the barricades and fountain in the middle of the roundabout outside the Savoy. She turns and gesticulates at the girls screaming and crying.

Max grunts to himself. *Ally. Mum's favourite. Always in control. Of me.*

He pulls himself away from the window to avoid one of the screaming girls looking up and seeing him.

Back in front of his wardrobe he peers at the clothes. It's clear which clothes are for him and which are for the fans. He moves to the fan section and picks out jeans and a plain black t-shirt that probably cost seventy-five pounds but looks like one you'd pick up for two at the charity shop.

Honestly, these clothes aren't even worth it.

He shoves his feet into his designer trainers, still stark white, and grabs his puffer jacket off the bed. He peers at himself in the mirror and runs a hand through his hair. *Straight as an arrow.* He lifts his chin and the false confidence from the cocaine hits with full force.

Performance time.

7

TOM

Tom walks back into the hotel lobby and the screams muffle slightly as the doors close behind him. He rubs his temples, trying to ignore the thirst erupting in his throat. He grabs a bottle of complimentary water and gulps as James strides towards him. *Not quite the kick I'm after.*

A throat clears behind Tom and he turns, peering at two men in black jeans, black t-shirts and dark shades. They both look like evolution skipped a step.

"Tom Grant?" The larger of the two grunts.

"Yes?"

"Barry." He sticks his hand out and Tom shakes it. Barry tilts his head towards his companion. "This is Paul."

"And you're Max's security, I imagine?" *Tweedledee and Tweedledum.*

"Affirmative." Barry nods once and Tom swallows the snort clambering to erupt.

"Right then… can I help you with something?" *Please fuck off.*

"No. Thought we should rendezvous."

"Aren't you a walking cliché?" Tom grins at Barry's confused frown. "Also… there's no sun in here."

"Excuse me?"

"Your shades. There's no sun. You look ridiculous." Tom twiddles his fingers next to his temple, indicating Barry should take his glasses off.

Barry lifts the shades and squints at Tom.

"Doesn't your mate speak?"

"I'm in charge of this operation." Barry lowers his shades again and Tom lets his snort out this time.

"Okay, Baz. Let me know if you need me." Tom clicks his tongue, turns and walks away.

How many more fools do I have to endure today?

James appears next to Tom and grabs his water out of his hand. "Did you see the talent out there?" *Oh, another one.* "Phwoar!" He takes a gulp of the water and goes to hand it back.

"Keep it," Tom snarls.

"Are you always this grumpy?" James cocks his head to the side and grins.

"Irritated."

"You what?"

"I'm not grumpy, I'm irritated."

"By what?"

"You. Mainly." Tom paces across the floor as Max steps out of the lift and strides to his security. "Made it then." Tom folds his arms across his chest, noticing the new spark in Max's dilated pupils. *Cocaine. Of course, you did.*

"Anything for the fans," Max nods.

Tom concentrates on keeping his face neutral as he looks Max up and down. *What the?*

Max is a completely different person; his voice has dropped a register and he strides through the lobby as opposed to flouncing. Not a single hint of who he was upstairs, no more than twenty minutes ago.

Max winks. "Time to protect me, Buttercup." *And there it is.* Max takes a deep breath before pushing the doors open.

The screams get louder—*if that's even possible.* Tom adjusts the uncomfortable shoulder holster Martha insists he wear with a suit and follows Max out. He watches Max interact with his fans. They scream, grab and kiss him and Max takes it all in his stride, appearing to love every minute.

"Who *is* that guy?" James whispers. "It's a completely different person."

Tom watches as Max saunters to the barricades, posing for pictures and signing autographs. Barry and Paul stick close to him. He lets the girls grope and tear at his clothing. *He's a security night-mare.* One girl plants her mouth right on his and he kisses her back, putting on a show for all the others. The girls whip themselves into a frenzy.

Tom grimaces, waiting for one of them to fall into the fountain standing in the middle of their screaming mosh pit.

"Wow," James mumbles.

Tom stops watching Max and scans the crowd of frantic females from his vantage point near the front doors. He spots a couple of boyfriends forgotten at the back and grins to himself. *If only you knew.*

Tom grabs James' sleeve and yanks him around the back of the screaming huddle. He spies a woman standing near the back, dressed in jeans and a t-shirt displaying Max's tour dates on the back. Black bobbed hair brushes her collar, and she wears heels. She holds an Australian flag, but it's dangles limply from her fingers. Tom's eyes drift to the people near her before landing back on her face.

All alone. Something's not right.

She glances around the crowd and back to Max. She checks her watch and shifts her weight from one foot to the other.

"Her," Tom mumbles to James.

"Huh?"

Tom squints at her, taking in the hard eyes and half-hearted waving of her flag. "She's not a fan."

She pulls a phone out of her handbag and answers it, she scans around and her eyes rest on Tom for a moment before she nods and ends the call. Her eyes flick back to Tom. She lifts her mouth at one end before turning and weaving herself through the hordes of females.

Something clicks and Tom scurries after her.

"What are you…" James' voice floats after him. Tom ignores James and tries to spot the woman.

Hands grab at Tom and he fends them off. He hears a rip and curses under his breath. *It's a fucking new suit.* Squeals and screams pierce his brain, and he looks up to see Max smiling and waving, heading back towards the hotel lobby. *Shit.*

"Oh my God!" A girl of about seventeen grasps Tom's jacket in both hands and her manic eyes fix on him. "You were on the other side before. Can you get me in? Can you?"

"Ah," Tom pries her hands off him. "No. I can't…"

"I'll do *anything.*" Her eyes are manic and fixed on his face. *"Any… thing."* She grabs at his trousers and slides her hand to his crotch and squeezes. Tom steps back and slaps her hand away.

Jesus.

He pushes through the crowd as she claws after him and grabs the back of James' jacket. James is prying a girl's hand off his shirt while fending her other hand away from his nether region. Tom rolls his eyes and yanks James away.

These girls are on heat.

Tom elbows bodies out of his way, knowing they are young girls but genuinely concerned they may rip vital body parts from him at any moment. Squeals and crying fill his ears and he keeps having to drag James along as he is accosted by more wandering hands. Moments later they are out of the jungle.

"Stay with Max."

"Where are you—"

"Stay with him." Tom runs in the direction the woman headed.

The Strand. He reaches the corner and looks both ways. He spies her fifty feet from him, getting into a cab. He runs but the cab pulls away before he can get to it. The woman turns and peers out the back window. They lock gazes for a moment and her eyes smile before she turns away. He stands and watches as the cab weaves into the traffic down the street and disappears.

Dammit.

Tom turns to get back to the hotel and sees a thickset man with black hair glaring at him from the corner. He makes eye contact with Tom and curls his top lip. Something about him makes Tom's skin crawl and within seconds the man stalks towards him.

Shit.

Without another thought Tom raises his forearm and cracks the man to the throat. He drops forward. Tom grabs his jacket, yanking him into an alcove before anyone notices them.

"Who the *fuck* are you?" Tom hisses, holding him up against the wall with his forearm still across the man's throat, as he gasps for air. "Take your time," Tom whispers. "I'm not going anywhere."

The man attempts to kick him, but Tom sweeps his leg out and the man lands with a thud on his back. Tom rolls him onto his stomach and digs a knee into his spine. He grabs one of his arms and twists it up his back, holding it there. The man groans as Tom pushes against the unnatural bend in his arm.

Tom searches his jacket pockets while the man shouts into the concrete as his arm is twisted tighter. Tom pulls a wallet out and scans the cards inside.

"Viktor?" Tom raises an eyebrow and peers at the panting heap on the ground under him. "Your name is Viktor?"

"Fuck you," Viktor spits with a heavy Russian accent. Ice forms in Tom's veins at the accented English.

He drives his knee harder into Viktor's back. "Why are you here?"

"I am fan."

Tom snorts. "Okay, Viktor." He pulls his phone out of his pocket and slaps it against his ear. "Judith. I need a car. Corner of Exeter Street and The Strand."

Viktor attempts to wriggle away, getting nowhere. *I don't think so.*

"What's happened?" Martha's voice is sharp.

"One moment." Tom lifts his knee, heaves Viktor onto his back and jabs him in the chin. Viktor yelps and his head slams onto the ground.

"Sorry about that. You were saying?"

"They're on their way. What shitfight have you—"

"Lovely, Judith. Always a pleasure." He pushes the phone into his back pocket and leans over Viktor. "Got a nice little room for you to chill out in. You might even get a lukewarm cup of tea if you're lucky."

"The fuck?"

"Unless of course you want to tell me what the hell you're doing amongst a horde of screaming females?" Tom pauses. "Are you looking for me, Viktor?" Tom's blood slows to a crawl through his veins. "Are you going to answer me?"

Viktor slams his mouth shut and glares at Tom, his nostrils flare.

"Didn't think so," Tom grins as a car lurches to a halt behind him. "Ah, here we go." Tom grabs Viktor by the jacket and yanks him off the ground. Two men approach and Tom throws Viktor at them. They drag him away and bundle him into their car without a word.

Tom tries to ignore the memory of Isabella being carried away by those same men, her limp body in the larger of the man's arms. He sucks in a breath and gives his head a little shake.

Tom's phone rings and he yanks it out, "He's on his way."

"I knew he was fool," Kat's Russian drawl slides into Tom's ear.

Tom's jaw clenches and his chest nose dives to his gut. "Kat."

"Ah! You remember me! I am flattered."

Tom stops walking and his heart pounds. "You're hard to forget." He glances around the street. "Where are you?"

Kat laughs. "Everywhere," she whispers before the line goes dead.

Tom stares at the phone in his hand a moment before turning and observing the street again. There are people everywhere, pushing and shoving their way past him. *Not good.* His hearing catches the screams and wails of teenage girls and it brings him back to task.

Tom approaches the pack of ravenous females. He spies James laughing and smiling while seven or eight of them flirt and grab at him, as he stands on the safe side of the barricade. Tom huffs out a breath and rolls his eyes. *Fuck's sake.*

He jumps the barricade and grabs James by the collar. "Having fun?" He jerks him backwards and pushes him towards the doors of the hotel. The girls squeal and shout promises and suggestions as they walk into the safety of the hotel lobby.

"What's your problem? I was just talking to them."

"Where's Max?" Tom folds his arms over his chest and raises both eyebrows.

"Ah, he went back upstairs."

"Did he? And you escorted him there, no doubt?" Tom rocks back on his heels and waits.

"Well, yeah. I mean… to the lifts… um."

"That's very interesting, James. Because I can see him as we speak, arguing with a bellboy." He nods over James' shoulder where Max is staring down a hapless bellboy.

James follows Tom's gaze. "Ah…"

"Lesson three. Follow my fucking instructions," Tom hisses.

"Maybe if you hadn't gone sprinting off down the street…" James inhales a breath and lets it out helplessly.

"So, I'm to blame for you being an incompetent drip?"

"Tom… chap—"

Tom's hand shoots out and he grabs James' shirt front in a bunch. "I swear, call me chap one more time… I fucking dare you."

Max saunters to Tom and James and puts a hand on Tom's arm. "Now, now. Tom. Buttercup. That's extremely macho of you. And I quite like it, but honestly… he can't help being useless." Max winks at James. "Cute, though."

Tom loosens his grip and shakes Max's hand off him. "You'll do as you're fucking told. Got it?" Tom stares at James, ignoring Max.

"Got it." James straightens his shirt and tie and holds Tom's glare. "Buttercup."

Tom curls his lip and eyeballs James.

"Boys, boys. Let's take this upstairs so people don't get startled… and I can watch the show." Max winks again and spins towards the lifts.

Tom steps into the lift and James goes to follow him when Max holds out a hand tapping urgently at the door close button. "No, no. You can get the next one."

James' mouth drops open and the doors slide shut. Tom finds himself trapped in the lift with Max and lets out an irritated sigh.

Max whirls around and corners Tom. "Do I make you nervous?" he whispers. His act is over and he's back to being sassy.

"Nope." Tom holds his stare without blinking.

Max's eyes drift down Tom's front. "Your jacket's ripped." He reaches across and Tom catches his hand before it touches him and throws it back at Max.

Max gasps and presses his other hand to his chest. "Fine," he sighs. "I'll admire from afar." He pouts and the doors open at his floor.

He sashays down the hall before tumbling into his hotel room with Tom close behind. Ally is on the phone and she startles as they walk in, fumbling her phone before composing herself.

"I've got to go," she whispers into the phone and shoves it in her pocket.

Tom frowns, watching her. A pang of uncertainty raises its head in his gut before settling again.

She stands and plasters a smile on her face. "How'd you go?"

Max walks straight to the drinks cart and pours himself a straight vodka. "It was a hoot," he mumbles. "I need a bath to soak away the claw marks and sloppy kisses." He turns to Tom, swirling his drink. "Care to join me?" He raises an eyebrow and smirks into his glass as he sips.

"I'll pass." Tom stares back impassively.

"You only had a shower an hour ago," Ally snipes.

"Who are you? Our fucking mother?" He whirls around and slams the door behind him.

"Again," Ally sucks air into her mouth through her teeth. "So sorry, he doesn't like being told *no*." She looks Tom up and down. "Even when it's quite clear the answer is... no."

"No apologies necessary." Tom watches as Ally paws through papers and schedules. "Must be difficult."

She jerks her head up. "What's that?"

"Keeping him on task."

Ally laughs, "You speak like some sort of military man."

"I was. Twelve years."

"Oh, of course you were... No, I mean..." She stops and stares at Tom. "Um..."

Tom holds her stare, waiting for her to blink. *Gotta keep them on the hook.*

Ally clears her throat.

In for the kill. Tom sits opposite her. "Who's the woman with the black bobbed hair and Louboutin heels?"

Ally's face drains of colour a moment before she regains herself. "You know what Louboutin's are?"

Tom watches her face and says nothing.

She squirms a little before shaking her head. "No idea."

"I don't believe you," Tom whispers.

A loud knock interrupts them and Ally breathes out a long breath. Tom stands and peeks through the peephole. He opens the door a touch and walks away back to his seat.

"What the fuck was that?" James grumbles as he halts in front of Tom.

"What was what?"

"The antics with the lift? You could have let me in, you know."

"True."

James' face turns crimson and he breathes faster. "I felt like a proper knob."

Tom leans back on the sofa and grins. "It wouldn't be the first time though, would it?"

"You're a right prick, you know that?" James throws himself into the chair opposite Ally and Tom.

"Well aware. Thank you." Tom squints at James before turning his attention back to Ally. "So, Ms Louboutin. Who is she?"

"I have no idea what you're talking about." Ally mutters, her voice strained. She coughs and picks up her water, taking a sip.

Tom's eyes travel down to her fingers as they fiddle with the corners of the papers in her lap. He leans forward so his face is inches from hers. "Again, I don't believe you," he whispers.

Ally gasps, biting her lip. "She turns up at all the events," Ally stammers. "She's a fan." Her fingers keep flicking the corners of the papers and she looks down at them, feigning reading.

"Didn't seem overly interested in him to me. Not to mention she has about fifteen years on half the girls down there." Tom inches forward to the edge of the sofa. "Girls who would struggle to pay for Adidas trainers, let alone designer heels."

Ally jerks her head up. "What's your point?"

"I don't have all the information. Do I?"

"I..."

"The thing is Ms Louboutin took a call down there earlier. A call that alerted her to me. And then she abruptly took off." Tom studies Ally's face, noting the colour rising in her cheeks. "Now, it certainly wasn't Max... he was busy having boobs shoved in his face. So that leaves... you."

Ally picks at the papers and tears the corners, refusing to look at Tom's face. Tom puts his hand over hers and she stills. She flicks her eyes up at his face and he stares straight back.

Ally lets out a breath and hunches over her lap. "Observant, aren't you."

"It's part of my charm."

"So, where *is* Max?" James' harsh tone pushes its way into the conversation.

"Bath." Tom answers, still watching Ally. She is very interested in the papers on her knee and Tom notices sweat across her top lip.

"He didn't ask you to join him then?" James chuckles.

"Yep." Tom's eyes slide to James. "I prefer showers."

Ally stands, gathering her folders and papers. "Right, well I might go to my room. Dead tired. Need a nap." She scurries to the door, pulling it open. Tom leaps in front of her, pushing the door shut. She gasps and looks up at him.

"I'm watching you," he whispers in her ear, opening the door and sweeping his hand towards the hallway.

Ally keeps her eyes to the floor and pushes past Tom. He watches her as she practically runs down the hall and disappears into her room.

8

MAX

Max dips his chin into the water and lets the bubbles tickle his nose. *God, that was hellish.* He slides up, grabs his vodka off the side of the bath and gulps the last mouthful.

"Vodka!" He throws his glass at the bathroom door. The glass shatters against the door and spreads shards over the floor.

"Max?" Tom's muffled voice is on the other side of the door.

Max grins to himself. "Come in."

"Ah, no. Thanks. Is everything okay in there?"

"It'd be better if you were in here with me," Max mumbles.

"Max?"

"Fine. I'm fine. I'm getting out." He grabs the plug with his toes and pulls it out. Stepping out of the bath, the room spins, and he grabs hold of the vanity. He looks at himself in the mirror and grimaces.

I fucking hate you.

His breathing intensifies and he whirls around, eyeing the glass shards on the floor. He crumples onto the tiles and picks up one of the biggest pieces.

The cocaine and alcohol play havoc with his brain, and he thinks about the tour. *Three months of hell.* He tries to focus on the shard in his hand but it's fuzzy and appears to be pulsating. Panic swells in his gut, working its way up his body. He grips the shard and squeezes his eyes shut. *Toxic mix*

"Who can tell me what happens when you mix cocaine and alcohol?" The group leader looked around the circle of six. Max scrunched further down in his seat, staring at the floor.

"Max? How about you?"

"You forget about how much you hate everything about your life maybe?" Max flicked his eyes up and noticed a couple of the others smirking at his response.

"Insightful as always," the group leader remarked.

Max slid his eyes around the group. Mary McKell, a soapie star who couldn't stay away from cocaine, Michael Westwood, celebrity chef that drinks away his demons, a few nobodies and Max. Court ordered rehab, after driving his Rolls Royce into a tree. Four more weeks to go...

"Actually, alcohol and cocaine metabolises into cocaethylene. The effects can be lethal and put immense stress on your kidneys, liver and heart..."

Max tuned out the boring man in his brown knitted pullover and gazed out the window. Four weeks to go...

A SHARP PAIN PIERCES MAX'S WRIST AND HE OPENS HIS EYES TO SEE he's pushed the shard into his skin, dragging it down his forearm. He gasps and drops the glass.

"Max?" Tom's voice is at the door again.

God don't come in here.

"Shit," Max mumbles, grabbing a towel and wrapping it around his waist. He stands up and pushes a hand against the wall to stabilise himself. He holds his wrist in front of his eyes and sees the cut he inflicted on himself. *I can't scar there. Oh God.* His heart jerks and he sucks in a deep breath. Sliding his hand to the door handle he pushes open the door.

Max spots Tom, standing in the doorway of the bedroom, arms folded, leaning against the doorframe. *Nowhere to hide now.* Tom looks him up and down, his eyes stopping on Max's wrist. Max follows Tom's gaze and notices the blood trickling down to his hand.

Tom stalks across the room and grabs Max's wrist, yanking it up and peering at the cut. He shifts his eyes to Max's and drops his hand. "Still alive. Excellent."

But am I? "Why wouldn't I be?"

Tom glances at Max's chest, his eyes appear to run over the myriad of scars that run down each side of his body.

"Matter for yourself. But know this. On my watch. You stay alive." Tom raises his eyebrows and walks out, shutting the door behind him.

Max flops onto the bed and stares at the ceiling. *He's no fool.* Max bites his lip. *Which could be a problem.*

Ten minutes later Max walks into the main room, his scars now covered with a t-shirt and jeans. Tom leans against the window on the phone while James sits on the sofa shooting daggers into Tom's back.

"Now, now." Max sits next to James. "Don't be angry at him. Bless." Max roams his eyes over Tom's back, landing on his back-side. He sighs. *It's perfect.*

"Maybe I should just shove off and he can do the job alone," James mumbles.

Max reaches across and grabs three glasses and a bottle of vodka. He pours. Picking up a glass he holds it out to James. James eyes Tom still preoccupied on his call.

James takes the glass from Max and clinks it into his. "Cheers." James throws the drink back and Max grins.

You're easy.

"What's that?" James peers at Max's wrist.

Max slams his hand down to his lap. "It's nothing."

James reaches across and grabs his wrist. "Doesn't look like nothing."

Max yanks his arm away. "Honestly. I'm fine. I dropped a glass and cut myself picking it up."

"Bullshit," Tom's voice cuts in.

Max lets out an exaggerated sigh. "I'm fine, Buttercup." He holds out the third glass. "Here, have a drink and relax."

Tom's eyes rest on the glass as he shoves his phone into his jacket. "Pass." He looks at James. "We have rooms. Four oh eight and four oh six. I'll go down and get keys."

Max and James watch as Tom disappears through the door.

"I'd tear him apart like a hot chook," Max sighs.

James laughs. "Ha. Good luck."

"Hmm… doesn't appear likely." Max swigs his drink and looks at James. "You two don't seem the best of mates."

James snorts. "Because we aren't. He hates me." James pours another vodka. "But I'm not overly fond of him either, so…" He shrugs and gulps from his glass.

"So, why are you here James?" Max settles back into the chair and smiles.

"Because I'm a screw up." James pauses, "And I have no choice." He polishes off the rest of his drink and looks out the window. "Next question?"

Max stands and walks to the window, peering at the crowd of girls still camping out downstairs. "We're all screw ups, darling. Some of us, just more than others."

"Let's *not* compare notes."

Max watches James for a moment. "So, I'm thinking of sneaking out tonight."

James looks at him. "And?"

"And… I'll need someone to come with me."

James pours another vodka and squints at Max. "What about Tom?"

"As much as I would prefer to stare at him all night... no offence," he tips his glass towards James. "Something tells me he wouldn't be impressed."

"No offence taken, and you're right. I don't know what all these stories are of him breaking the rules and being spontaneous. He's a right stuffy suit."

"A rule breaker?" Max sucks air in through his teeth. "I do love a bad boy." Max jiggles his glass and downs the last of his drink. "So, you'll come with me tonight and make sure no one shoots me?" He winks. "And maybe, you facilitate me doing what I want, the whole tour?"

James stares at Max. "What do I get out of it?"

Max grins and slips a hand into his pocket, wrapping his fingers around a small bag of white powder. He slips it out and dangles it in front of his face. "Let's start here."

James grins.

Max sits back down next to James and tips the bag out on the smooth surface of the marble coffee table. He pulls out his gold-plated straw. "Not to mention, your pick of any of the screaming females down there." He juts his chin towards the window.

"Excuse me?"

"Pick one. And I'll arrange it for you." He pulls out his credit card and taps at the powder. "Hell pick two... or three. It's not like I want any of them." He snorts along the table and hands the straw to James.

James takes the straw, peering at Max. "Are you serious?"

"As a heart attack."

James snorts two lines, stands and looks out the window. "My friend, you have a deal."

9

TOM

Tom turns away from the reception desk, slipping the two room cards into his pocket. His mind flashes to Paris.

Only one room key required.

His chest gives a jolt, and he swipes a hand across where his heart beats. He pushes thoughts of what *she's* doing in Belgium and if he crosses *her* mind. *Of course, I do. The letter.* Tom shakes his head and exhales the pain from his chest. *A goodbye letter.*

He glances around the lobby and spies the way to the bar and his mouth waters. *Don't be an idiot.* His phone rings and he pulls it out of his pocket, peering at the screen he sees Martha's code name **Judith**. He rolls his eyes and slaps the phone to his ear. *Definitely has a radar.*

"Martha."

"Supreme Order isn't behind the threats."

Tom rubs a hand across his forehead. "What?"

"The emails haven't been coming from them. They have active cells across Europe and the USA. But these emails have origins in Australia."

No shit. "Remember when you told me this would be an easy job?" Tom looks at the ceiling, blowing out a long sigh. "We were in your office? And you said Tom, this is an easy job. Do you remember?"

"Yes. Now, may I continue?"

"Oh, please do. There's nothing I'd rather hear more in this *exact* moment." He plonks on a chair and watches as people roll their suitcases past him, swallowing the thirst in his throat. "And by the way, James is a bigger pain in my arse than I anticipated. And you owe me. Again. But… do go on."

Martha lets out an irritated breath and Tom grins to himself. "As I was saying… the emails originated in Melbourne and then Sydney. They stopped for thirty-six hours before a couple more were sent." Martha pauses. "From London."

Tom leans forward in his chair. "Thirty-six hours? Enough time for, say… a plane ride with a stop over."

"Yes. So, it would seem."

"Fucking knew it." Tom mutters under his breath. "I don't suppose we have IP addresses?"

"Yes. Wireless. Last email sent from The Savoy. Eight thirty-seven this morning."

Tom looks up and sees Ally getting out of the lift, her phone to her ear. "Well, well…"

"What?"

"I've gotta go."

"Yes, but Tom—"

Tom ends the call and watches Ally as she stands outside the lift, engrossed in her conversation. He stands and walks towards her, stopping behind a pillar, watching. His phone goes off in his pocket and he ignores it.

Ally shakes her head furiously and appears to hiss something into the phone before shoving it in her pocket. She claws her hands on her hips. She wanders towards the revolving front doors and peers out before looking around the lobby. Tom slides behind the pillar, out of her line of sight.

Moments later, she stalks across the lobby towards the bar. *Ugh, not the bar.* Tom follows her into the Beaufort Bar as Ally takes a seat, tapping her fingers on the bar top. Slinking into a corner at the back, he sits, leaning forward over his knees. Ally orders a drink and looks towards the entrance of the bar.

She's waiting for someone.

Twenty minutes pass and Ally appears more frustrated with each passing second.

Tom peers at his watch. *Nearly seven.* He looks up to see Ms Louboutin walk in and stop next to Ally. *Surprise surprise.* A drink is put in front of Ms Louboutin before both women pick up their glasses and walk to a small table at the opposite corner of the room.

Tom pulls his phone out, ignoring the four missed calls from Martha and takes a photo of the two women sitting together. Tom waits until Ms Louboutin leaves before he walks towards the entrance. As he passes Ally's table, he makes eye contact with her and smiles. She coughs and pushes her hand into her chest.

Tom stops and leans in and stares at Ally. "I *do* look forward to having a chat."

Ally gasps and slops her drink over the edge of the glass. "Umm, Tom. What are you…" she clears her throat. "Shouldn't you be—"

"Upstairs fending off your brother. Yes. Yes, I should. But… I saw you and thought this looked far more interesting."

Ally rubs her forehead.

"You have a headache?" Tom asks.

"No… why?"

"Maybe conspiring to bring your brother's tour down from the inside is taking its toll?"

"Excuse me?"

"Oh, I'm sorry. Was I not clear? You're trying to harpoon your brother's tour."

Ally stares at Tom a moment before he lets her off the hook.

"I know about the emails," Tom whispers, winking before sauntering off towards the lifts.

He walks through the lobby and gets in the lift, proud of himself for not caving and ordering a drink. Tom watches Ally rushing to the lift doors as they close on her startled face. He smirks. *This'll be fun.* He notices he now has six missed calls from Martha. The lift dings at Max's floor and he steps out. Instead of going to Max's room he stops outside Ally's and leans against the wall.

Three, two, one.

The second lift dings and Ally stomps out. She looks down the hall and locks eyes with Tom. He pushes himself off the wall and grins. "Fancy seeing you here."

"It's not what you think," Ally grabs her card and opens her door. "Come inside before Max sees you."

Tom doesn't move. "What are you concerned about?"

"He's the jealous type." She raises an eyebrow.

Tom snorts and walks into the room. The desk is piled with papers and schedules, her bed perfectly made and the whole room has an order to it that is non-existent in Max's room. Tom leans against the edge of a desk and folds his arms.

Ally sits on the end of the bed and rubs her forehead again.

"You really should do something about that headache."

"Look, I don't know what you *think* you know. But I'm not trying to sabotage Max."

"Is that right?" Tom's phone rings again in his pocket and he answers. "Judith."

"Are you with someone?"

"Obviously… Judith."

"We need to talk. Can you extricate yourself?"

"Yes." Tom ends the call and stands up. "Seems it's your lucky day." He bends down so his nose is practically touching Ally's. At the same time, he slides a spare room key for Max's room off the desk and into his pocket. "But we aren't done," he whispers.

Tom presses Martha's number as he stalks up the hall to Max's room. The call isn't answered and Tom huffs, pressing redial. This time the phone is engaged.

"Fuck's sake." He shoves the phone back into his pocket as he reaches Max's room.

Tom pounds his fist on the door. He hears Max's muffled voice on the other side. "You even look good through the peephole."

"Open the fucking door before I shoot the lock."

"Okay, calm down, can't have you getting all hot under the collar." The door swings open and Max walks backwards into the room with his arms out. "Missed you."

"Indeed." Tom spies his cabin bag next to James' at the door where he left it earlier. He picks it up. "Where's James?"

"Indisposed." Max winks.

Tom steps into him and notices his pupils. "Cocaine eyes," he mutters.

"Flattered," Max fans himself with one hand while covering his mouth with the other.

Tom looks up at the bedroom door. It's shut. He stalks across the room while Max tries to follow but trips over a chair leg and giggles in a heap on the floor. Tom observes Max a moment before opening the bedroom door a crack and peeking in.

He sees James standing with his back to him, a female is on her knees in front of him, topless.

Tom slips into the room unnoticed. "Enjoying yourself?"

James jumps. "Fuck!" He pulls up his trousers and jiggles the fly.

The blonde scrambles to the bed grabbing her shirt and bra.

Tom stalks across the room, grabs James by the back of the neck and pushes him onto the bed. He turns to the blonde and jerks his head towards the door. "Off you go." He waits until the girl leaves before he grabs his pistol out of his jacket and pushes it into James' cheek. "Lesson four. Keep it in your fucking trousers."

"Or what," James counters, his voice muffled in the duvet.

"Or I shoot you in the head." Tom pushes the pistol hard into James' face before taking the pressure off his neck. He stands back, stuffing his pistol into his holster. He watches James stumble off the bed and finish doing up his belt.

"You have a giant stick up your arse, you know that?" James twitches his nose and stares back at Tom.

Tom leans forward, peering into James' eyes. "More cocaine eyes," he huffs. "Been partying in my absence, have you?"

"Well, I—"

"Don't bother." Tom jerks his thumb over his shoulder and James scurries past him into the main room. Tom slaps a keycard against James' chest as he stalks past. "Room four oh six." He picks up his cabin bag and spins around to face James and Max. "Oh five hundred tomorrow. Be ready and be fucking sober. This is your first and last warning." Tom slams through the door and paces to the lift. "Fuck me," he mumbles under his breath.

TOM THROWS HIS BAG ONTO THE BED AND FLOPS NEXT TO IT. HE calls Martha. She picks up on the first ring.

"Tom."

"Martha."

"What's with the delay?" Martha's voice is sharp and irritated, and it makes Tom's blood pressure rise.

I'm not in the fucking mood. Tom opens his mouth, ready to complain she didn't pick up when he called but thinks better of it. *Best I don't.* "James."

"What?"

"James is the delay."

"I see."

"I don't think you do," Tom grunts. "Anyway, what's the big drama?" *She doesn't need to know about the cocaine... yet.*

"I saw you on the news earlier."

"What?"

"Phone footage aired from Max meeting his fans outside the hotel today, and your face made an appearance."

Tom pushes his thumb and fingers into his eyes and rubs. "Fuck."

"Yes." Martha takes a breath. "It's fine, it was only a few seconds but thought you should know."

"Right." Tom eyes the mini bar and the small bottles of spirits on the shelf. "Anything else? I mean... so far for an easy job, I've got an inside threat, an agent that thinks it's party time and a pop star that keeps trying to get into my trousers."

Martha laughs. "He what?"

"Don't ask," Tom smiles in spite of himself. "It's a fucking nightmare."

Martha's cackle dies and she pauses a moment. "Maybe it's a good distraction."

"I don't need a distraction."

"You keep telling yourself that, and I'll keep bringing you back to reality. Your mate from the alley earlier hasn't said a word."

"Disappointing." *But not surprising.*

"Call me tomorrow when you get to Copenhagen." Martha orders. "In the meantime, I'll keep working on him."

"Yep."

"Oh, and Tom?"

"Yes?"

"Stay away from the mini bar." Martha hangs up.

You know I won't.

Tom tosses the phone on the bed and stands, looking around the hotel room. He squeezes his eyes shut as memories of the last hotel room creep into his mind and he claws at his stomach.

"I THOUGHT I'D LOST YOU," TOM BREATHED.

"I'm not going anywhere," Isabella promised. He tangled his hand in her hair, kissing her as she ran her fingers over his chest, making his skin tingle.

TOM INHALES AND GRABS THE TINY WHISKY OFF THE SHELF; HE cracks the seal of the cap and tosses it on the desk. He gulps. Two mouthfuls won't cut it. He grabs the phone and dials room service.

"Blue label Walker." Even as the words leave his mouth, he's disgusted with himself. He hangs the phone up and scrubs his hands through his hair. Martha's face, with her puckered cat's bum mouth fleetingly invades his thoughts before he pushes her away.

His phone rings again and he rolls his eyes to the ceiling and grabs it without checking the screen. "What now?" he huffs.

"Now, now Tom. That is very aggressive of you."

Tom's blood stands still, and he sits up on the bed. "Kat."

Tom says nothing more, gripping the edge of the mattress with his other hand. He waits.

"I saw your handsome face on the news earlier. It reminded me to check in and say hello."

Tom finds his voice. "Watching the news, Kat? How grown up of you."

Kat giggles. "Indeed Tom. Now tell me. How are you? You must have been devastated to see your lover shot dead in front of you."

Tom swallows. "What do you want?"

"To say hello. Oh, and remind you that I intend to avenge Natasha as well. So, I'll see you soon."

The line goes dead.

Tom squeezes the phone in his fist and pushes Martha's number.

She picks up before it rings. "Tom."

"I need you to look up a number that just called my phone." He pulls the collar of his shirt away from his neck.

"Why?"

"Because it was Kat."

Martha is silent.

"Martha?"

"I see."

"Let's add it to the pile of shit I'm already wading through, shall we?"

"Leave it with me. Watch your back."

"Yeah." Tom ends the call and throws the phone onto the bed.

He lays back, waiting for his whisky to turn up, so he can feel nothing for a few hours.

10

JAMES

Max and James sit behind the deeply tinted windows in the back of a Range Rover. The adrenaline courses through James' arms mostly on account of the cocaine sharing his bloodstream. The butterflies erupt, the way they always do when he's doing something he shouldn't. *Which is most of the time.*

I'm supposed to be earning Tom's trust. Ha!

"Tom's gonna rip my head off," James mumbles, staring out the window as they pull away from the back of the hotel.

"He's not gonna know about it, Gumnut." Max hands him a bottle of premixed vodka and leans back in his seat, closing his eyes. "We go out, I get what I need," he pauses. "And then we are back in our hotel rooms by one a.m., a quick snooze and up, bright eyed and bushy tailed for five." Max sips and grimaces, "Ugh, five a.m. Tom's an early riser. Luckily I've got a pill for that." Max smirks, coughing as the drink goes down the wrong way.

"You okay?" James peers at Max.

"Fucking great."

James frowns which appears to irritate Max and he clenches his jaw. "I get sick of answering questions sometimes." He gives James a pointed look.

The Range Rover rolls to a stop in an alley in the West End. Max climbs out of the car and sticks his head in the driver's window. "Come get us around two."

"Two?" James yelps. "You said we'd be back in our hotel by one." *God, I'm regretting this already.*

Max blows an air kiss and skips past James, towards an innocuous set of steps. "I lied," he throws over his shoulder. "Are you coming or not?"

James follows Max down the steps to a black door. "What is this place?" James looks at the stairwell. Bubbles of anxiety simmer in his gut.

"It's sweet," Max grins. "Don't stress."

"It's what?"

"The Sugar Fix," Max furrows his brows at James, "Don't you live in London?"

"Well, yeah but I was on and off a ship for five years and then…" He shakes his head. "Now, I'm not." *Not that I ever wanted to be.*

"Hmm… Max pokes a finger into his cheek and grins. "I look forward to hearing *that* story."

James grunts, chewing on his lip as the cocaine wears off.

Max watches him for a moment. "Cheer up, Gumnut." He pulls James' sleeve, and they walk into the underground bar. Max sweeps his arm out. "Enjoy," he nods towards a booth at the back where a man sits wearing red glasses and a black beret. "Ha, there's my date." He slides an arm around James' shoulders and whispers in his ear, "Give me one hour. Then I promise we can leave."

"Wait a second," James raises an eyebrow, "You've already arranged a meet up?"

"Oh, Gumnut, of course I have. I can't mess about. It's only a matter of time before someone recognises me, regardless of this getup." He gestures at his clothing, glasses and blonde wig. "I mean… I look ridiculous." He juts his chin towards the bar. "Now go play on your own awhile and I'll find you soon." He winks and shoves a bag of cocaine into James' hand before skipping off towards the back booth.

James looks down at the bag and up at Max's back as he weaves through people with ease. *If only they knew who it was.* James shakes his head and shoves the cocaine into his pocket. He sits at a table as a couple get up and walk away. He makes sure he can still see the table Max has perched himself at.

JAMES SLAMMED THE SHOT GLASS ONTO THE BAR, GRINNING AT THE *blonde standing next to him.*

"Do you have to be back on your ship right away?" she whis-pered in his ear, running her fingers down his torso.

"I do what I want," he winked at her and downed the last of his

beer. He pulled a small plastic bag out of his pocket that contained four green pills. "You keen?" He grinned, not caring if he got caught under the influence and charged for being AWOL. Again.

She pouted, dragging her index finger to her chin and traced her neck to her ample chest.

James felt a jolt below his waist and followed her through the throng on the dancefloor towards the bathrooms.

Moments later she was against the wall in the disabled stall, her head thrown back, her knickers halfway down her left leg. The stall swirled into a tornado of tiles, porcelain and steel handrails as James slopped his mouth against her neck clumsily and groped under her dress.

Her hands fumbled with his belt buckle before his trousers dropped around his ankles. She wrapped both legs around his waist as he lifted her onto the small washbasin.

"Moore!" a voice shouted on the other side of the cubicle door.

"Fuck," he mumbled against her neck. She pushed her face into his and caught the rest of his words in her mouth.

"Don't stop," she whispered.

His vision swirled and his breathing hastened.

"He's not here," James called out, knowing the moment he walked out of the stall he would be arrested.

A BOTTLE OF GREY GOOSE AND A GLASS IS PLONKED IN FRONT OF James by one of the bar staff.

"Courtesy of the booth over there," the barman nods towards the table Max sits at. Max raises a glass and gives James a cheers from across the room.

James gives him a tight smile and pours himself a glass. *It could be worse.* The cocaine burns a hole in James' pocket, and he slurps his drink. Slapping the empty glass onto the table, he dips his face towards his lap and pulls out the bag. *This is a stupid idea.*

He sticks his head below the table and snorts a bump or two before looking up.

Max is gone.

The hell? The booth is empty, and James' swings his head, trying to make sense of the jumble of people in every direction. *Shit.*

James leaps to his feet, shoving the plastic bag into his pocket. He stumbles away from the table and pushes his way through the people.

He can't have gotten far.

James runs to the toilets and pushes open the door. He smashes his fists against the stall doors, each of them slam open with a bang and bounce off the wall. The urinal has two men standing at it; neither of them are Max. *Fuck!*

Back inside the club it's hot and musty and cluttered with more sweaty bodies than it was before. James pushes back through the writhing bodies dancing and swaying against each other. Other people's sweat flies through the air along with spilt drinks. He avoids being drunkenly groped as he stands in the middle of the club, looking back and forth.

The vodka and cocaine speed his heart up and it thumps against his rib cage. The sweating and panting begin, and he curses making a bad decision. *Yet again.*

James resorts to grabbing random strangers and peering into their faces. Panic crawls over his skin and he pushes people away when they aren't Max. Coloured lights and music hit him in the skull and he makes a dash for the exit. *Please let him be outside.*

Scrambling up the steps onto street level, he stumbles and falls forward.

Shit.

He clambers forward on his hands and knees before gathering the mindset to stand up. Letting out some deep breaths, he squeezes his hands against his hips. He scratches at his cheek where Tom had jammed the gun earlier and practically feels it pushed against his face a second time.

I'm fucked.

The street is full of people, but none of them look like Max. The Range Rover is nowhere to be found. He turns back towards the club.

Where the fuck is he?

11

TOM

Tom's eyes snap open and he squeezes them shut again a second later as pain splinters through his eyeballs. *Fuck.* Pounding on his hotel room door encourages Tom to sit up.

"Ugh, shut up."

"Tom? Tom, open up," James shouts.

His voice is higher than it should be, and the pounding intensifies in Tom's head.

"Tom!"

Tom peers at his phone screen. *03.36. Are you fucking kidding me?* Tom isn't sure what time he passed out, but he knows the room is spinning through the darkness. He stumbles out of bed. "Okay, okay shut up," he barks through the door.

Tom yanks the door open and James is leaning against the doorframe, resting his head on his forearm. He pushes past Tom into the room.

"Do come in." Tom slams the door and leans against it. "Where's the fire?"

James spots the bottle of whisky with a third still in the bottom and turns to Tom. "Did you...?" He picks the bottle up.

Tom rubs his face with both hands and snatches the bottle out of James' hand. He tosses it into his open cabin bag and folds his arms across his chest, trying to focus on James' face. "Why are you here?" Tom notices James' clothing and hair for the first time. "Dressed like that?" *Wait a minute...* "What the fuck have you done?"

"I, umm... Tom, don't get psychotic but... I kind of lost Max."

Tom stares at James and clenches his hands into fists. His stomach lurches but he can't be sure that's not the whisky. "You what?" He swallows the wave of nausea that sweeps over him.

"You see, he ah... well, we went out and I—"

"You went *out*?" Tom grits his teeth and leans into James' face. "Out?"

"Okay, tear my balls off for that later, yeah? Because right now... we need to find him. I have no idea where he is."

Tom stares at James, saying nothing. *Dilated pupils. Of course.*

James peers into Tom's face. "But, holy shit, Tom. Are you drunk?" James' mouth stretches into a grin and he juts his chin towards the bottle Tom threw in his bag.

"Marginally, however I feel that we have bigger fish to fry at this moment," Tom blinks a couple of times to get James back into focus. *This is not ideal.*

"Yeah… yeah we do. He left the club, and I don't know—"

"You went to a club? With one of the most famous pop stars... apparently… in the world?"

"Yes."

"And you lost him."

"Yes."

Tom nods. "The thing is, I'm not even surprised."

"He disappeared. Into thin air, Tom."

"And how much coke had you snorted at this point?" Tom's anger outweighs the lingering effects of the whisky and he peers into James' face.

"Well, I…" James looks at the floor. "A bump or two," he mutters.

Tom flicks James in the forehead with his fingers, "Fucking moron."

"Can you kill me *after* we find him?"

Tom is already halfway out of the room before he remembers he isn't wearing a shirt or shoes. He stalks back in and rummages through his bag.

"Yeah, I was gonna mention—"

"Shut up," Tom snarls. He pulls a shirt over his head and pushes James out the door. "Have you checked his room?"

"His room?" James brows pull together and he squints at Tom.

"Yes, yes, his room, James. The place he would go back to sleep in. And… whatever else he may want to do." Tom hops on one foot while he tugs his trainers on.

"Well, no."

Tom gets to the lift and hammers the button. "If he's in there, I'm going to shoot you. Just so we're clear."

"Fuck," James mutters under his breath.

The lift arrives and Tom marches in, slamming the floor button with his fist.

The lift dings, opening, and Tom paces up the hall to Max's room. He pulls the keycard he lifted from Ally's room earlier and swipes in.

"How did you…?" James' voice trails in as Tom stalks through the room and slams his fist on the bedroom door.

"Max?" He hammers. "Max?" He puts an ear to the door. *Silent.* Tom opens the door and flicks on the light. *Empty.* Looking to the left he sees the bathroom is open and vacant.

Fuck. This.

Tom spins and slaps his hand in the middle of James' chest and pushes him backwards.

"Where did you go?"

"Um, some club? I don't know? Sugar Place or something?"

"The Sugar Fix?" Tom's voice is low and dangerous.

James swallows and nods. "Yes, that's it. That one."

"At what point did you decide this was a great idea?" Tom widens his eyes and glares into James' face. "Was it before or after the cocaine? The vodka? The female with the hospitable mouth?"

James' nostrils flare as he stares back at Tom. "Maybe if you had shown me more respect and trusted me, this wouldn't have happened."

Tom curls his lip and squints. "What?"

"I said—"

"I heard what you said, I *just* can't believe you said it. Where I come from, respect is earned. Trust as well… come to think of it."

"How much whisky *did* you drink before passing out earlier?" James steps into Tom and narrows his eyes. "Don't make out you are some kind of saint. You aren't. And I know it. So how about we call it even?" James' eyes glint and he smirks.

Tom's mouth presses into a thin line.

"Well, well, well." Max's voice fills the room and Tom looks up to see him standing at the doorway. Relief floods Tom's veins and the tension in his shoulders loosens. "If I'd have known you'd be here waiting for me Tom, I'd have come home *a lot* earlier." Max smiles at James. "There you are, Gumnut. You left without me." He pouts.

"But you… you disappeared." James' voice comes out squeaky.

"Oh darling, I went out for… a quickie." He winks and sits on the sofa.

"A quickie?"

"Yeah you know a—"

"We know," Tom grunts. "I'm going back to bed."

Max gasps. "Ohhh, can I—"

"No." Tom slams the door behind him and stalks down the hall.

Ally's door opens as he approaches and she steps into the hallway wearing a long coat and scarf, holding a beanie in her hand.

"Going somewhere?"

She jumps a foot into the air at Tom's voice. "Oh my God," she pants, falling backwards into the wall. "What are you… it's four a.m."

"Yes. I guess going back to bed is no longer an option. Maybe we finish our chat instead." Tom walks towards her, practically pinning her to the wall with his presence.

"Oh. I was about to…"

Tom waits. "Go on."

"Ah…"

"Let me take a wild stab in the dark here, Ally. You've never been found out before have you? You've been doing whatever you want until this point and now you're completely adrift and don't know which lie to tell me." Tom slams his palm into the wall above Ally's head. "Yes?"

Ally slides from under Tom's arm.

"Walk with me," she hisses, powering to the lift.

Tom huffs and rubs his face. Following her into the lift, he waits for the doors to close before punching the emergency stop button. The lift goes dark and he corners Ally against the back wall. "Speak."

"Despite what you might think, I love my brother and I'm trying to stop him from completely destroying himself."

"By?"

"By…" Ally sighs. "I wanted him to cancel the tour and go into rehab. He refused. So I…"

"Posed as an extremist group, sent him threats and hoped for the best."

"Something like that," Ally mumbles. "Only, he wouldn't cancel, somehow you got roped in and now…"

"Jesus," Tom grunts. "You didn't think this was a bad idea? You didn't think an agency like ours would become involved given the nature of the threats?"

"Obviously not." Ally crosses her arms over her chest and kicks a toe into the floor. "God, what a mess." Ally peers up at Tom. "Maybe you guys should go. I'll hire extra private security and we'll be out of your hair."

"Do you understand the penalties for what you've done?"

"Well… no."

"If we pulled out, questions would be asked. And you'd probably be arrested…"

Ally rubs her forehead again. "What a disaster."

"One word for it." Tom leans his shoulder against the wall. "Where are you going?"

"Nowhere."

"In a coat, gloves and beanie? At four in the morning?"

"Jogging."

Tom chews on his bottom lip. "Again, in a coat and gloves? At four in the morning?"

"I like the quiet." Ally wrings her hands. "Seriously Tom, I'm having some me time. I don't get much of it. And I hate flying so I need to burn off the nerves."

"Is that so?"

Ally swallows and her face breaks. "It's not what you think."

Tom decides to let her off the hook for the moment. *We are gonna be on a plane together for two hours.*

"I hate it when my time is wasted." He gives her a hard glare before punching the start button on the lift and facing the doors.

12

JAMES

J ames climbs the steps into the Lear jet. The perfectly flamboyant attendant gives a little flourish of his wrist, inviting James inside. His eyes land on Tom, already in his seat, resting his head against the window.

James slides into the seat opposite. "You're welcome," he says, clicking his belt in.

Tom's eyes open to James' face, but he keeps his head against the window. "What?"

"You're welcome. I helped you avoid a hangover."

"Not all heroes wear capes," Tom mumbles, closing his eyes again.

James opens his mouth then slams it shut. *Not the right time.*

"Buttercup! Gumnut! Look at you gorgeous humans." Max sweeps into the plane, wide eyed and bushy tailed as he promised he would be. *The uppers would be helping.* "I'll be up the front in the swishy section." Max winks at the attendant who covers his mouth and giggles.

"Enjoy," Tom mumbles, burying his chin into his jacket.

Max bends down, his face inches from Tom's. "Feel free to join me."

Tom opens one eye and pushes Max's face away with an open palm to the face. Max chuckles and heads to the front of the plane.

James watches as Max starts flirting with the attendant before turning back to Tom. "How do you get away with that?" James leans forward over his knees. "Actually, how do you get away with any of the shit you do?"

"Practice." Tom's eyes remain closed.

"Huh." James leans back in the seat. *Test the waters.* "So tell me. The senator. What happened?"

Tom's eyes snap open and he pierces James' face with them. He straightens in his seat and cracks his neck. "I was drunk, James."

"You what?"

"Drunk… how you were last night. Minus the coke."

James swallows. "How did Martha let you anywhere near a senator while you were drunk?"

"She didn't know."

"But how?" James' mouth drops open.

"You ask too many questions, James."

Don't blow it. "So, enlighten me and I'll shut up."

Tom rolls his eyes and stares at the roof of the cabin. "I'd been drinking all night. Woke up in a hotel room with…" Tom stops and bites his lip. "Was late, got there in time. But…" Tom shakes his head. "Why are you even asking?"

"Tom, chap—"

Tom's head snaps up and his eyes shoot lasers.

"I mean, Tom… it's legendary. Who else in the history of the agency could have a senator shot dead on his watch and keep his job?"

"No one." Tom folds his arms over his chest and resumes looking out the window. "Now, maybe you can go to sleep or something."

"Why?"

"So, you stop talking." Tom closes his eyes again.

James leans his head against the headrest and smiles to himself. *It's a start.*

"He's so cute when he sleeps," Max's is back, and he leans over James' seat. James can smell the alcohol from the night before, seeping out of Max's pores.

James puts a finger to his lips. "I'm fairly sure he can—"

"I can hear you," Tom grunts.

"Buttercup needs his beauty sleep." Max laughs. "Come up the front and hang." He pulls at James' shirt.

James shoots a look at Tom who still has half his face buried in his jacket. *Why not?* James stands.

"Water."

James turns and frowns at Tom.

He glares at James. "He'll be drinking water." Tom's eyes slide to Max. "Or pink lemonade."

James purses his lips and fights the urge to snarl at Tom. *He's such a git.*

"Sh, sh, Buttercup, go back to sleep." Max winks and James lets himself be dragged down the aisle by the shirt.

At the front of the plane James sits as the engines start to get louder and more intense.

Max pours a vodka and holds it out to him.

James goes to grab it and stops. *Better not.* "Ah, maybe I'll have water."

"Now, Sir," the attendant says. "Not until we are cruising. You know the rules." He winks and waggles his finger at Max.

Max smirks and throws the vodka down his own throat as James reaches for bottled water. He cracks the seal and gulps a mouthful. *Boring.*

"We can bend the rules this once can't we?" Max leans forward and squints at the attendant's name badge. "Justin?" Max grins and pulls out a small bottle he had concealed in his chair pocket.

Justin huffs and turns to walk away. "I haven't seen anything." He perches himself in his seat, buckles up, and inspects his nails.

Max leans back in his seat as the plane speeds up for take-off. "Tell me Gumnut, do you always do as you're told?" Max raises his voice over the roar of the engines.

"Clearly not. Last night wasn't my finest hour."

Max looks at the ceiling as the plane lifts off the ground. "Oh, don't feel bad. I was on heat. I was liable to end up anywhere." Max chuckles. "Now... let's talk about when we get to Denmark."

Anxiety creeps up the back of James' neck. "What about it?" As the plane ascends, James' stomach rolls with it. He slaps a hand over his gut and squeezes his eyes shut.

"Well, clearly I'm going out again this evening." Max carries on, oblivious to the take-off rush.

"Fuck, Max. I can't. Not right away. Tom will blend my balls into a smoothie and make me drink it." James takes another gulp of water. "Or shoot me in the head."

"Or both," Max smirks.

"Exactly."

Ally is asleep in a seat to James' left and she snorts and mumbles as she turns towards the window. Her hair is all over her face and she hugs herself with both arms.

Max rolls his eyes and juts his chin towards his sister. "Don't mind her. She snores when she's taken a sedative. She hates flying." Max observes his sister for a moment with a soft smile before sipping his drink. He turns his smile back to James. "Anyway, Gumnut. Tell me about you."

"What about me?"

"Everything. You got family? How did you end up here with us?"

James pushes himself backwards into his seat, hoping he sinks right into it and can avoid this entire conversation. He blows air out of his mouth and taps his foot.

"Humour me," Max leans forward jiggling his glass so the ice clinks. "I like hearing about other people's lives so I can ignore the disaster that is mine."

Your life? A disaster?

James heaves a breath in, noting how constricted his lungs are in this moment. "I've got a brother. And a father. Mum has a whole wing of the house to herself. My father took a number of lovers over the years and Mum got sick of it." James ran a hand through his hair. "He's a bastard."

"Oh intriguing," Max cradles his chin into his hand as he leans on the armrest. "Go on." He gestures his glass towards James.

"He's Lord Oliver Moore," James mumbles.

Max jerks an eyebrow, "Lord?" He splays a palm against his chest. "Oh my!"

"It's all inherited wealth. Didn't work a day in his life for it." James gulps more water so he can stop talking.

"You hate him."

"Like I said, he's a bastard. His brother is the fucking king of the Navy so of course that's where they shoved me." James rolls his eyes and pulls his collar away from his neck. *Why the fuck am I telling you this?*

Max gasps. "I do love a man in uniform." He winks

again and flaps his hand to encourage James to keep talking.

"Well, don't expect me to be in uniform again. Ever."

"What did you do?" Max's tone is sing-song, and it causes James' pulse to ratchet.

I should shut up. "I got caught dealing drugs. More than once. But the last time… a couple of sailors ended up in hospital." James slams his mouth shut.

. . .

"*Sub-Lieutenant Moore. You are charged with one count of using violence to a superior officer. One count of offering to supply a controlled drug to another. One count of possession of a controlled drug with intent to supply. One count of unfitness or misconduct through alcohol or drugs.*" The MP flicked his eyes up from the paper, resting them on James' face.

James stared straight ahead.

"*And being AWOL.*"

The appointed advocate sitting in the chair next to James sighed as he read through the paperwork.

"*Your investigation took eighteen months. My client won't be answering any questions at this time.*"

James dropped his eyes to the man sitting next to him. "*Sir?*"

"*Shut up, Moore.*" He pulled out the chair next to him and pointed at it. "*Sit.*"

The advocate waited until James sat before looking at the MP.

"*Could we have the room please?*"

The MP spun on his heel and left the room.

"*Fuck,*" James dropped his face into his hands.

"*My name is Lieutenant Jenkins; I'll be your legal representation. But, before all that, someone wants to speak with you.*"

James jerked his head up from the table. "*Who?*"

Seconds later the door swung open and Admiral Peter Moore marched in. James' lawyer jumped to his feet.

"*Fuck!*" James dropped his head backwards and stared at the ceiling.

"What happened to standing when a superior enters the room?" *Admiral Moore's voice was low and even.*

"You aren't in uniform and you're just Uncle Pete." James smirks at the Admiral.

"Watch yourself, James." Admiral Moore sat and folded his hands on the table. "I have a proposition for you."

"I bet you do." James eyed his Uncle.

"I want information. And you're going to get it for me."

James let out a slow sigh and balled his hands into fists under the table. "Hit me."

"Gumnut?"

James snaps his eyes to Max. "What?"

"Did the sailors die?"

"Ah, no they didn't."

"Cause for celebration!" Max pours another vodka and pushes it into James' hand. "One won't hurt." He winks. "We have two hours before we land. Drink up."

James grips the glass and looks at Max. *Nothing to lose.* He swallows the vodka as Max looks on with glee.

James holds the glass up and Max claps his hands.

"Isn't this fun, Gumnut?"

It's a goddamn blast.

13

TOM

"Hey," a soft voice is at Tom's ear. His eyes blink open and Ally sits back in James' seat.

Tom sits up in his seat and stretches. "What's up?" he asks through a yawn.

"Ms Louboutin." Ally rubs her drowsy eyes before looking back to Tom. Her fingers fiddle with the hem of her jumper.

Tom watches her squirm a moment before tilting his head. "What about her?"

"She's ahh…" Ally blows her fringe off her face. Tom's eyes remain on hers. "She…" Ally sighs and sits forward. "She's black-mailing me. Well… Max. Only he doesn't know."

Can this job get any more annoying?

Tom leans forward. "Go on."

"She's threatening to out him."

"Out him?"

"As being gay. Out him." She sucks on her lip. "She has photographs and everything."

Tom quirks a brow and sits back. "Do people really not know?"

"He's good at pretending."

"The moment he saw us he was out and proud. I don't get it."

"He wants into your trousers, Tom," Ally laughs. It was the first time Tom heard her laugh freely and it irks him that he enjoys the sound. "He won't pretend around you."

Tom smiles despite himself, "It's never gonna happen."

"I know, and so does he." Ally smiles. "He's harmless."

"I know." Tom sees in Ally's eyes the love for her brother and understands why she did what she did. "I'm not going to report you, by the way."

"Report me?"

"The fake threats?"

Ally inhales and nods her head. "Thank you. I was only trying to…"

"I get it." Tom leans forward again until Ally looks up at him. "But no more lies. I can't help you if you lie to me."

"Okay," Ally mumbles, fiddling with her hands in her lap. "I can't tell him about the blackmail. Max doesn't know. And if I tell him, he will lose his shit."

"And when you say… lose his shit…?" Tom raises his eyebrows.

"He'll have a meltdown. His career is built on a lie. If it's exposed, he's done. And he can't handle that." Ally's eyes fill with water and she sniffles. "He'll hurt himself." She gives a little shrug, "He thinks I don't know he's still doing it… but I do."

"What about all those photographs of him with his shirt off? The scars and cuts?" Tom remembers the fans holding huge posters of Max posing in jeans and not much else.

"Photoshop, makeup…" Ally smiles at Tom's furrowed brows. "Welcome to show biz. Nothing is real."

"Who is this Louboutin woman?"

Ally pulls out an iPad and hands it to Tom. A website for a PR company is displayed. "Melissa Jones, PR." Tom reads. "PR?"

"She owns the largest PR firm in the UK. The fact she's doing this is bizarre to say the least."

"She's on the rich list. She doesn't need your money." Tom bites his lip.

"She wanted to rep Max in the UK. But we went with a different firm. She's crazy. Hates being rejected, clearly." Ally takes a breath. "She doesn't want money. She's blackmailing us for Max's contract. He's a huge star. It's a massive feather in her cap to get him."

"So why don't you use her?"

"I don't trust her. I didn't from the start. I wasn't wrong."

Tom closes the folder and hands it back to Ally. "She won't be releasing anything."

"How?"

"When we land, I'll make a call. All her systems will be blocked, and I'll have her held in a comfy little room with no windows for a while."

Ally tilts her head and raises a brow. "You can do that?"

"Not personally. But I know someone who can." *Martha can do anything.* "But, in fairness. Max should know."

Ally sighs heavily and wraps her arms around her stomach. "He won't take it well."

"Then, we reassure him." Tom leans forward and waits until Ally looks at him. Her eyes are gentle and tears swim at the corners.

No going soft, Grant.

14

MAX

Max throws himself on the bed inside the main bedroom of the penthouse suite. He picks up a room service menu and reads it aloud. "Nobis Hotel welcomes you..." He throws the menu down to the floor and stares at the window in the roof. "Fancy," he mumbles. *Whatever.*

"Max?" Ally's voice filters up the stairs.

Max sighs and rubs his face. "Up here," he calls back. He flops his arms above his head and his hands dangle off the side of the bed.

"Max. There's something you should know." Ally's voice is in the room now.

Max closes his eyes and blows air out of his mouth, making his lips vibrate. "Wow, straight into business. This sounds serious."

"It is." Tom's voice startles Max and he sits up.

"Buttercup!" Max sees James over Tom's shoulder. "Gumnut!

The whole crew is here. This should be good." He smirks and swings his legs to the edge of the bed, crossing them.

"Max... Um..." Ally pulls a folder out from her handbag and thrusts some photographs onto the bed.

He picks them up and his blood freezes. He sees himself in compromising positions with another male at a club in Sydney, days before flying out to London.

"Oh my God," he looks up at the three of them. "Where did you get these? Who saw me?" His heart leaps against his ribcage and he jumps off the bed. He holds the photographs out and his hand trembles. It's clearly him, despite the cheap wig and hat. His breathing runs away from him and he pushes a hand to his chest.

"Melissa Jones." Ally sits on the bed and pats next to her. "Sit down, can you?"

"No, I cannot." He whirls around and looks at Tom. He runs across the room and grabs him by the shirtfront. "Make it go away. Please? Can you do something?"

Tom pries Max's hands off his shirt. "Sit down, Max." Tom's voice isn't gruff; it's consoling—sympathetic, and it throws Max into a panic. His heart dances to a beat too fast to keep up with and his head is too light.

Tom grabs Max's shoulders and steers him to the bed, sitting him down. He squats in front of him and looks him in the eye. "Take a breath and drink water." Tom hands him a bottle.

Max takes the water and gulps.

"Now, Melissa Jones will not be releasing any photographs or information about you."

"How do you know? You can't stop her." Max wipes his forearm across his nose.

"You underestimate me, Max." Tom raises a brow and grins, and Max's insides disintegrate. His nose tingles and his throat aches. He tries to stop the tears, but they force their way out the corners of his eyes. "She's currently sitting in a tiny room with no windows, drinking room temperature tea," Tom continues.

Max sniffles and hiccups. "What does that mean?"

"It means I pulled some strings. Her office is being tossed and she's had blocks put on all electronic communication."

"But how?"

"I lied." Tom stands up. "Thank me later."

Ally hugs her brother. Max leans against her and kisses her cheek.

"It's too hard Al. I can't…"

"It's alright Max." Ally's voice soothes him, and in that moment, he needs his sister more than anyone else. He curls into a ball and cuddles into her.

"Why couldn't Mum comfort me like this?" he mumbles into her neck.

"Because Mum didn't know how," Ally whispers.

A soft click of the door tells Max that Tom and James have left and for a moment it brings him relief. Until the problem at hand worms its way back into his mind. Max leaps out of Ally's arms and off the bed.

"Has he really fixed this?" He screws his face up and stares at his sister, willing her to come up with a magic solution. His body trembles and the urge to press something sharp into his ribs floats to the surface.

"Tom said he can handle it." She stands and puts both hands on her brother's shoulders. "We need to trust him."

"But she won't be sitting in a tiny room drinking tea forever."

Ally pulls him into her again and hugs him. "It'll be ok."

"Yeah," Max mumbles into her shoulder. He pulls away. He wipes his nose along his arm. "I'm going to have a bath."

"Okay, but Max?"

Max turns to his sister. Her face is pale and eyes wide. "Yeah?"

"Please don't lock the door."

Max meets his sister's eyes a moment and sees her tears brimming. He walks into the bathroom and leans against the door, resting a hand on the door handle. He sniffles and gives his head a shake. With a click he turns the lock.

15

JAMES

James closes his room door and leans against it. He throws his bag on the bed and shakes the lingering fog from the flight out of his head.

He checks the screen of his phone and sees four missed calls and a text from Uncle Pete. Rolling his eyes his hits call and sits on the bed.

"You were supposed to call me two days ago."

"Geez, not even a hello? How are you doing, my favourite nephew?"

Peter doesn't say anything.

James flops back on the bed and stares at the ceiling. "I'm doing my best, okay? He really hates me." *Though, I do keep fucking up.*

"Try harder." Peter ends the call and James sighs to himself and rolls over, switching the TV on. A news report shows Max arriving at the hotel while flimsy orange barricades hold back the hordes of screaming fans. Luckily neither he nor Tom are featured.

"Insane," James whispers to himself. Uncle Pete's words fly around in his head as he sits up. "Okay, okay," he mutters. He grabs his wallet and room key and shuffles out the door.

Moments later he is in front of Tom's door. He stares at it with his hand poised to knock. The door swings open and Tom walks straight into James as he checks his phone.

"The fuck?" Tom glares at James.

"Ah… hey." James observes Tom in workout gear, carrying a towel. "Heading to the gym?"

Tom blinks and stares at James. "What do you want?"

"A… chat?"

Tom breathes a slow breath in closing his eyes.

"But you know… it's fine we can chat… later."

As Tom squints into James' face, a hotel worker walks down the hall, obscured by a huge bunch of red roses.

"Tom Grant?" The woman peers at James.

"No, not me." He points at Tom who stares at the roses as though they may bite his face off.

The woman smiles at Tom and holds the bunch out. "For you."

Tom grasps the roses and takes them out of the woman's hands. He stares into the bouquet, unmoved.

"From lover boy?" James smirks.

Tom fumbles behind him and opens the door. James follows him in. Tom throws the roses onto the bed and stands with his hands on his hips, biting his lip.

"What gives?" James peers over Tom's shoulder at the bouquet.

Tom grunts and rifles through the bunch, picking out a small envelope. He rips it open and reads the message inside. He jerks his lip up in a snarl and James can't help but let his curiosity get the better of him. He plucks the card out of Tom's hand and reads it.

"See you soon?" James looks closer. "Wow, she actually kissed the card?" He points to the bright red lipstick.

Tom snatches the card back, rips it in half and throws it on the bed. He picks up the roses and tears them apart, red petals fly around the room.

"Fuck!" Tom kicks the bed and scrubs both hands through his hair.

"Okay. Tom. What the hell?" James' heart ratchets up and the adrenaline from Tom rubs off on him. He grabs a bottle of the over-priced water out of Tom's mini bar and gulps. "Seriously, who is she?"

Tom already has his phone to his ear. "It's me." He paces the room. "I've been sent a bouquet of roses." His eyes flick up to James. "Are you kidding me?" His voice lowers and he glares at James. "But I *don't* trust him. Do I?" He is saying it into the phone but it's clear to James that the words are directed at him. *With good reason.*

Tom prods the phone with his thumb and shoves it in his pocket. He swipes up his gym towel and stalks to the door. Pausing, he turns and glares at James. "Are you coming or what?"

"To the gym?" James scrunches his face up in confusion.

"You wanted to chit chat, did you not?" Tom sweeps his hand towards the hall and jerks his head towards the lift.

Inside the lift Tom's jaw clenches and unclenches.

"So…?" James asks.

Tom stares straight ahead at the closed doors, his arms are crossed over his chest. "They're from Kat."

"And she would be…"

"She's a crazy Russian assassin, James."

Russian? Hello.

"Russian assassin?" James furrows his brow and hopes Tom can't hear the erratic thump of his heart. James swallows. "I thought Isabella was dead? Or was it this Kat person?"

Tom's eyes snap to James' face as the lift doors open. The force Tom's eyes hits him with pins James against the wall of the lift. Tom slams a palm into the wall next to James' head before stalking out of the lift.

James scurries after Tom. "Isn't she though?"

Tom stops at the door of the gymnasium and turns to James. "Kat is the psycho bitch that killed Isabella. Do not *ever* get the two mixed up. Do you understand?"

James holds his breath a moment before exhaling slowly. "So, Isabella… she's dead?"

Tom's eye twitches and he steps right into James' space. "That's what I said," he whispers.

James notes the twitch but powers on. "So, why is this Kat bird sending you roses?"

"She misses me." Tom looks James up and down. "Are you working out or are you fucking off?"

"Yeah I'm gonna..." James pokes his thumb over his shoulder. "Fuck off."

Tom glares at James' a moment longer before he spins, pushing open the gym door and disappearing through it.

James watches the door swing shut and lets out a breath that had been filling his lungs uncomfortably. He pulls his phone out and sends Uncle Pete a text.

We have lift off.

16

TOM

Tom slams weight plates onto the leg press and narrowly misses jamming his finger between them. *Calm down.*

He throws himself onto the seat and positions his feet on the plate. The evil, ice cold blue eyes of Katarina Ivanov flash in front of him. He squeezes his eyes shut as he releases the weights and pushes his legs out.

*K*AT PUSHED THE YOUNG BOY SHE HAD HELD AGAINST HERSELF AS A *human shield aside and aimed her gun at Isabella. BANG! Tom had no time to get to her. It happened so fast.*

Isabella let out a grunt, dropping to her knees. She fell forward, her face landing in the dirt.

Kat grabbed the boy by the arm, and they ran, disappearing into the night. Tom's feet were glued to the spot. The scene playing out in front of him didn't seem real.

TOM'S OPENS HIS EYES. *BECAUSE IT WASN'T REAL.* HE EASES HIS LEGS back before pushing against the weights again. Ten reps and he drops his legs to the floor and sits up. Kat's cackle invades Tom's thoughts. His heart rate spikes and it has nothing to do with the exercise. He sits against the backrest and repositions his feet. The weights may be a touch heavier than usual, but he needs to zone out. He pushes against the plate and punches out another ten before sitting up.

The conversation with James at the door of the gym replays in Tom's head. *Why is he so interested? Why did he ask about—*

Tom leaps up from the leg press and grabs his towel. He stalks to the door of the gym.

"OPEN THE FUCKING DOOR," TOM BARKS, POUNDING ON JAMES' hotel room door with his fist.

The door swings open and Tom plants his hand in the middle of James' chest, pushing him backwards into the room.

"Tom? What the—"

"How do you know who Isabella is?"

"What?"

Tom shoves James onto the bed and stands over him.

"I said…" Tom takes a breath and watches James' face as his eyes widen and sweat glistens on his top lip. "How do you know who Isabella is?"

"I d... don't."

"You asked about her."

"Yeah well… you said her name…"

"How did you know she was dead?"

"I didn't."

"You knew she was a Russian assassin. And that she was dead. That's a lot of information to be aware of if you don't know who she is."

James swallows and stares at Tom. "No, but… Kat's the assassin, right?"

What the fuck is going on? Tom peers into James' face. "What are you playing at?"

Tom's phone rings in his pocket, he ignores it and glares into James' face.

"Are you… gonna answer that?" James squeaks.

The ringing stops. "Guess not." Tom grasps James shirt and lifts him to a standing position. "What. Are. You. Up. To?" His phone rings again and he lets out an irritated sigh. "Fuck's sake…" He swipes the phone out of his pocket and barks into it. "Yes?" He pushes James back onto the bed and spins to face the window.

"Tom?" Ally's voice is frantic. "I need help. It's Max.

Tom's gut plummets. "Where is he?"

"He's locked himself in the bathroom and—"

Tom ends the call. He points at James. "This isn't over."

 He stalks out the door slamming it behind him.

ALLY GRABS TOM'S ARM AND PULLS HIM INTO THE ROOM. "I'M sorry, I didn't know who else to call and I can't get the door open and..."

Tom scrubs a hand through his hair and exhales. "What's happened?"

"He's in the bathroom, but he's been in there too long. He said he wanted a bath..."

Tom paces to the bathroom door and tries to open it. *Locked.* "Max?"

Silence.

Tom backs up a couple of steps and slams his shoulder into the door, it breaks open and Tom sees the bathwater. *Fuck.* Max's head lolls onto his shoulder but he isn't underwater. *Thank Christ.*

He leaps across and drags Max out. Red water slops over the bath onto the floor. He grabs a towel and wraps it around Max's left wrist. A gash goes from the heel of his palm to halfway up his forearm. *Jesus.*

"Get over here," he shouts at Ally. She runs to them, her knees hit the floor with a thud and she slides to a stop next to her brother.

"Oh my god, is he..."

"He's alive. Put pressure on this. Keep it tight." He grabs Ally's hands and wraps her fingers around the towel on Max's wrist. Tom bends down and listens to Max's breathing. It's shallow but it's there.

Tom looks to the side of the bath and sees a couple of bottles of pills and a half-drunk bottle of vodka. His heart jitters at the sight of the bottle. He understands that part too well. He shakes his heads to clear his own demons before focusing back on Max.

"He needs his stomach pumped." Tom stands and pulls his phone out. "Stay with him and don't let up on that pressure."

Tom waits for his call to be answered and leans his face against his forearm on the wall.

This is not what I signed up for.

🌸

TWO HOURS LATER TOM IS ON HIS BED, LYING AMONGST THE shredded roses holding an unopened bottle of whisky. Saliva pools on his tongue as he tries to convince himself he doesn't need it. *But I want it.*

A soft knock at the door interrupts his inner argument and he plonks the bottle on the bedside. A quick peek through the peephole before he pulls the door open and leans against it.

"Hey, um… hope I'm not interrupting anything." Ally wrings her hands.

"Ah…" Tom glances back to the room at the torn up roses and the whisky bottle. *I look like a psychopath.* "No, I was …" He steps back, gesturing Ally in. "Don't mind the mess."

He follows Ally into the room. She tilts her head, staring at the bed. "Remind me not to buy you roses as a thank you." She grins. She takes in a deep breath, raising her shoulders up under her ears. "It smells divine though."

Tom runs a hand through his hair and smiles. "Yeah, but... no thank you required." He brushes past Ally and clears a spot amongst the roses for her to sit.

"You don't like roses?"

"I don't like who sent them."

"Ohh, interesting. Jilted lover?"

"No. Though... that would be easier to deal with." Tom grabs the chair from under the desk and straddles it.

"Since when is a jilted lover easy?" Ally laughs.

"Trust me." Tom taps his hands on the back of the chair. "How's Max?"

"He's sleeping. We got back half an hour ago." Ally crosses her ankles. "I wanted to say thank you. And apologise."

"Apologise for what?"

"You're a government agent... you deal with spies and fancy stuff. Not mentally ill pop stars who try to off themselves in a bathtub." She drops her face into her hands.

"I'll admit, it's not my usual job. But I'm here now. And if we leave, your lie will be exposed, so..." Tom shrugs.

Ally flicks her head up and sucks a breath through her teeth. "About that—"

"Don't worry about it. It's done. I see why you did it."

Ally nods and her eyes rest on the unopened bottle on the bedside table. "God, I'd die for one. Were you about to indulge?" She raises an eyebrow.

Indulge is the wrong word. Medicate more like.

Tom reaches behind him on the desk and grabs a glass. He holds it out to Ally.

"Help yourself."

"You aren't having any?" She takes the glass.

Later. Straight from the bottle.

"No." Tom clamps his mouth shut before he says anymore.

Ally puts the glass on the bedside, next to the bottle and stands up. "I should go. I wanted to say thank you. Max is hard work and…" Her voice cracks and she shakes her head.

Tom stands and whisks the chair out of the way. He is about to pull her against him and hug her when he remembers she isn't Isabella. He puts a hand on her shoulder and peers into her face, waiting for her to look up.

"One day at a time, yeah?" He smiles at her.

Where have I heard that before?

Ally nods and squeezes Tom's hand before dropping her eyes to the floor and leaving.

Tom stares at the closed door a moment before throwing himself on the bed and grabbing the bottle of whisky.

17

JAMES

James paces his hotel room, digging his fingers into his hips. *Too far, you dickhead.*

He sees Tom's snarl in his mind's eye. *He knows. He fucking knows.*

The rolling waves of terror intensify in his stomach. He slaps his hand to his gut and sits on the end of the bed.

I'm cooked.

He flops back on the bed and glares at the ceiling. He hates that he's in this position and he hates his Uncle more for putting him there. His heartbeat gets louder and his chest tightens.

Rolling onto his side, he grabs a small plastic bag out of his trouser pocket. He peers at the white powder, bites down on his lip and inhales deeply.

"Fuck it." He sits up and pours the cocaine on the bedside table before haphazardly pushing it into a line. He holds one nostril closed and snorts along the table.

Sitting up he takes a couple of deep breaths and rubs his nose, before standing and shaking his shoulders out.

"This room's too… fucking… quiet."

He whirls around and sweeps an arm across the bedside table, knocking the lamp and alarm clock to the floor. He picks up the clock and hurls it at the TV, smashing the screen. He stops and runs the back of his hand across his wet eyes. Gritting his teeth he lets out a groan and leans forward over his knees.

"How the fuck did I end up here?"

His phone rings from the desk and he stalks across to answer it. Reading the screen and seeing Uncle Pete's name flash up ignites a second wave of fury. It starts in his belly and blazes up his body, intensified by the cocaine. He squeezes the unanswered phone and hurls it at the wall. It falls to the floor, continuing its incessant ringing.

"Fuck off!"

He crouches and digs his hands through his hair and into his scalp. *Why can't they all leave me the fuck alone?*

"I'M NOT ARGUING WITH YOU, JAMES. YOU WILL TAKE UP YOUR OFFICER training placement at Dartmouth and accept the commission that's been arranged for you. I won't have you moping about here, making the place look untidy. Your mother and I are in agreement on this. No negotiations."

James glanced across at his mother, sitting on the too soft sofa, sipping a gin and tonic.

"Mum?"

His mother jumped as though being scared from behind and dragged her gaze to her son. "Sweetheart?"

James neck prickled and he clenched his hands into fists. "Are you even in the room, Mum?"

"Of course, sweetheart." She gave him a drowsy smile. "Now, do as your father says. There's a good lad."

James gritted his teeth and glared at his parents. "No. I won't. I don't want to be a Naval officer and I certainly don't want to have to deal with Uncle Peter any more than necessary. Christmas is bad enough. At least I can get rat arsed and ignore the smug bastard." He folded his arms across his chest and looked out the window at the rolling green manicured gardens.

His father stalked across the room and grabbed him by the throat.

James gasped and fell back against the wall. "What are you—"

"This family has an impeccable reputation. I will not have you tarnishing it with your lax attitude and hooliganism." His father's face was red and sweat dribbled down his temples.

James grabbed his father's hand and ripped it away from his throat. He stood toe to toe with him and glared into his face, curling his lip.

"With all due respect... Father... fuck you."

His father's face turned purple and he grabbed James with both hands by the shirt and threw him to the floor.

James glared at his father. They eyed each other for an age before his father walked to the door. He stopped.

"The papers are on my desk. Sign them." He walked out without a backward glance.

JAMES' PHONE RINGS AGAIN AND HE DROPS ONTO HIS BACKSIDE AND squints at it across the room. *Maybe it's Tom. No... it's been a few hours. He's probably drunk by now.* James huffs at Tom's hypocrisy and crawls across the floor and peers at the now cracked screen. *Uncle Pete. Fuck.*

James sighs and grabs the phone, knowing Peter won't stop calling.

"What?"

"Excuse me?"

"What do you want?" James clunks his head against the wall and stares at the ceiling.

"I want you to follow the orders I gave you."

"I'm trying."

"Try harder."

"Do you know how vicious Martha gets when she's crossed?"

"Leave Martha out of it. This is about Tom and that Russian killer."

"Yeah well, Tom doesn't like being crossed either."

"You know what you are, James? You're a god damn disappointment."

"Yeah. So, you and Dad keep saying." *Whatever.*

"So, take this opportunity to do something worthwhile and stop quitting when things get too hard!"

James holds the phone away from his ear and massages his forehead. "Worthwhile?" His pulse jumps and he sits forward. "How is *this* worthwhile? You're on some witch hunt to nowhere. Tom's too smart to play this stupid game. I mean... fuck. Do you even know him? Do you know the things he's done? *And* gotten away with?"

"I don't care, James. Complete your orders."

James hurls the phone across the room again and lets out a strangled groan. He gets off the floor and pushes a chair over, before kicking the lamp off the desk.

I hate my fucking family.

James paces the room again as anxiety crawls all over his skin. Tom knows he's up to something. Uncle Pete won't stop pressuring him and Max expects him to go out and party behind Tom and Ally's back.

"Can't everyone fuck off." He squeezes his eyes shut as they water and his nose tingles. "I never wanted this bullshit." He slumps onto the bed and grabs one of the pillows. He smooshes his face into it and screams, punching the mattress with his fist.

18

TOM

Tom sits in the middle of a row of seats, looking at the empty stage. Max is gesticulating at his sister down on the floor of the arena. Tom has to admit, when it comes to business, Max is nothing if not professional. The bright white bandage around his wrist catches the blacklight on the edge of the stage, making it more visible than it needs to be.

Someone thuds down into the seat next to him and the row of seats shudders.

"Left without me," James mumbles.

"Because I didn't want to look at your face," Tom grunts.

"Why?"

"Because I may punch it." Tom chews on the inside of his mouth to stop himself saying anything else.

"We should talk abo—"

"I'm not talking about anything with you, outside of this job. Got it?" Tom keeps his eyes straight ahead.

Tom's phone rings and he gladly stands and pulls it out. "Martha." He walks away from James, down the rows of seats.

"Tom. Your friend Viktor has finally confirmed he's working for Kat."

"And?"

"And, he has been cut by her. She's changed her number and thrown him to the wind."

"So, he's useless."

"Essentially. Though, no doubt she'll find him and kill him."

Tom's insides grow cold. He sits on a chair ten rows from James and throws daggers at the back of his head. "Have you tracked her yet?"

"She's in Denmark."

"So, she's following me."

"Appears so." Martha takes a breath. "Tom, you need James to be aware of this threat. You may need him."

"No fucking way."

"Tom—"

"No! He already knows things he shouldn't."

"What things?"

"He knows Isabella is dead. And that she was a Russian assassin."

Martha says nothing.

"Martha?"

"How does he know that?"

"Exactly." Tom kicks the seat in front of him.

"I'll be in touch." She hangs up and Tom taps his phone against his forehead as Max walks towards him. He perches on the seat in front of Tom and looks at him.

Tom stares back and raises an eyebrow. "Can I help you?"

Max grins. "You've helped me enough for a while." He tilts his head. "Won't you join Ally and I for dinner and drinks? As a thank you?"

"Thanks, but no." Tom leans back in the chair and folds his hands behind his head.

"Do you ever have any fun?" Max smirks.

"I have fun," Tom mumbles, not meeting Max's eyes.

"I bet you do."

"What's that supposed to mean?"

"Well… look at you. You are one hot piece of—"

Tom's head snaps up and he glares at Max.

"My point is… it would take you T-minus five seconds to pick up any pretty little thing you like." He grins. "And I bet you do just that."

"Really." Tom neither agrees or disagrees with Max and it makes Max lean forward like an excited little puppy.

"Yeah, new girl every night I'm guessing. Blondes, brunettes, redheads…"

Tom observes Max a moment and leans forward. "Do you think it's worth it?"

"What?"

"Picking up a nameless person every night and taking them home?" Tom surprises himself with the question.

Max's grin fades and he tilts his head to the side. "It's not?"

Tom shrugs and gazes across the stadium. "It's better when they're not nameless."

Max gasps and clutches at his shirt. "Buttercup's in love!" He bounces in the chair. "Aren't you?"

Tom bites his lip and says nothing.

"What happened?"

Tom shrugs, looking back across the arena at nothing. "It's complicated."

"Ha! It always is Buttercup." Max winks. "Maybe you should try to escape too."

"Like you?"

"It helps." Max shrugs, staring at Tom.

"Until the drugs wear off and the alcohol dries up. And then you're … empty."

"Well yeah, that's when it gets unbearable and I hurt myself…" He glances down at his bandaged wrist and wraps an arm around himself. He jerks his face up to Tom who is staring intently at him. "I could have died last night."

"Yep."

"You saved me."

"That's my job." Tom immediately regrets saying this as Max's eyes fall to the floor and he nods gently.

"Yeah… your job."

"I meant—"

"I know what you meant." Max glances up with a half-smile on his face, "Everyone around me has a job. No one's here because they want to be." He grimaces. "Even me."

"So why do you do it?"

Max gazes at Tom a moment. "Because who am I otherwise?"

"Do you need to be someone?"

"Everyone needs to be someone, Buttercup."

"How about trying to be yourself?"

"Because I don't even know who that is anymore." Max looks at Tom. "Do any of us really know who we are?" He winks. "I bet you had it all growing up. Mum, Dad, puppy. Picket fence." Max's eyes fix on Tom's face.

"Bet you're wrong."

Max raises an eyebrow. "You had no one to care about you?"

"I had my Mum… but she died when I was eleven." Tom scratches a hand across his chin.

"And then what?"

"And then…" Tom shrugs. "I was looked after. Eventually." Tom leans forward in his chair and stares out at the stage, making it clear he is done talking.

TOM FOLLOWED THE WOMAN FROM FAMILY SERVICES OUT OF THE HOUSE. *Her name was Carol, apparently.*

His foster father punched a hole in the wall as the front door closed. Tom knew he had, because he'd done it before, and it sounded the same. He flinched as the plaster cracked.

"Fuck!" His foster father roared.

Tom's gut clenched and he rubbed a hand over his chest, trying to make his heart stop flipping.

"He wants the payments for having me," Tom mumbled, shuffling behind Carol.

Carol put her hand on his shoulder once they reached the front gate and bent down to look at his face.

"I'm sorry Thomas. This should never have happened."

Tom looked at the ground, "Yeah."

"Why didn't you say anything?"

He lifted his head, flicking his hair out of his eyes. "What am I meant to say?" he mumbled. "He hit me. I'm thirteen. No one cares what I have to say."

Carol put an arm around his shoulder and walked him into the street. Tom turned towards her car, but she pulled in the other direction.

"This way." She strode ahead, to the other end of the street. She opened the front gate of the house with the shrubs Tom liked to hide inside.

Tom scurried along beside her. "Why are we here?"

She knocked on the door and turned to Tom, she brushed his shirt down and lifted his chin up. "Don't slouch, big smile."

"But I don't—"

The door opened and Martha stood in the doorframe.

"Ah," she smiled, and her eyes crinkled. "You're here. I was beginning to worry." She stepped back and gestured them inside.

Tom walked past her, peering into her face.

"You already know each other I believe, but Thomas," Carol turned and bent forward again. "You will be living here with Martha for now."

For now?

"Here?" his voice squeaked, and he cleared his throat. "But..."

"Would you rather live with a stranger?" Carol raised an eyebrow. "I think you've been through enough in the last little while. And Martha here has very generously offered to have you in her home." Carol's eyebrows dipped into a frown as Tom continued to stare at her. "You should be grateful."

"Now, now," Martha stepped forward and put her hand on Tom's shoulder, even though he was already a few inches taller than her. "Give him a moment, it's probably a bit of a surprise." She swept a hand toward the sofa. "Sit down, Tom. Have some cake."

Carol turned as she tightened her scarf around her neck, "Now Thomas, if this doesn't work out, I'll have to find somewhere else for you." She pursed her lips together. "Keep that in mind." She nodded at Martha and walked down the front path.

Tom watched her through the window, as Martha walked over and stood beside him.

"I'm sorry," Tom whispered.

"What for?"

"Bothering you." Tom walked back to the sofa and sat, clawing his fingers into his knees.

"Bothering me?" Martha sat beside him. "Whatever are you talking about?"

"Did Carol make you take me?"

Martha smiled at Tom and the warmth in her face released the tension Tom was holding in his shoulders. He sank a little lower into the sofa cushion.

"Make me? I offered."

"Why?"

"Because you need me."

Tom stands and shakes his shoulders out as Max is summoned to the front of the arena by an overweight man wearing headphones.

"Thanks for the chat, Buttercup." Max grins before bounding down to in front of the stage.

Tom watches him stick a set of headphones over his spiked hair and sway his head about. Last night is a distant memory to him.

"Tom?" Tom turns and finds Ally standing behind him. She smiles. "Are you busy?"

"I was about to do a perimeter walk if you feel like a stroll."

Ally looks across at James, as he prods at his phone screen. "And James?"

"Far too busy playing Words with Friends, though I doubt he can spell." Tom gestures ahead and Ally walks out into the aisle. As they pass James, Tom kicks his feet off the chair he has them propped on.

"What—?" He glares at Tom.

"I'll be back."

"Whatever," James mumbles looking back at his phone again.

Tom bites his tongue and continues past James. He and Ally leave through a side door and out into the sunshine. Tom squints and puts sunglasses on.

"So, um… thanks for listening to me last night." Ally looks at Tom as they walk down the front step towards the manmade lake, out the front of the Royal Arena.

Tom shrugs. "Must be hard dealing with him all the time."

"Can be."

"You said last night that your mother didn't know how to comfort Max."

Ally sighs and smiles into the distance. "That's one way to put it. She was pretty self-centred."

"Was?"

"She's in a care home. Early on-set dementia. She doesn't even know who we are."

Tom lets out a low whistle. "That must be difficult."

"Is what it is." Ally presses her lips into a straight line and stares ahead. "She has the most famous son in the world and has no idea." Ally huffs out a half chuckle.

They walk around the outside of the arena in silence a few moments before Ally stops and looks up at Tom. "Did Max ask you to have dinner with us?"

"He did. Though, it's probably not the best idea."

"Why not?"

"Well, I have terrible table manners. Not to mention, I'm afraid Max will want to play footsies." Tom grins and Ally laughs.

"What if I tell him to be on his best behaviour?"

Tom stops walking and tilts his head, looking at Ally.

"Let us show you that we're grateful?"

Tom rolls his eyes and starts walking again. "Okay fine. But I don't do McDonalds."

"Right, new reservations then."

Tom laughs as his phone rings in his pocket. He plucks it out, still chuckling as he answers. "Grant."

"Ahh Tom! You sound so happy."

His throat squeezes and the chuckles stop. "What the fuck do you want?"

Kat's trademark cackle softly trickles down the phone line. "Is that any way to greet a lady? I do like your sunglasses."

"No, it's not. But you're no lady." Tom spins in a circle, taking in his surroundings. *Where the fuck are you?*

"The blonde is cute. I must admit I did not expect you to replace Irina so quickly."

Tom's eyes rest on Ally and she raises her chin, quirking a brow in question. He wraps his fingers around Ally's bicep and steers her back towards the arena.

"What—"

"Walk," Tom hisses.

"Oh Tom, what are you afraid of?" Kat whispers.

They get to the door and he pushes Ally ahead. "Get inside and stay there."

"What's going on?" Ally stands with both hands outstretched as Tom pulls the door shut and turns back around. He scans the fore-court area. *Nothing.*

"Show yourself Kat, get whatever this is, over with."

"Why? When we are having much fun."

"You killed Isabella. What more do you want from me?" He hisses, squeezing the phone against his ear.

"It did not fill me with the joy and elation I expected."

"You're a sick twist, Kat." Tom ends the call and looks around the forecourt one more time before shoving his phone in his pocket and storming into the arena. Ally is standing at the doors and goes to speak. Tom brushes past her. "Give me a sec."

Tom spies James sitting exactly where he left him.

I can't believe I'm doing this.

He stands in front of James, who looks up, flicking his hair out of his face.

"I need your help." Tom swallows back the acid in his throat.

"My help?" James raises his eyebrows.

"Unfortunately."

19

JAMES

J ames grins at Tom and sweeps a hand at the seat next to him. Tom curls his lip and runs his tongue across his teeth.

"What can I do for you, chap?" James throws an arm across the empty chair next to him. *This is killing him.*

Tom closes his eyes a moment. "The Russian…"

James' heart stops for a millisecond before kicking back into gear. *It can't be this easy. Surely.* He leans forward. "Go on."

"She's here."

What? "What?" James looks around the stadium.

"No not here, you moron." Tom swats James across the back of the head. "In Denmark."

James runs a hand across where Tom swatted him. "Why?"

"She's playing cat and mouse."

"With you?"

"Yep."

"Okay, Tom. You're gonna have to give me more than that. What the actual fuck is going on?" James leans on his knees and rests his chin in his hands.

Music blasts from the front of the arena and both James and Tom's heads snap up. Max is in the centre of the stage with one hand on the microphone, the other shot straight up in the air. He sways his head from side to side and sings into the microphone. His voice echoes around the empty arena.

The back of James' shirt lifts and Tom drags him out of the seat. He points to the emergency doors. "Outside!" he shouts over the music.

They emerge into the ticket area where Ally is helping to set up one of the myriads of merchandise tables. She turns her head and watches them as they walk outside.

"You're telling me that we have another threat besides Supreme Order?"

"Shit." Tom runs a hand through his hair and bites his lip, wincing at James.

"What?" James holds both hands out and widens his eyes at Tom.

"Supreme Order isn't a threat. It was faked." Tom blows air out of his mouth. "I got caught up with Max almost offing himself and forgot to fill you in…" Tom raises an eyebrow.

"Forgot? Or didn't think I warranted the effort?" James drills his eyes into Tom's face and waits. The phone call the previous night from Uncle Pete resonates, and he clenches his jaw. *I'm not worthless.*

Tom nods. "That's fair."

"Generous, I'd say. But…" James flips his wrist. "Do go on." James has the upper hand, and he doesn't intend to lose it.

Tom looks into James face and sighs. He pulls his phone out and flicks the screen a couple of times. He holds the phone up and James sees the face of a thirty something woman with a blonde pixie cut and startling blue eyes.

"Katerina Ivanov." Tom says. "Crazy Russian assassin with a penchant for sending roses to her favourites."

"Favourites?"

"Those she intends to kill," Tom purses his lips. "My mistake."

James eyes widen further until he's sure he resembles a cartoon character. "She wants to kill *you?*"

Tom nods

"But why?"

Tom sits down on a bench seat and James stands in front of him, crossing his arms over his chest. He's enjoying suddenly being more in control than Tom.

"Because I killed her sister."

"You killed her…" James shakes his head. *None of this was in your briefing Uncle Pete.* James bites his tongue. "Go on." James sits next to Tom on the bench.

Tom squints and leans towards James, piercing his face with his stare. "Can I trust you, James?"

James swallows. "Yeah, 'course. I wouldn't be here otherwise. Would I?"

"You're a useless git."

"Correct."

"But Martha seems to think you're worth the effort."

James laughs. "No, she doesn't. She's under direct orders and we both know it."

This elicits a wry grin from Tom, and he ducks his head forward, running both hands through his hair before standing up. He stares out at the manmade lake and forecourt for a few moments before turning back to James.

"Kat's *assassin* sister, Natasha, killed my fiancé. So, I killed Natasha. Six months ago, in Paris, Kat killed my charge. Isabella Wirth." Tom stops and clears his throat. "And now she wants to tie up loose ends."

"You're next." James states, standing next to Tom.

"Seems that way."

"And this Kat bird is in Denmark?"

"I believe so."

James studies Tom's profile. "That must have been shit."

"Which part?" Tom continues to stare straight ahead.

"Both? Losing your fiancé and watching your charge be killed. And not being able to stop either of them from happening."

Tom pushes his hand into his chest, and he grasps his shirt. "I've had better days." He shrugs. "Anyway, watch your back. Kat's nasty."

"Right." James watches Tom as he walks back inside.

Once the door shuts, James pulls his phone out and walks down the forecourt. "C'mon, pickup…"

"What have you got?"

"You really need to work on your phone manner."

"I haven't got time for your bullshit, James. What is it?"

"Some Russian bird is stalking Tom."

Uncle Pete says nothing, and James cranes his neck forward and pushes the phone harder against his ear.

"Hello?"

"Yes. How do you know this? And is it her?"

"No, it's not her. To be honest I'm fairly sure she's dead. Tom hasn't balked on that."

"So, who is it?"

"He says her name is Kat Ivan-something"

"Ivan-something? That's what you're giving me? Ivan-some-thing?" Uncle Pete's voice climbs with every word he says.

"She's not the one you're interested in, so why do you care?" James scoffs.

"Sub-Lieutenant Moore. You show some respect."

"Sub-Lieutenant Moore? I'm your nephew—who, by the way, has been discharged. How about showing *me* some respect first?"

"I don't know who you think—"

"I know exactly who I am. And frankly, this bullshit task you've given me is stressing me out. Maybe I'll take the five years inside instead?" He hisses into the phone.

James hears his Uncle draw in a breath before sighing it out down the phone line. "Find out what you can about Miss Ivan-something. And keep pressing on Isabella Wirth. Something doesn't add up."

James rolls his eyes. "She's fucking dead." *I'm done with this.*

"Apparently." Uncle Pete ends the call.

Fuck!

20

MAX

Max replaces the microphone into the stand and stretches his arms above his head. Yawning, he peers down at Ally.

"I'm done. I want to go take a nap." He sits on the edge of the stage before climbing down to the floor level. He stands next to Ally who is gazing at Tom as he speaks into his phone.

"Hands off, I saw him first," Max whispers in her ear.

"Ha, ha. I'm not perving. Not that you've got a hope in hell."

"I know. But it's fun watching him squirm." Max winks.

"Maybe you should give him a break. He's helping you out and he really doesn't need to."

"What do you mean by that?"

"Well, a threat by some PR maven to release pictures of you with a bloke isn't exactly his charter. He deals with terrorists and spies and stuff like that."

"What about those Supreme people?" Max arches an eyebrow and sips from a bottle of water. He grimaces. "Ack, boring." He glares at the bottle in his hand.

Ally stares at Max a moment, chewing on her lip. "Well, yeah them too."

Max peers at his sister. "What's going on?"

Ally sighs and stares at the lighting fixtures above their heads. "Supreme Order isn't a problem anymore," she mumbles.

Max rests his weight on one foot and juts his hip out. "What?"

"Max I—"

Tom appears behind them. "Time to go?"

"What's the deal with Supreme Order?" Max stares at Tom.

Tom looks at Ally and then back to Max. "Ahh...you haven't...?" He rubs the back of his neck and exhales.

"Haven't what?"

Tom sucks a breath through gritted teeth and walks backwards a couple of steps. "I might leave you both for a moment."

Max wags his finger at Tom. "No, no. What are you two cooking up?"

Tom's phone rings and he grabs it. "Grant..." Tom walks away up the aisle and Max spins to stand directly in front of his sister.

"Out with it." He folds his arms.

Ally nods and holds both hands out, patting them downwards in a calm down motion. "Okay, Max. Listen...." She takes another breath and fixes her eyes on Max's. "Supreme Order never sent any threats."

Max tilts his head and peers at Ally. "What?"

"It was me."

"You?" Max steps into Ally. "You?" he repeats in a low voice.

"I was scared. Okay? I was worried about you and I—"

"You faked threats from some international supremacist group?" Max's voice grows louder with each word he spits at her. "Are you fucking mental? Why would you do that?" His heart leaps against his ribcage and heat rises up his back and shoulders, into his face.

"Because you need help. And you won't get it. I thought if you were forced to cancel your—"

Max spins and walks away from Ally. His breaths may as well be on fire. He stalks towards Tom who raises his brows and finishes his call.

"Max! Wait!" Ally screams up the aisle.

Max stands in front of Tom and crosses his arms. "I'd like to leave now." He tosses his head back. "Without *her.*"

Tom's gaze slides over Max's shoulder before his eyes dart back to Max. "Max, don't overreact she was only trying to—"

"Are we leaving?" Max leans into Tom's face.

Tom purses his lips a moment before jerking his head back and walking towards the exit. Max follows him, feeling Ally's eyes stuck on his back. He knows she's crying and distraught.

I don't give a fuck.

IN THE CAR TOM SLIDES INTO THE BACK SEAT NEXT TO MAX.

"She was only trying to help," Tom says quietly.

Max whips his head around and glares at Tom. "Don't try to

defend her. She lied to me. And got a government agency involved. What the fuck was she thinking?"

"I don't think she expected us to get involved. And furthermore, she's trying to protect you."

"From what?" Max throws his hands up and grabs a bottle of vodka from the small ice bucket between them. He rips the lid off and gulps.

"Yourself."

"Myse… I don't need protecting from myself."

Tom grabs Max's arm above the bandage and holds it up. "You wanna rethink that?"

Max yanks his arm away from Tom and stares out the window.

"You're unhappy and spiralling down a rabbit hole of pain."

"How would you know?" Max grumbles, gulping from the bottle again.

Tom's hand grabs hold of Max's jaw and turns his face.

"Takes one to know one." Tom's eyes are hard and Max swallows.

Tom lets go and leans back in the seat, folding his arms.

"You have no idea," Max mumbles.

Tom snorts.

The car ride falls silent. Max refuses to look at Tom. He doesn't want to admit he has a problem. *I know I have a problem.* The fact Tom can see right through him makes his insides squirm.

Max blows out a breath and turns to Tom who is staring out the window.

"Sorry." Max presses his lips together. *God, I hate apologising.*

Tom lifts his head off the headrest and turns to Max. "For?"

"Being a dickhead."

Tom smiles. "Which time?"

Max grins. "You've been counting?"

"I keep a tab."

Max chuckles. "That's fair. I can be a right pain in the arse."

"So, what about Ally?"

"What about her?" Max grabs the vodka again and Tom yanks it from him.

"Give it!"

"What about Ally?" Tom repeats.

Max notices the grip Tom has on the bottle, his knuckle turning white. "Do you always grip things that tight? I might keep trying to seduce you after all." Max smirks.

Tom looks down at the bottle and huffs. He holds it out to Max. "Make the whole situation ten times worse. Doesn't bother me."

Max opens the bottle and leans towards Tom. "It does though. Doesn't it?"

Tom looks at Max and says nothing.

Max takes a swig and wipes the back of his hand across his mouth. "You want to drink this as much as I do right now. Don't you?"

"Why would you think that?" Tom adjusts himself in the seat, turning his body towards the door.

"The way you gripped the bottle. To make sure you didn't take a gulp of it yourself." Max jerks forward as the car comes to a stop at the back entrance to the hotel.

Tom takes his seatbelt off and gets out without looking at Max.

Max grins to himself. *I knew he had skeletons.*

Max climbs out and the screams from the girls behind the chain link fence fill his ears. He pulls his jacket sleeve down over his wrist and taps Tom on the shoulder. "I should go say hi. Can you hang for a minute?"

Max raises a brow and Tom grunts, standing against the car with his arms crossed over his chest.

21

JAMES

The car James and Ally are in pulls up behind the one Tom is leaning against. James peers at Tom and can see his face is less than amused. *Here we go.*

Climbing out of the car, James stands next to Tom. "What's going on? Ally said about three words in the car. She's pretty upset." James watches as Ally walks straight into the hotel without talking to anyone.

"Yeah, Max is being his usual bastard self." Tom pushes himself off the car with one foot. "Stay with him." Tom juts his chin at Max and paces away.

James sighs and walks towards Max. Standing a few feet away, he watches as Max signs pictures of himself and poses for selfies. James scans the crowd.

There are around fifty girls clawing at the fence. Some of them are crying and others fan themselves with their hands, shrieking.

Pathetic.

Max blows a few kisses towards the girls before whirling around and sauntering towards James. James keeps his eyes fixed on the crowd and for a split second thinks he sees a platinum blonde pixie cut and bright blue eyes. The pulse in his neck throbs and he darts forward towards the fence.

Max laughs. "Oh darling. I don't think they're here for you."

James ignores him, scanning the crowd but coming up empty. *I swear I saw…*

A hand curls around James' bicep. "I'm going out tonight and you're coming with me." Max's voice rasps in his ear. James is still watching the girls. They become more frantic and louder as Max retreats.

"Did you hear me?" Max barks.

"Yeah…" James gives the girls another scan before turning to Max. "I heard you. I don't think it's a good—"

Max sticks an index finger over James' mouth. "Shhhh… you're all in. Remember?" He nods at the door. "Let's get away from the ferals."

Max pulls James inside.

James yanks his arm out of Max's grip. "I need to speak to Tom."

Max rolls his eyes. "Fine. I'll be in my room. Getting pretty." He winks at James and strides to the lift.

James waits for the lift to close and shakes out the weight on his shoulders. He pulls his phone out and dials Tom.

"What?"

"You know, a nice *hello James* wouldn't go astray."

"What do you want?" Tom's voice is directly behind James and he turns to see Tom standing there with his phone to his ear.

"Ah," James ends the call and smiles. Tom doesn't smile back. "Your friend was outside a moment ago."

Tom rolls his eyes. "Which friend would that be?"

"The hot Russian. Kat Ivan-something."

Tom's stare turns icy. He reaches across and grabs James by the shirt front. "Don't play fucking games with me, James."

"I'm not! I saw her." James rubs the back of his neck as Tom loosens his grip. "She was amongst the girls screaming at Max. But, as soon as I saw her, she disappeared."

Tom breathes out, staring at James. "Where's Max?"

"Upstairs… he thinks he's going out tonight."

Tom marches to the lift and hammers the button. "No way in hell," Tom mutters as James stands next to him.

"Well, good luck trying to stop him."

"He'll do as he's fucking told. For once."

The lift arrives and Tom stomps in as James trails behind.

James' phone vibrates in his pocket and the doors close. He pulls it out and sees that it's his Uncle. *Not a good time.* He slips the phone back into his pocket and folds his arms across his chest.

Tom glances sideways at him and raises an eyebrow.

"Old girlfriend," James shrugs. "Won't leave me alone."

"You're a crap liar, you know." Tom says as the lift arrives, and he walks out.

James blows a breath out and follows him into the lounge of Max's suite. Tom calls to the upstairs room. "Get down here, Max."

Max peers at them from the top of the stairs before creeping down. "Gumnut. Buttercup. Are we all going out together?" His eyes are glassy, and he giggles.

James catches Max as he hurls himself at him and wraps an arm around his shoulder. "My playmate," he whispers in James' ear.

"Max, what have you taken?" James squints into Max's eyes.

"The whole supply by the looks," Tom grumbles. "Max, you aren't going anywhere." Tom steers him back up the stairs and points at the bed. "Get in."

Max flops onto the bed and presses his hand to his chest. "You don't know how long I've waited to have you order me to bed, Buttercup." He winks.

Tom rolls his eyes. James' phone rings again and he huffs out a sigh.

Tom peers at James. "Maybe you could tell your ex you're busy?"

James looks at the screen, seeing Uncle Pete's number he pushes the phone screen against his chest. "Yeah, she's persistent. Sorry." He backs out of the room as Tom watches his every move.

James closes the door behind him and answers the phone. "Can you wait until I call you, maybe?"

"Say the name Alexei Petrov in front of Tom."

"What?"

"You heard me."

"Why?"

"Do it. And then call me back." The phone call ends and James stares at the screen. *What on earth?*

Max's door opens and Tom slams it shut behind him. "He's a royal pain in the neck," Tom mutters.

"Um…" James watches Tom.

Tom stares back at him and holds both hands out, palms to the ceiling. "What?"

"Alexei... Petrov." James winces.

Tom steps towards James, his left eye twitching. "What did you say?"

"Alexei Petrov." James straightens his shoulders and stares back at Tom.

The muscles in Tom's jaw tighten. He walks into James, making him stumble back into the wall. Tom slams both palms on the wall either side of James' head and glares at him.

A well opens in the pit of James gut as he stares back, having no clue what to say next. "Ah, I take it you know him. Or is it her? Um, I don't know…"

Tom reaches into James' pocket and pulls out his phone. He holds it in front of James' face. "Unlock it." His voice is low and dangerous.

James swallows. "Why?"

"Because if you don't, I'll shoot your kneecaps out."

"But—"

"Unlock it!" Tom punches the phone into James' chest.

James' heart throws itself against his ribs and sweat trickles down the centre of his back. "Jesus Christ," he mumbles. He fumbles with the phone and presses the first two numbers to unlock it. He stops and looks at Tom whose glare hasn't shifted. "Maybe I can tell you wha—"

"Unlock the fucking phone."

James stares down at his phone with the two numbers of the four punched in. A wave of defiance swells from his gut and he flicks his eyes back to Tom's. "You first. Who's Alexei Petrov?" The moment he asks the question, he holds his breath.

Tom purses his mouth and slams his palm into the wall. James jumps, and hopes Tom didn't notice. Tom pushes the lift button and grabs James' shirt as the doors open. He throws James into the lift.

James stumbles, bumping the back wall with his face. "Fuck."

"Why are you asking?" Tom advances on James and pins him against the wall with his glare.

Anger bubbles in the pit of James' gut and he pushes Tom with both hands to the chest. Tom stumbles a little before flooring James with a right hook to the jaw. James lays on the floor of the lift and massages his cheek as pain laps at his face. Tom leans over yanks James up with both hands and slams him against the wall so air huffs out of his lungs. He stares into his face and James feels the red-hot anger radiating off him.

The fuck?

James holds both hands up as Tom seethes in his face. "Okay, Tom. Stop." James pants and attempts to regain control of himself. "Back the fuck up." He gives Tom a shove and steps away from the wall.

"I don't want to hear that name come out of your mouth. Ever again. Are we clear?" Tom still has hold of the front of James' shirt.

James glances down at Tom's fist and slowly creeps his eyes back to Tom's face.

Tom twists his fist, tightening James' collar around his throat. "I said—"

"Clear!" James grabs hold of Tom's wrist and rips his hand off him. "Fucking clear!"

Tom and James both breathe heavy breaths and ignore each other as the doors open into the lobby.

James stalks out of the front doors and throws himself into a waiting cab outside. *No more.* "Downtown, *behage*." The cab pulls away from the hotel and James leans back into the seat.

He punches the call button for his Uncle and waits.

"So?" Uncle Pete waits.

"He damn near beat the shit out of me. You mind telling me what the fuck that was all about?"

"Excellent."

"Excellent? Are you serious? Who the *fuck* is Alexei Petrov and why the *fuck* did I nearly get my front teeth knocked out?"

"I'll be in touch."

The line goes dead and James kicks the back of the seat in front of him. "Fuck!"

The cab swerves to the side of the road and the driver turns in his seat. "Out. Out." He flicks his hand at the door.

"Yeah, yeah," James grumbles, sliding over to the door and jumping out. *Can't blame him.*

The cab peels away from the curb and James kicks at the gravel in the gutter. He looks around, spots a couple of bars and stumbles across the road.

He flops onto a bar stool and slides his fingers through his hair while he rests his elbows on the bar top. "Beer, *behage*." James says to the barman and glances around the half empty bar. The drink is put in front of him and he nods in thanks. He climbs off the stool and chooses a table in the back corner where it's dark.

He sits and pulls his phone out of his pocket. He taps it on the table.

"Is this seat taken?" A female voice with a Russian accent purrs.

James looks up and sees the face Tom showed him on his phone earlier that day. His heart jerks and he puts his beer down before he drops it.

Kat sits without being invited and folds her hands on the table. "You seem lonely."

You're a killer. You're dangerous. You're fucking beautiful.

"Not lonely. Fed up." James grimaces. "What are you drinking?"

"Water." Kat leans forward, her cleavage on full display. "What has Tom told you about me?" Her eyes send ice through his veins.

"Tom? You? No... nothing." James shrugs and sips his beer. "Should he?" James' voice is higher than it should be, and he takes another sip to soothe his throat.

Kat smiles and runs her finger along her lips and chin. "Have you been in scrape?"

"Tom," James grunts, rubbing a hand along his jaw.

"Ah, hot headed as always." Kat runs her hands across the table and over James'.

James stares at Kat's hand and slides his from underneath it. "Aren't you an insane killer?" James jerks his head up and fixes his eyes on hers.

"Did Tom tell you this?"

"You killed Isabella Wirth." James holds his breath. "Right?"

Kat's eyes shift and she sits back in her chair. "Irina Petrov you mean."

Petrov?

James' heart starts its double time thumping and he scratches a hand across his chest. "Who is Irina Petrov?"

Kat smiles. "Ah, Tom has kept many secrets." She pushes her index finger into her cheek and studies James a moment. "Irina is Isabella." She leans forward again, her nose practically touching James'. He swallows, hoping to fix his dry throat. "Isabella is trashy European name she gave herself when she ran away from Motherland."

"I see," James' voice is husky. *Except I don't see.* "And you killed her?"

Kat sits tall and smiles again. She holds her fingers out like a gun and points it. "Straight through heart." She pokes her finger hard into James chest, and her touch sends a shudder through him. "I never miss."

He grabs her hand and holds it against him, staring her in the face. "So, she's dead." James holds her stare.

"Burning in hell, I'm assuming." Kat whispers, leaning forward so her lips are within a breath of his. "She killed so many."

James closes his eyes a moment and tries to remember what Tom said about Kat being a crazy Russian assassin. The sweet perfume on her neck and her breath brushing his face do nothing for logical thought.

"We leave?" she whispers, her lips against his.

James nods, standing and leaving his half full beer behind.

22

TOM

Tom paces towards his room. He sees Ally sitting on the floor of the hall, next to his door. *Shit.* He stops and observes her a moment.

She wipes tears off her face with both hands. "Hi." She stays on the floor.

God, I'm thirsty. Tom sits on the floor next to her. "Hi." He drops his head against the wall.

Ally sniffles. "I should have told him straight away."

Tom stretches his legs out in front of him and rolls his head towards Ally. "Would it have made a difference?"

"Doubt it."

"So why beat yourself up? It's done."

"I've made everything ten times worse now. He'll give me the silent treatment for days over this."

"Really?" Tom raises both eyebrows and grins. "How do I get him to do that for me?"

Ally laughs. "Ha, good luck." She smiles at Tom. "You're probably the only one he *will* keep talking to. Oh, and James. James seems to facilitate his bad behaviour."

Tom grunts. "James doesn't know how else to behave. That's his problem." Tom hauls himself off the floor and offers to help Ally get up. She takes his hand and stands.

He opens his door and moves back to let Ally inside first. Ally turns and smiles as she stands at the foot of the bed. "No more roses?"

"I prefer hard liquor."

"Hear, hear." Ally nods.

Ally's eyes roam around the room. He doesn't want her there but at the same time, he does. *Jesus.*

Her phone chimes and she grabs it, peering at the screen. "Oh, my god," she gasps.

Tom peeks over her shoulder. One of the pictures of Max with his friend in a compromising position is splashed across the phone screen from a British tabloid website, *The Daily Roundup.*

"Well, fuck." Tom bites down on his tongue. "Let's add that to the mix."

"I thought you said you blocked her?" Ally squeals. She fans her face with her free hand.

"I had her arrested. And blacked out." Tom grabs the phone and peers at the website. "She sold this prior. It's the only explanation." *Always have insurance.*

Ally whirls around and sits on the edge of the bed. She leans over her knees and gasps in large breaths. Tom grabs a bottle of water and cracks it open. He kneels beside her. "You and Max are far more alike than you care to admit." He grins grabbing her hand and pushing the water bottle into it. "Drink."

She lifts a trembling hand and sips from the bottle, her eyes remain on Tom. "If Max sees that, he will literally jump off the roof of this building."

"So, we make sure he doesn't see it."

"The fans have already seen it." She points to the comment section. "There are over three thousand comments!" She pants and puts the water bottle on the bedside table. "He's *going* to find out."

Tom pulls his phone out and calls James' number. It isn't answered and Tom huffs out a frustrated sigh and pushes the call button again. The call isn't answered again, and Tom lets out a grunt.

"*Fuck's sake,*" he whispers.

23

MAX

Max lies on his bed as the ceiling contorts and spins above his head. He holds a hand out in front of him and his fingers leave trails as he waves them back and forth. *Pretty.*

His phone pings on the table across the room and he does his best to ignore it. *No social media while under the influence!* He rolls over and shoves his head under the pillow. *Wait, I'm going out tonight. Aren't I?*

He sits up and glances around the room and down at himself. He's in track pants and nothing else. He thinks back and remembers Tom and James putting him to bed. *Was that today?* Max always goes out the night before his first show in any city. Tonight, would be no different. He edges to the side of the bed and swings his legs over to the floor. Standing, he sways a little before righting himself.

He hears the lift arrive at the Penthouse and wanders downstairs to the lounge. He sees Tom walk into the room and pushes both hands into his chest and bats his eyelashes.

"Hey, Buttercup." Tom opens his mouth. "Wait!" Max holds a finger in the air. "I'll answer for you. Oh, hey babycakes. I thought I'd come up and check on you." Max slurs, giggling as he falls down on the sofa, he stands next to. "And give you a back rub. It's been quite a tense day." He winks as Tom watches him with a grimace on his face. "Oh, relax Buttercup. I know." He sees movement behind Tom and Ally peers at him. "Oh. You brought that." He flicks his bandaged wrist towards his sister.

Ally sighs and walks over to Max. "Where's your phone?"

Max looks past Ally to Tom. "Can you tell this… person that I'm not speaking to her?" He raises an eyebrow.

Tom folds his arms over his chest. "Where's your phone Max?"

"Why? Are you gonna send me a dick pic?" He dissolves into giggles on the sofa. Tom closes his eyes and purses his lips.

"Call it," Tom looks at Ally as she pulls her phone out.

"Hey! What's the big deal? It's upstairs," Max flicks his head towards the bedroom and Tom marches up the stairs. Max jumps off the sofa, and after a second of gripping the edge of it as it wobbles and undulates, he blinks and follows Tom. Max turns as Ally arrives behind him and slams the door in her face.

Tom spins around. "Was that really necessary?" He squints at Max.

"Yes. I'm angry and don't want her anywhere near me." Max sweeps across the room and stands in front of Tom. "You, on the other hand." He raises a hand with every intention of dragging it down the front of Tom's shirt. *There are muscles under there.*

Tom catches his hand and squeezes his wrist. "I wouldn't."

Max rolls his eyes and snatches his hand out of Tom's. "Fine," he huffs. "My phone's over there." He nods towards the table, but the phone isn't there. He frowns and pushes past Tom. "But I left it there. It was making noises." He looks up at Tom.

"Unfortunate."

"But. Do you have it?" Max raises an eyebrow. "Do I have to... search you?" He runs his tongue along his top lip.

Tom leans forward so he's looking directly into Max's eyes. Max's stomach flip flops. "I dare you to try." Tom stands up straight. "Now, shouldn't you be in bed?"

"I'm going out, Buttercup. Remember?"

"You're going to bed. Remember?" Tom points at the bed. "And maybe when you wake up, you'll stop being such a bastard to your sister."

Max climbs into bed and scoffs. "Doubt it." He flips onto his pillows and crosses his arms pouting.

"Sweet dreams, princess." Tom walks down the stairs.

Max drops his head to the side and watches Tom leave.

God, I'll regret all of that tomorrow.

24

TOM

Tom stalks down the stairs and shoves Max's phone into Ally's hands.

"Let's go," he mutters.

Ally follows him into the lift and Tom pretends not to watch as her face cracks and she purses her lips, trying to hold it all in. A pang of softness towards her hits him in the gut and he immediately pushes it away. *When did I get so pathetic?* He leans on the wall with his shoulder.

Ally thumbs the phone screen, reading the messages and social media comments, scrolling at warp speed. Tom steps forward as the lift opens on their floor and guides her into the hall. He pulls the phone out of her hands and holds it against his chest.

"Don't read this shit. What's done is done. We can deal with it tomorrow when Max is sober and alert." Ally rolls her eyes and Tom laughs. "Yeah, I didn't realise how hopeful that sounded until I said it."

Ally shakes her head and glances around the hall. "The minute he switches the TV on tomorrow morning, all hell is going to break loose." She gestures to the phone Tom still holds against his chest. "Taking that off him is a tiny Band-Aid."

"Agreed. But it stops him doing something idiotic while under the influence."

Ally's chest starts to heave, and she flaps her hands at her face again, "Oh God, he's supposed to play to a sold out arena tomorrow night. What's going to happen? Tom?"

Tom steps forward and puts both hands on her shoulders, leaning down to make her look at him. "Go and get some sleep. And we deal with it in the morning." Tom jerks his head towards her room door and smiles.

Ally sags her shoulders forward and nods. "Okay."

Tom holds up Max's phone. "I'll keep this. I have no desire to read it." He raises an eyebrow. "God knows what I'd come across."

Ally pats Tom's arm. "You're a good egg, Tom Grant." She smiles and shuffles towards her room.

Tom waits until she disappears into her room before stumbling into his own. He throws himself onto the bed and scrubs both hands over his face. "I should have dumped this job when I had the chance," he mumbles into his hands.

He sits up and glances at the bottle next to the bed. As he leans across to grab it, his phone rings. He drops his head and squeezes his eyes shut a moment before picking it up. He sees James' name and grunts.

"Where the hell are you?" he barks into the phone.

"Uh, I'm… jus…"

Tom stands up. "James?"

Tom hears a breath being sucked in and incoherent mumbling.

"James? Where are— "

"Hello Tom," Kat's voice slithers down the phone line. "It's always so nice to hear your sexy voice."

Tom's gut drops through the floor and his throat closes up. "What have you done?" His voice comes out raspy and he clears his throat.

James, you fucking idiot.

"Nothing. James was sleepy. So, I gave him place to rest."

Tom's heart jerks as his pulse breaks clear out of his neck. "Where are you?" He asks the question knowing she won't tell him.

Kat laughs.

"It's me you want. Tell me where you are, and I'll come to you." Tom grits his teeth and hopes his voice sounds steady and menacing. *Doubt it.* He grips the phone, pressing it harder into his ear. "Well?"

"I would simply love to see you again, Tom. It has been far too long."

"Where?"

"Well, first I must deal with James. He followed me with such high hopes. I do not wish to disappoint him."

Tom closes his eyes and images from Paris, of Jack, his almost father-in-law with a choke collar around his neck, flash past. "Kat let the stupid git go. He's a fool, but he doesn't deserve your treatment."

"But it will upset you, Tom. And let me be honest… I love seeing you at your angriest. It makes me giddy." She hangs up and Tom hurls the phone at the wall.

"Fuck!"

Tom plants his hands on his hips and stares at the phone, the battery dislodged and on the other side of the room. He puts it back together and calls Martha.

"Tom."

"I need you to trace James' phone."

"Why?"

Tom sighs and scratches his head. "Because Kat has him."

Silence.

"Martha?"

"And how… pray tell… did this happen?"

"Because he's a moron who thinks with his dick. Now… can you trace his phone?"

"I can try. You think it's still on?"

"Yep. She wants me to find her."

"Okay. Second question…"

Tom rolls his eyes. "Yeah?"

"Do I need to come down there?"

Tom huffs. "No Martha, I'm perfectly capable of dealing with the shit fight you dropped me in. Thanks."

"It was an easy job."

"Was." Tom hangs the call up and stalks out of the room.

TOM PACES AROUND THE LOBBY TWIRLING HIS PHONE IN HIS HANDS. The concierge keeps shooting him quizzical looks and Tom returns with a tight-lipped smile.

Conspicuous? Yes. Do I give a damn? No.

His phone pings. Coordinates and a blunt message.

Don't get killed.

Tom scoffs and slams through the front doors.

He slides into a cab. "Refshaleoen Island, *behage*." He slides a hand across his back feeling his pistol and making a promise to himself that the moment he sees Kat, he'll shoot her in the head. It's because of *her* he can't see Isabella; it's because of *her* Jack is dead. *Not that I miss him.*

The ten-minute cab ride feels like ten hours. Tom trains his eyes on the phone screen, waiting for Kat to call again. She doesn't. The cab jerks to a stop and Tom jumps out. He looks at the warehouses and factories sprawled out in front of him and walks. The chill off the water in the bay behind him is nothing compared to the chill running through his bloodstream.

He presses on James' number and waits. Kat picks up on the third ring.

"You look ready for business, Tom."

Tom's eyes dart around the buildings as he continues to walk. "Where are you?"

"Close by. I could shoot you from here."

Tom's gut contorts and he peers up at the windows.

"But I will not. I want to see your handsome face first. Straight ahead of you. Steel steps. See you soon." The line goes dead.

Tom focuses on the zig zag steps leading to a red door at the top of a warehouse. He climbs the steps and the door is ajar. He sucks in a breath and pulls his pistol from his waistband.

He pushes the door open and the room is dark. Moonlight shines through the dirty square windows running around the top of the walls. He halts and gives himself a moment to adjust to the darkness. The room is empty save for an old rusty table and a couple of vinyl chairs. He stays close to the walls and walks to the door at the other end of the vast room.

The second room mirrors the first, but with a staircase in the middle leading down. Tom sweeps his eyes around the room and back behind him. Satisfied there's no one there he edges to the top of the stairs. He crouches and peers down the spiral staircase made of rusty steel.

"Come out to play, Kat," he calls into the open room below. His voice echoes. He waits. No reply.

Tom taps his pistol against his leg and jiggles his jaw back and forth. *We're doing this the hard way.*

He swallows, moving onto the top step. He waits. *Nothing.* He moves a couple more steps down and peers into the room. *Dark.*

His breathing is thunderous in his ears as he creeps to the last step. The darkness envelops him, and he finds himself disoriented at the foot of the staircase. He swings around to check behind him, gripping his pistol with renewed strength.

"Fun game, Kat. Isn't it time to pounce?" His voice bounces off the walls.

Light floods the space and he squints as his eyes adjust. Movement at the other end of the room draws his attention and he focuses on the scene in front of him.

He inhales a sharp breath as his stomach tumbles into a pit.

25

TOM

James is slumped in a chair atop a makeshift platform. His hands are tied behind his back and he has a noose on his neck. Tom's eyes travel up the rope to see it attached to a beam on the ceiling above his head. No one else is there.

"James," Tom hisses, inching forward. He keeps scanning the room. *No, this is too easy.*

"Stop right there, Tom." Kat's voice floats through the darkness from above and he sees her at the top of the staircase. *Where the fuck were you hiding?* She struts down the stairs and her heels clack on the steel of the steps. A man descends behind her. *Goon.*

"You never said we could bring friends." Tom watches the goon ignore him and march straight to James, whose head lolls on his shoulder.

Kat observes James a moment and pouts, "Aw, he is still sleeping. Adorable."

"What did you give him?"

"Something to help him rest." Kat grins and crinkles her nose. "Only enough to incapacitate him for short while. He should wake soon." She tilts her head and looks at Tom. "Just in time for big show." She winks and pulls a Beretta from the waistline of her pants.

Tom grimaces and points his gun at Kat. She looks to the ceiling and laughs.

"Oh, Tom. If you shoot me, your little friend is dead." She nods towards James and the goon grabs him out of the chair, holding him up. He rests one foot on the box beneath James' feet.

Tom's throat constricts and he sucks in a breath. He sweeps his hands out either side of him, still holding his pistol. "Here I am." He nods towards James. "You don't need him anymore."

"Oh Tom. You know me better than that." She steps towards him. "Always have insurance."

I knew I'd heard that before.

Tom presses his lips together and glares at Kat. His hand twitches and he wants nothing more than to shoot her right between the eyes. He slides his glare to the monster of a man holding James up like he's a rag doll.

"*Pokazhi yemu svoye oruzhiye.*" Kat orders her goon.

Show him your weapon. The goon raises his arm and points a Glock at Tom. Tom holds his breath and stares down the barrel of the gun.

"You see, Tom. You shoot me. He shoots you and then lets go of your friend." She shrugs. "I win, even in death."

Because that's what it's all about for you. Tom peers at Kat, the hatred he feels for her is hard to contain. "How do you make these idiots do whatever you want?"

Kat smiles and steps forward, teetering on her stiletto heels. "Because Tom," she whispers, bending forward so her top gapes. "Men think with only one thing." She winks.

"You're nothing more than a Russian whore who gets a lucky shot off every so often."

Kat's smile falters a moment and ice flashes through her eyes. "It is means to end."

"The... fuck?" James rasps.

Tom's head whips up as James falls against the goon holding him. He blinks a couple of times and goes to move his arms.

"*Pust' sidit.*" Kat orders her goon to let James sit.

The chair is slid across the platform and shoved beneath James, who collapses into it.

"Shhh..." Kat holds a finger over her lips and grins at Tom. "Let us watch him for moment."

Tom's arms are at his side. One hand grips the pistol while the other balls into a fist. He watches as James focuses on him and realises there is a rope around his neck.

"Sit still, James." Tom's eyes slide back to Kat. "It'll all be over in a minute.

"Tom? What's g... going on?" He stretches his neck moving his head side to side. "Fucking headache."

Kat giggles and drags her fingers down her neck to her cleavage. "I would say that is least of your troubles."

Tom tries to calculate whether he can get to the other side of the room before James is knocked off his platform or Kat shoots him in the back. *Not quick enough.*

"So, how does this end Kat?"

Kat stares into Tom's eyes. A smile creeps across her lips, and she licks her lips.

Tom hears James' breathing intensify and he glances up at the platform. James' eyes are wide now and he's staring at Tom with urgency.

"Let him go," Tom says, still watching James. Kat's goon keeps his gun trained on Tom.

"I tell you..." Kat steps towards Tom and closes her hand over the one he holds the pistol in. "You give me that. I let him go. And you and I chat... and..." Kat runs a hand down Tom's torso. "Whatever else I feel like."

Tom's hatred bubbles over and he pushes Kat away and she falls to the floor.

"*Ne strelyay v nego!*" Kat screams. "*On moy.*" *Don't shoot, he's mine.*

Tom grimaces. *I'll never be yours.*

She raises the Beretta and adrenaline spikes through Tom's blood. He kicks the weapon from her hand and kneels over her.

He wraps a hand over her jaw and squeezes. "Let James go," he hisses in her face. He feels the presence of the goon in the room but knows he won't leave James unattended.

Kat spits in Tom's eyes and he loosens his grip enough that she pulls away. He remains on his knees and wipes his face.

He trains his gun on her.

Kat waggles a finger from where she lies on the floor. "Uh uh, remember what I said." She nods towards James. "I die. He dies." She narrows her eyes at Tom. "And so do you."

Tom's nostrils flare as he runs through every possible scenario that can happen from this point.

"*Podgotov' yego!*" Kat shouts at her goon.

He sweeps the chair out from under James, who stands on tiptoes, barely reaching the platform.

"Fuck," James gasps. "Tom… please." He totters on his toes and drills his eyes into Tom's.

Jesus.

"You misunderstand our meeting here tonight, Tom." Kats voice is low and blunt. "I am not going to kill you. This time. I like to toy with my prey a while." She juts her chin towards James. "Though, I cannot say same for your little friend."

Tom snaps his eyes back to James.

"*Sdelay eto!*" Kat shouts.

Do it. Shit.

The goon pushes the box away from James and he drops. His eyes bulge and he toes the cement trying to find solid ground.

Tom scrambles to stand as Kat jerks her knee back and kicks him in the face. Tom grunts and falls on his backside. Pain slices through his head and he grasps above his left eye. Every colour of the rainbow flashes against the black spots as blood trickles down his face.

Fuck!

He remembers James and runs to him, blinking through the one eye not covered in blood.

Kat's goon advances on him.

Tom raises his gun, points and pumps his trigger, while running towards James. The lump of a man hits the floor. Dead.

Should have shot me first. Idiot.

He ignores the pain thundering through his head as Kat's footsteps clatter up the steel staircase and she's gone.

Again.

James squirms as his face turns purple and his eyes bulge. He totters on the very tips of his toes, gurgling and fighting to breathe. Tom lifts James up and he flops over Tom's shoulders. He stumbles as James' weight throws him off balance. He reaches behind his own head to loosen the knot around James' neck but gets nowhere. He shoots the rope, and it breaks as James wheezes and splutters. He drops James to the floor and works on the knot. His fingers pick and pinch at the thick rope, bits of it fray off and sweat dribbles down Tom's back.

C'mon!

He finally pulls it loose and slips the rope off James' neck. Tom rolls onto the floor and catches his breath. James pants and rubs at his throat. Tom pushes the heel of his palm into his head, tilting his face to the ceiling.

"What… did she…" James sucks in air as he lies on his back, sprawled on the gritty floor.

"Kicked me in the head. Fucking stiletto." Tom squeezes his eyes shut and groans. "Fuck."

"I would have…. died." James gasps. "If… you…"

Tom groans and rips the sleeve of his shirt, pushing it against his face. "Forget it."

"I'm an idiot," James mumbles.

"One word for it. Did I not tell you she's insane?" Tom glares at James with his good eye. "Did I not make that clear?"

James leans forward over his knees. "Yep."

"And you let her lead you off somewhere?"

"I did."

"Lesson five. Don't follow crazy women to dark places." Tom stands up and adjusts as dizziness takes hold. "Let's get the fuck out of here."

"What if she's…"

"She's gone. For now."

26

MAX

Max kicks the comforter off himself and peers at the clock on the wall. *Eight am.* He stumbles to the bathroom. Leaning against the vanity, he peers into the mirror. His gaunt cheeks and bloodshot eyes make him squirm. *Pull it together. You have a show tonight.* The thought of performing sends a zing through his body. There's no feeling quite like it. *Not even cocaine makes me feel that good.* He grips the sink and gives his body a shake.

He hears the lift arrive and walks downstairs.

Ally stands in the middle of the room.

Max crosses his arms over his chest. "What do *you* want?"

Ally stares at him a moment. "Hey. You okay?" She raises a brow.

"Yeah? I mean... until you showed up." He rolls his eyes and throws himself onto the sofa. He grabs the remote and points it at the TV.

"Wait!" Ally jumps across and grabs it out of his hand.

"What the hell are you doing?" He goes to snatch it back and she holds the remote above her head.

"You should go shower and get ready. We have another sound check this morning."

"You should fuck off and leave me alone. Send Tom, or even that idiot James if you want to tell me something." Max turns his back on her.

Ally sighs which makes him tighten his crossed arms against himself.

"Max, they aren't my errand boys. They're government agents. Maybe treat them with a little more respect?"

"Well, I need someone *else* to assist me, then."

Ally stands in front of Max. "*You're* the one who didn't want a huge entourage remember? *You're* the one who likes to hide who you are from the world."

"I'm not hiding," Max mumbles.

Ally purses her lips, before her expression softens. "Max. Listen I need to tell you something."

Max leans forward. "I'm not talking to you." He looks at the ceiling and ignores Ally. *Go away.*

"Fine, don't talk, listen."

Max scoffs and continues to stare at the ceiling.

"The photographs that Melissa has…"

Max's chest squeezes shut, and he turns his head to Ally. "What about them?" Max whispers. He claws at the arm of the lounge chair.

"She sold them to The Daily Roundup. She must have done it before Tom blacked her out."

Mist forms at the edges of Max's vision and he blinks, trying to focus on his sister. "What?"

"It's all over the media, Max. I'm so sorry."

Max jumps off the sofa and sways on his feet. Ally lunges forward to help him and he holds a hand up to stop her. "Don't touch me," he spits.

His body trembles and he backs toward the stairs. Nausea hits him in waves before he claps his hand over his mouth and runs up to the bathroom.

He leans over the toilet bowl and vomits. He heaves until every single skerrick in his gut has been expelled. He slumps to the floor and draws a breath in, swallowing the burn at the back of his raw throat.

"Max?" Ally is at the bathroom door.

Max blinks at her through blurry, tear filled eyes. "Don't come in here. Don't look at me." He curls into a ball on the bathroom floor. "… don't." He hides his face in his hands and tries to slow his breathing, so he doesn't hyperventilate.

He hears Ally rattling around the vanity top, and peers through his fingers. She is taking his razor and nail scissors out of his toiletry bag.

She catches him watching her and turns to face him. "I can't let you hurt yourself, Max." Her eyes brim with tears. "Not again."

Max's nose tingles and tears topple onto his cheeks. He hugs his knees to his chest and backs against the wall. "Please leave me alone," he croaks.

"Max—"

"Fuck off!"

Ally scurries out of the bathroom, shutting the door behind her.

Max lays on the tiles, keeping himself curled into a ball. He runs his fingers over the bandage around his wrist and a shiver runs down his back. A hole in his chest opens and he gasps breath in.

I can't do this.

MAX ISN'T SURE HOW LONG HE HAS BEEN LYING ON THE BATHROOM floor, but the tiles aren't cold anymore. He rolls onto his side and picks at the bandage over his wrist. Pulling it apart, he scratches his fingernails along the raw cut and sobs. He scratches again, and again until blood runs down his arm and cakes under his nails. Tears seep out from under his closed lids and he sniffles.

A loud knock at the door pulls him out of his trance. He wipes his arm along his nose and shakes his head. "If that's you Ally you can fuck off!" He coughs and cries. "Leave me al—"

"It's Tom."

Max heaves a breath in and keeps his eyes scrunched shut. "Don't come in," he whimpers. "I'm fine. … leave me here." He sits himself up against the wall.

"I owe you an apology."

Max opens his eyes and stares at the door. "For what?"

"I told you I'd handle it." Tom pauses. "Open the door, Max. C'mon."

Max hauls himself off the floor and creeps to the door. He leans his head against it. "I'm sure you did your best," he mumbles.

"Open the door. It's only just been repaired from when I broke it last time. Don't make me do it again."

Max pushes a palm against the door and clicks the lock. "It's open." He retreats and sits on the edge of the bath.

Tom walks in, Ally is right behind him. Max sees a bruised cut above Tom's left eye. "What happened?"

"She must have sold the pictures, in case…" Tom sits on the closed toilet and leans over his knees.

"No, your face…" Max frowns and stares at Tom's eyebrow.

"A bad night." Tom gives Max a tight-lipped smile before his eyes drop to Max's wrist. "What are you doing?" He grabs a fresh hand towel and wraps it around Max's wrist, all the while Max's eyes are fixed on his cut.

"Should you get stitches for your head?"

"Probably."

Tom grabs Max's other hand and makes him hold the towel around his wrist before sitting back again.

"But how —"

"I'm not here to talk about me." Tom's eyes fix on Max's and it makes him slink back against the bathroom wall.

"There's nothing to talk about." Max sucks on his bottom lip. "I'm finished."

"Why?"

Max rolls his eyes at Tom and gapes his mouth half open. "Are you serious? People are gonna hate me. My fans will turn on me. I lied to them. I'm done. It's over."

"You don't know that."

Max raises a brow and huffs out a laugh. "You watch. I bet the arena tonight… The *sold-out* arena... will be half empty. If not completely empty." Max runs a hand over his stomach. "I wish I was normal," he whispers.

Tom tilts his head. "You *are* normal."

Max snaps his eyes up. "What?"

"You *are* normal," Tom repeats. "I mean, you can't take a hint and your fashion sense leaves a lot to be desired but…"

Max lets a small smile slip. "Did you ever imagine that your job would have you in a penthouse bathroom, talking a pathetic outed pop star off a ledge?"

Tom chuckles. "Nope. But it keeps things interesting." Tom stands up. "Make it your own Max."

"My own?"

"Yeah… own it. Be who you are. Fuck everyone else."

"But what if—"

"What if they love you anyway?" Tom nods once and walks out of the bathroom, shutting the door behind him.

"But what if they don't?" Max whispers to himself.

MAX EMERGES INTO THE LOUNGE. TOM AND JAMES ARE BOTH THERE. James appears worse for wear with a red mark circling his throat. Max looks from James to Tom and back again. "What the fuck happened to you two last night?"

"Don't ask," James grumbles into his bottle of water.

"James got himself a date." Tom glares at James, before wandering to the other side of the room and peering out the window.

"She likes to play hard ball?" Max smiles, despite feeling like the world is caving in.

"Something like that." James sips his water. "You alright?"

"No. Not at all." Max drops his smile and stares at a spot on the wall above James' head. "Tell me, is there a crowd outside the hotel?"

Tom looks at Max and says nothing.

"Thought so."

"We can leave through the back for your sound check," James offers, sipping more water.

"There will be media everywhere I go today." Max drops his face into his hands. "And I don't want to face any of them."

Ally sits on the sofa next to Max and inches her hand across to him. He looks down at it and back to her face. His chest softens towards her, but he doesn't let her know. "You have to stop getting Tom to sort me out because you can't." He moves into the corner of the sofa and stares at her.

"I agree. But you wouldn't talk to me and I was worried."

"I can't believe you tried to derail my tour by making false threats Ally. That's another level of mental."

"I know." She nods. "I was so worried about you." The end of her words come out in a squeak and her eyes are full of tears again.

Max huffs out a sigh and he looks at the ceiling.

"And now I'm worried again." Ally pulls a tissue out of her sleeve and blows her nose.

Max refuses to look at her. He isn't done being mad at her yet and doesn't want to accidentally hug her.

Tom wanders back over. He glares at James and Max grins, sitting up. *Let's distract myself a moment.*

"Okay spill. What's going on?" He raises an eyebrow and looks at Tom.

"Nothing. James learnt a lesson. Didn't you James?"

James' eyes slide to Tom and he flares his nostrils before nodding and looking back to the ground.

Max feels the ice wall between them and makes a show of shivering. "Brrrr… is it cold in here?"

"Freezing," James nods.

Max sits back on the sofa, enjoying the distraction from his own problems. He claws a hand into his stomach as it comes flooding back. *It's all over the media.* He gives a little squeak. Tom and James stop glaring at each other and look over at him.

"Sorry," Max whispers. "I …" He looks at Ally. "I'm not going this morning." He stands up.

Ally's quirks an eyebrow. "What? But you have to do another sound check—"

"I don't *have* to do anything." He reaches and picks up the half empty vodka bottle before spinning and waltzing to his room. He turns at the stairs and addresses Tom. "I want to be left alone. Unless you care to join me?"

Tom stares at him impassively.

"Didn't think so," Max mutters, stomping up the stairs.

Max stands in the middle of his bedroom as his chin quivers. His eyes fill with tears and they topple down his face. The tingling in his nose and the pain in his throat take over. He crumples to the floor and sobs. He digs his fingers into the floorboards and wishes it would splinter and pierce his skin.

"Max?" Ally's voice is at the top of the stairs.

"Leave me alone," he whispers.

"I can't."

Max scrunches his face up and claws himself up onto the bed. He flops into his pillow and ignores Ally. The bed dips and he knows she's perched herself next to him. He buries his face further into the pillow and scratches at the open wound on his wrist.

"Stop!" Ally leaps across and slaps both her hands over his and holds tight.

Max coughs before trying to swallow back the sobs jostling to escape from the back of his throat. The sobs win. "I… don't want to be here, Ally." He gulps air as the tears slide down his face.

"In Denmark?"

"Anywhere."

27

JAMES

James sits at the Marble Bar inside the hotel and half-heartedly sips a beer. He trains his eyes straight ahead and the labels from the bottles on the shelf blur.

He scans the near empty room and rubs at his throat, remembering the air huffing out of his lungs as he flopped over Tom's shoulder. *Tom's shoulder.*

He shakes his head and takes another sip as he presses Uncle Pete's number on the ancient brick phone Tom hurled at him that morning.

"Where the fuck have you been?" Uncle Pete barks down the phone and it makes James' temper flare.

"Tied up."

"Where are we at?"

James takes a breath and closes his eyes. "Nowhere." He swallows.

Silence sits on the other end of the line.

James sips and waits.

"I'm sorry?" Uncle Pete's voice is dangerously quiet.

"I'm not doing it."

"You'll do as you're goddamned told."

James springs up off the bar stool and grips the side of the bar. "No. I fucking won't." He takes a breath. "There's too much of this bloody job I know nothing about. So, unless you care to enlighten me on who all these Russians are and what Tom has to do with it…" He takes a breath. "Ms Ivan-something nearly fucking killed me last night." *Not that you'd care.*

"What?"

"I was hanging in a noose."

"Is that so?"

James waits and grips the phone. Uncle Pete says no more.

"Would I say it if it didn't fucking happen?" James hisses.

"James, you say a lot of things. Most of which turn out to be lies. So, I wouldn't know." Peter pauses and James hears ice clinking in a glass. "I'd have let you hang for getting in such a stupid position in the first place."

"Fuck you."

"And how James, did you get yourself out of this… noose?"

James sees the fuzzy image of Tom running towards him. Seconds from blacking out.

"Tom."

Uncle Pete scoffs. "Didn't want any more blood on his hands."

"What does that mean?"

"Stop asking irrelevant questions and do the job I tasked you with."

James sucks in another breath and sits back down. "I'm out." He pauses. "Unless you tell me more about this whole story other than, 'find out if Isabella Wirth is still alive'."

"James you don't need—"

"I'll be the judge of what I need." *For once.*

Uncle Pete clears his throat but doesn't speak.

"Right then," James takes another sip of beer. "I'll be on my way."

"Stop! James. Don't be an idiot."

"Fine. Speak."

Uncle Pete lets out a rough sigh and James grins to himself. *Irritated much?*

"Jack Ford was killed in Paris six months ago."

"And he is?"

"He was a Commander alongside me. And a damn good one. He made some… questionable decisions about helping a Russian girl, and now he's dead."

"This Russian girl…?"

"Irina Petrov. Otherwise known as Isabella Wirth."

"The dead one."

"Apparently."

James rolls his eyes. "Tom says she's dead, and this Kat Ivansomething claims to have shot her through the heart. She's. *Dead.*" James downs the last dregs of his beer and slams the glass onto the bar top. "Can I get the fuck out of here now?"

"No." Uncle Pete grunts. "I don't believe she's dead. And I believe she killed Jack and Tom helped her."

"Why would she... or Tom do that?"

"Because Jack is the reason she got found out. She had a motive. And I lost a damn good unit leader. And friend. She pays."

"She's dead!" James springs off the barstool again and the barman raises an eyebrow as he polishes a glass. James clears his throat and walks to a table at the back of the room. "I think she's paid enough don't you?" He slumps onto the table. "And what about Tom?"

"He and Jack despised each other. He helped her finish him. No doubt."

He's a git. But... kill a naval officer?

"I want no part of this," James mumbles. "I'll take the jail time."

"When did you become so weak?" Uncle Pete's voice creeps down the phone as though stalking him.

James bristles and sits up. "Weak? I'm not weak."

"You'd rather languish in a filthy jail cell?"

James bites his lip. "Who's Alexei Petrov?"

"Irina Petrov's father."

"Isabella."

"Whoever." Uncle Pete pauses. "Get it done." The call ends.

"Bye." James mutters at the silence. He drops the phone on the table.

JAMES SHUFFLES DOWN THE HALL TO HIS ROOM. HE SEES TOM standing against the wall with one foot up. James rolls his eyes. *So not in the mood.*

"Hey," James says as he unlocks his door.

Tom turns. "Out looking for stray cats again?"

"Ha, ha. No… needed a drink. Figured you wouldn't be up for it." James sits on the bed and looks at Tom. "So, what do you want?"

Tom squints at James a moment and shrugs. "Checking you're not having a breakdown."

"A breakdown?"

"You had a noose around your neck, James."

"Yes, I recall." James rubs at his throat again over the rough red bumps left by the rope.

"And I figure that's the first life or death scrape you've found yourself in?"

James cocks an eyebrow. "I was in the Royal Navy, Tom."

"So was I, James." Tom grabs the desk chair and throws himself onto it. "Only difference is that I saw active combat. You cooked in the galley because you couldn't behave yourself."

Busted. James' gut sinks and his eyes drop to the floor. "Well... yeah."

"Not much life or death going on in a large vat of watery eggs."

James crosses his arms over his chest. "Did you come here to mock me?"

"No." Tom leans on his arms over his knees and looks straight into James face. It makes James squirm. He unfolds his arms and fiddles with his hands. "I wanted to check on you. I can only deal with one mentally deranged person at a time. And Max is mentally deranged enough to cover four people."

James flicks his eyes up to Tom. "You wanted to check on me?" *I matter now?*

"Yes. If we're working together, I can't have you falling in a heap after one close encounter."

"I'm not falling in a heap," James mumbles.

"Excellent." Tom stands up. "You're lying through your teeth but…" He shrugs. Tom walks to the door.

"Tom?"

"Yeah?"

"Did you kill Jack Ford?"

Tom remains facing the door. "Why would you ask me that?"

James holds his breath a moment. "You hated him."

Tom turns his face to James and peers at him. "I'm not overly fond of you either, James." Tom stares at him a few seconds. "We leave at eighteen hundred." Tom opens the door and disappears.

James stares at the back of the door and covers his nose and mouth with his hands.

My own Uncle would have let me hang.

28

MAX

"Max, how do you feel about deceiving your fans all this time?"

A microphone is shoved in Max's face as fans scream and reporters — *vultures* — jostle for the soundbite they're after. The back alley to the hotel is crammed with bodies all pushing forward towards Max.

He ducks into the waiting car. James is inside.

"Oh. Gumnut." Max gives him a half smile.

"Yeah. Sorry it's not lover boy."

Max chuckles. "You're cute. Don't worry." He winks, before turning to squint out of the heavily tinted windows as they pull away from the rear of the hotel.

"Where *is* Tom?"

"He went ahead with Ally." James turns to Max. "How are you?"

"Shit."

"Yeah, that makes sense." James nods.

"There's been reporters trying to call my room all day. One even got into the lift." Max shakes his head. "I'll be making my thoughts known to the manager on that one."

"You seem… upbeat? Considering?"

Max turns and grins. "It's chemical. I'm fucked." He shrugs.

"You always turn up at the venue this late when you play?" James rubs at his throat and Max stares at his neck.

"No. But I didn't really want to get out of bed to be honest." He reaches across and pulls James' hand away from his throat. He sucks in a sharp breath through his teeth. "Ouch! Gumnut! You need more practice at rough play."

James shrugs away and looks out the window. "Yeah…"

"What happened?"

James shakes his head and keeps his face turned away.

"Humour me, Gumnut."

James sighs. "I got hoodwinked. I ended up in a noose and Tom… rescued me."

"What?" Max laughs. "Nice one Gumnut. I needed that laugh." Max shakes his head, still chuckling. "A noose."

"A noose." James leans into Max's face with a snarl on his face. "I. Nearly. Fucking. Died." He breathes heavy breaths through his nose as his eyes bore into Max's.

Max gasps and puts a hand on James' shoulder. "Okay, Gumnut. Okay." Max's chest aches as he thinks that James was lucky to be in that position. "Don't be scared of death."

"Why not?"

"Because living is a fuckload scarier." Max's throat constricts and now it's his turn to massage his throat.

"But please tell me how you ended up in that position?"

Before James can answer, something thuds against his window and explodes with globby white lumps. Max's heart jumps to his throat and he shies away from the window.

"What the fuck was that?" he squeals, backing himself right against James.

James cranes his neck over Max to inspect the window. "Looks like… flour?"

Max pulls himself back towards his side of the car. "Could have been worse," he mumbles.

Shouting, screaming and voices invade Max's ears as the car arrives at the arena. Max shuts his eyes. *I don't want to see them.*

James gasps and pokes Max in the shoulder.

"What?" Max keeps his eyes shut.

"You should look."

Max opens one eye and looks at James.

"Trust me."

Letting out a long sigh Max peers through the dark windows. He sees rainbow flags and happy faces. He hears "We love you Max," and "Marry me Max."

What?

Confusion muddles his thoughts. "But… online…" he mutters.

"Online isn't real Max," James scoffs and points at the window. "That is."

A smile spreads across Max's face. His mind races and the smile halts.

But the haters still exist. They always will.

*

MAX STANDS AT THE MICROPHONE AND LOOKS OUT AT THE CROWD AT the colour, joy and happiness. But a solid, invisible wall still separates them.

I wish I could feel what they feel.

He grips the microphone with both hands and rests his lips against it. He glances at his leather wrist band, covering his cut and slides his eyes back to the crowd.

"Can I have the house lights turned up?" His voice echoes through the arena.

The crowd appears before him like magic and he sees the arena is bursting with people. The noise is incredible. He can't make out a single voice — they are one.

What if they're shouting hate?

His heart aches against his ribcage as it becomes apparent to him that his mind is still tortured. He dips his head and takes in a breath.

"This next song is currently number one in eleven countries," he starts, and the crowd roars. "I wrote 'Me' some time ago."

He stops and picks up the water bottle at his feet and takes a gulp.

"When asked about it in interviews I would say it is about hiding my insecurities, self-doubt, my shyness." He pauses and runs his eyes over the crowd. "It's not."

The crowd's roar swells to deafening levels.

"It's about me. The real me. That I hid from you all for too long." His voice cracks as he wipes his mouth along his arm as he holds the microphone. "And...I'm sorry." The last words come out as a whisper.

Wow.

Max takes a moment, staring at the floor and taking deep breaths. The crowd screams and shouts, filling his ears with white noise. He turns his head and nods to his band. The first bars of music resonate in the arena and the crowd appear to move as one pulsating wave.

Max swallows his emotions and opens his mouth.

29

TOM

Tom stands in the wings of the stage with Ally.

"Ten minutes. Then he'll do the encore before running off and out the back." Ally says to Tom. She adjusts her earpiece. "Is the car ready at the back door?" she barks into the microphone.

Tom smiles to himself as he listens to Ally ordering people around. He watches Max. He holds the crowd in the palm of his hand. *He's a pro.*

"How do you think this will make him feel?" Tom asks.

Ally watches her brother, the anxiety palpable. "No idea. Max can be quite the good actor." She smiles up at Tom. "You may have noticed."

"The crowd doesn't seem to care."

"No. But the final count of scanned tickets shows over four thousand fans didn't show."

"And?"

"And… that will be what Max focuses on. Not the thirteen thousand that *did* come."

"So, don't tell him."

"He already knows. He always asks about numbers before he goes on."

Tom turns back to watch Max as he holds the microphone stand up above his head. The noise from the crowd is thunderous. Tom can't help but be impressed.

Seconds later Max runs offstage towards them. He grabs the towel Ally holds out and wipes his face.

"You have eight minutes to get changed before the encore."

She's all business.

"Yeah, yeah, make sure I have chilled drinks in that car."

"It's under control. Get sorted." Ally points him to the other end of the backstage area.

Max doesn't move and winks at Tom. "What did you think?"

"Impressive."

Max raises his eyebrows and grins, taking a sip of water.

"For an arrogant prat," Tom finishes.

Max scrunches his nose up. "Cute." He flings his towel over an unused microphone stand and scrambles to his wardrobe rack.

Tom's phone vibrates in his pocket and he yanks it out. James' new number flashes up on the screen.

"Yeah?" Tom sighs into the phone. He blocks his other ear to drown out the interlude still playing onstage.

"This phone is shit by the way. Who even knows what a Nokia is these days?"

"You lost your good one. So, you get what you get." Tom chews the inside of his mouth and waits.

"It was taken by a psychopath, actually."

"After you got led astray by your dick."

"*Anyway,* everything is fine out here. There's nutty females everywhere but no other threat that I can see."

"Excellent. Another few perimeter walks should do it."

"What? C'mon Tom—"

Tom ends the call and shoves his phone back into his pocket.

"Is he still outside?" Ally asks.

"Yep. He's doing laps around the arena."

"Looking for?"

"Nothing. I'm keeping him out of my face."

Ally throws her head back and laughs. "You're evil, Tom."

"He'll survive."

"How's your head?"

Tom presses the lump above his eye. Pain shoots into his head but he plays straight. "It's fine."

"How did you even—"

Max appears in between them. He bounces on the spot like a boxer waiting to enter the ring. "Okay, good to go?" He waves out at his band and the lead guitarist gives him a thumbs up. "See you in ten!" He dashes out to the middle of the stage and his fans go ballistic.

This is insane.

The crowd pulses and jumps as one entity. Cuddly toys and bras are thrown on stage. Max starts with a singalong, getting the crowd to repeat after him and the noise is deafening. The band kicks in and he launches into his encore performance, strutting around the stage brandishing the microphone stand like a sword.

Three songs later he finishes and sprints off the stage, he throws a towel over his shoulders and wipes his face with it as he runs down and out the corridor to an open car door.

Tom follows and slides into the seat next to him. The car lurches forward and they are away.

Max pants and gulps water.

Tom eyes the ice bucket.

Max follows his gaze. "Take one, Buttercup."

"Pass." Tom looks out the window. "So, how did that feel?" He doesn't turn around.

"The show? Yeah, good."

Tom notes the tone in Max's voice and turns his head. "But?"

"Well, we were still short a few thousand people." He grabs a bottle of vodka and snaps the lid off.

"So?"

"So… it matters." He swigs from the bottle. "To me." He holds the bottle out to Tom. "You sure?"

Tom eyes the bottle and swallows down his thirst. "Positive," he mumbles looking back out the window.

"Okay, time's up. Spill."

Tom squeezes his eyes shut. "Spill what?"

"What's the deal? Do you drink? Or do you not? And do you have a partner? Or do you not?"

Tom hears Max take another swig and swallow.

"You know all about me. Besides, might be nice to hear of someone else's car wreck for a while."

Tom turns and gives Max a wry smile. "Flattered." He inhales and holds it a moment. "But there's nothing to tell."

"Okay, I'm a messed-up pop star with an alcohol and drug problem. But I'm not an idiot."

Tom says nothing.

Max holds a fresh bottle out for him. "Thirsty?"

The back of Tom's throat floods and he swallows, shaking his head. "Nope."

"Because?"

Tom huffs. "Because I won't be able to stop." He peers at Max. "Is that what you want to hear?"

"No." Max lowers the bottle and buries it in the ice. "I don't wish addiction on anyone," he whispers and waits a beat. "At least you can say no."

Tom snorts and rolls his eyes. "Yeah, sometimes."

"Sometimes?"

"Not when I'm alone. Or sitting in a bar that I shouldn't be sitting in."

"I never would have thought." Max rests an elbow on the ice bucket and cups his chin in his hands.

Tom slides his eyes back to Max's face. "Like I said… takes one to know one." His voice croaks and he clears his throat before gazing out the window.

"And what about the partner."

"Don't have one." Tom takes a breath. "Right now."

"But?"

"But..." Tom shrugs and irritation prickles the back of his neck.

"You love someone?" Max's voice is barely above a whisper. "A *she* I'm guessing." He chuckles.

Tom nods before he can stop himself. *Shit.*

"Well, that's cute, Buttercup. What's her name?"

Tom sighs and rubs his face. He looks at Max and raises his eyebrows. "Can you stop?" He looks ahead through the front windscreen. "We're back, anyway. So... to be continued."

"Really? Continued?"

"Probably not." Tom opens the car door. "Let's go."

Tom steps out and for the first time since they arrived in Denmark there isn't a crowd of over one hundred girls waiting to catch a glimpse of Max.

There's fifteen.

Max emerges from the car and they squeal. He smiles and Tom notes it doesn't reach his eyes. He shuffles over to where they are and lets them hug him and he poses for selfies. He resembles a rag doll being pushed and pulled.

His energy — or lack thereof — seeps across to where Tom is leaning on a wall next to the back entrance to the hotel. He slumps forward a fraction and takes in a breath.

Why the fuck did I tell him all that in the car?

Max wanders over to Tom and gives him a half smile. "I'm done, Buttercup." He walks into the hotel, and Tom's eyes linger on the fifteen girls still standing behind the fence.

Well, shit.

UPSTAIRS, MAX CATCHES TOM'S ARM AS THE LIFT DOORS OPEN. HE glances at the vice-like grip Max has on his forearm. "What?"

"Thanks for... putting up with my shit." He lets go of Tom and creeps back against the wall.

Tom furrows his brow and stands between the doors, so they don't close. "Um... you're welcome?" Tom waits and Max stares blankly at him. "I'm sure there's more to come. So maybe keep your apologies til the end of the tour?"

"Maybe the end is closer than you think."

Tom's gut takes a nosedive. "What?"

Silence lingers a moment before Max shrugs. "I mean... no one is gonna come see me in concert anymore."

Tom nods as he studies Max's face. "I see." Tom sucks his bottom lip in. "Best go to sleep. You've got another show tomorrow night."

"Goodbye, Buttercup."

Tom steps out of the lift and watches the doors slide shut. He walks up the hall, trying to ignore the nagging voice in the back of his mind, whispering words he can't make out.

He reaches his room, and he swipes the key card as his phone sounds. He clunks his forehead into the door, forgetting about the cut over his eye.

"Fuck's sake." Pain volts through his skull. He rips his phone out. "Martha."

"You need to get back to London." She's blunt and she's angry.

"Excuse me?"

"Why are you still there? Kat nearly killed the pair of you."

"Okay, calm yourself down, you'll have a stroke." Tom opens his door and stumbles into the room, falling onto the bed. *You had no issue 'til Kat turned up.*

"A str…" Martha stops, and Tom hears her take in a breath. "You don't need to be on this detail anymore. Supreme Order has nothing to do with it and there's no threat."

"Correct," Tom pushes a hand against his throbbing head. "Although there is a threat. And I feel obliged to see this through, now."

"What threat? Kat's a threat to *you,* Tom. Not Max. You."

"Not her."

"Then who?"

"He's a threat to…" Tom sits bolt upright. *Himself.*

"Tom? A threat to who?"

"Fuck."

MAX

Max sets a half full bottle of vodka and a tiny vial with a few drops of GHB in the bottom on the edge of the pool. He dangles his legs into the water before sliding in. He glides across the water for a moment on his back, staring at the ceiling. Reaching the opposite end of the tiny rectangular box, he turns and floats back to his vodka.

Sitting on the steps he opens the bottle and gulps down a mouthful before opening the vial and tipping the contents down his throat. He chases it with more vodka.

Lethal combination.

"Because I'm me... it's who I'll always be..." he sings to himself as tears prickle the corners of his eyes. He sniffles and lays back in the water again. He stretches his arms out either side of him and waits.

Time to fly.

TOM

Tom taps his foot as the lift climbs higher. He pulls his phone out and looks at the eight calls he placed to Max's phone on the short walk to the lift from his room. All unanswered. *Shit.*

The lift arrives after what feels like a century and Tom bursts out of it.

"Ally!"

Ally turns around and smiles. She's in the middle of the room watching a news report about Max's show. "Hey," she peers beyond Tom. "Where's Max?"

"He isn't here?"

Ally frowns, tilting her head to the side. "I thought he was with you. Or James?"

"No…" Tom bounds up the stairs to Max's room. *Empty.* "Max?" Tom stalks to the bathroom and throws the door open. "Shit." He runs back down the stairs and grabs Ally by the shoulders. "We need to find Max. Now." He drills his eyes into hers.

"Um, yes I thought he was with…"

Tom shakes his head. "He's not. Where would he go?" *Don't say anything. She'll freak.*

Colour drains from Ally's face and her chin quivers. "What's going on?"

"I'm …" Tom blows a breath out. "Concerned."

Ally nods. "Okay um, maybe he went to the sauna? He likes a sauna after using up so much energy."

"Great, okay. Let's go." He grabs Ally's arm and stalks into the lift, dragging her behind him. *I'm always in this goddamn lift.*

"Tom?" Ally's voice shakes and she steps into Tom, staring at him. "What is it?"

Tom resists the urge to plonk his forehead against hers and comfort her. He swallows the mountain peaking in his throat.

"He… said something that worried me. I'm sure it's nothing." The lift arrives and Tom jerks his head to look over Ally's shoulder. "Let's go."

Tom slams his keycard into the lock for the sauna room and marches in. The first thing he sees is a vodka bottle on its side beside the cooling pool.

Tom's insides erupt in flames as he spies the pool.

And Max.

"Jesus." Tom sprints to the pool and jumps in.

"Max!" Ally screams and it makes Tom's blood curdle. "No!"

He scoops Max into him, cradling him like a child and pulls him from the water.

He leans over him and listens for breath.

"It's your lucky day…" Tom mumbles. He tilts Max's head back, gives him a rescue breath and pushes both palms into his chest. *Thirty compressions, two breaths…*

Tom flicks his eyes up to where Ally is crumpled in a heap on the floor. "Call an ambulance. Now!" Tom finishes the compressions and breathes for Max. *Nothing.* Tom's chest constricts. Sweat dribbles down his back as his breathing intensifies. He pushes against Max's limp frame, feeling no response. "C'mon!"

He breathes for him again.

Ally speaks into her phone, but it's a jumble of words Tom can't make out. His eyes are fixed on Max's blank face, blue lips and wet skin.

Ally drops to her knees next to Max and grabs his hand. She holds it against her face. "C'mon Max." She coughs and gulps air. Tears drip off her chin.

"…twenty-nine, thirty," Tom whispers to himself, leaning down to breathe for Max again. Sweat beads across Tom's lip and trickles down his forehead. He starts the compressions again. "C'mon Max. I'm not snogging you for fun."

Max coughs a little and water trickles out of the corner of his mouth.

Tom's heart leaps to his throat. "Max?" Tom rolls him on his side and leans over him. Max wheezes and gurgles softly. Tom keeps his head down next to Max's mouth. Water continues to run out of his mouth, down the side of his face.

Tom glances at Ally. "He's breathing…"

Ally places her hands either side of Max's face and rests her forehead against his. "Wake up, Little Bear," she whispers.

Tom rocks onto his backside and gulps in deep breaths. He notices the vial on the side of the pool and picks it up. "What was in this?" He holds it up.

Ally looks up, tears stain her face. "Oh Max," she shakes her head and looks down at her brother. "It looks like Fantasy."

"Fantasy?"

"Liquid ecstasy. GHB."

"I see."

A new wave of tears erupts from Ally and she slumps across her brother.

Tom scrambles to her and lifts her off him. "Watch his airway."

Ally sits up and wipes her eyes with the sleeve of her shirt. "He did this on purpose."

Tom's insides shudder. *I know.* He looks at Ally and says nothing. She stares back at him a moment and Tom's heart softens. *Stop.*

Banging at the doors draws Tom out of his trance and he jogs across to let the paramedics in.

"Vodka, liquid ecstasy and a pool. He's breathing. Thirty compressions, two breaths."

One paramedic starts working on Max while the other looks at Tom quizzically. *Of course, you don't speak English.*

Tom makes a compression and breathing motion to show he

performed mouth to mouth. The paramedic nods and drops down next to Max.

Tom pulls Ally off the floor and away from Max. "Let them help him."

Ally leans into Tom's chest and wails. He instinctively holds her, letting her cry.

Holding her like that, Tom realises he feels sorry for her. Pity. His heart reaches out to her because she's sad. *Definitely losing my edge.*

The paramedics load Max onto a gurney and the one that Tom didn't speak to earlier approaches him.

"Hospital. Now." He points between Tom and Ally.

Tom gently pushes Ally forward. "Go with him," he whispers to her.

Tom watches as they disappear through the doors, Ally grabbing Max's limp hand from under the white blanket.

He sits on the edge of the pool and scrubs his hands over his face.

Fuck me.

TOM STANDS IN THE MIDDLE OF HIS BATHROOM AND PEELS HIS WET clothing off. Dumping it in a heap on the floor he steps into the shower and turns it on too hot.

He winces under the water a moment before becoming accustomed and letting his shoulders drop. Images of Max floating face down in the tiny pool swirl around in the steam from the shower.

Tom shakes his head.

Jesus Christ.

He slides down the cold tiles until he's sitting on the floor.

He contemplates the one thing—person, he wants. She's in Belgium, surrounded by chickens and cows. He smiles to himself, imagining Isabella in a pair of filthy jeans and a checked shirt.

There'd still be a knife in her waistband.

But she's with her father. *Where she should be.* She can't come back.

Looking up at the shower head as water rains down on him he lets out an aggravated huff. And drops his face into his hands.

I need you here. Right now.

He hauls himself off the floor of the shower and turns the water off.

Walking into the room, scrubbing his head with a towel, he flicks the TV on. Images of an ambulance leaving the hotel he currently stands in, makes Tom's blood run cold. The news reporter speaks in Danish. *I need to learn Danish.* But the photographs of Max flashing up on the screen along with snippets of the article in *The Daily Roundup*, tells Tom all he needs to know. He grimaces and turns the TV off.

He flops onto the bed and stares at the ceiling as his thirst creeps up the back of his throat. He reaches across for the bottle in his cabin bag.

Sitting up he looks at the bottle, and it morphs into the bottle beside the pool. Laying on its side.

Max is floating.

Face down.

Tom scrunches his eyes shut and stalks to the bathroom. He cracks the lid and pours the contents of the bottle down the sink. He crumbles to the floor, head in hands, heaving in breaths.

I'm nothing like him.

32

MAX

Blinding white light pushes its way into Max's eyes as he flutters them open. He blinks a couple of times as his vision adjusts.

Am I...?

"Max!" Someone grabs hold of his arm and kisses his forehead. Blonde hair brushes against his face.

"Ally..." he croaks. His throat grates and he brings a hand up to massage it.

"Hey," Ally smiles. "Sore throat?"

Max nods and peers around the stark room he finds himself in.

"Yeah well, you had a tube down your throat the past two days to help you breathe." Ally's voice inflects at the end and Max flops his head to the side to see her face. Tears roll down her cheeks. She wipes her nose with a tissue.

Max pulls his eyes away from her to curb the bubbles of sadness multiplying in his chest. "Two days?" his rasps.

I don't even sound like me.

"Yes. They had to keep you sleeping so your brain had time to recover. You nearly caused irreversible damage. If Tom hadn't..." She gulps in air and sniffles again.

Max's head snaps back to his sister. "Tom?"

Ally nods. "He had a feeling you were... and we looked for you. He had to give you mouth to mouth. Oh, Max..." Ally holds Max's hand and rubs his fingers. "I thought you were going to die."

"He gave me mouth to mouth?" Max raises an eyebrow and gives a little grin to his sister.

Ally giggles. "Yes. But this is no time for jokes."

Max plummets back to earth. "You should have left me there," he mumbles.

Ally gasps and the tears jostle for position on her cheeks. "Don't you ever say anything like that to me again." The sniffle in her nose sounds like there's little room left for air.

Max wants to argue. He wants to scream at her; shout the hospital down, but his throat is too raw. He shakes his head and looks at the tiny television mounted above his bed. Tears take over his vision and he blinks, sending them down his face.

"You said two days?" Panic stabs him in the chest. "I had another show..."

"No. It's cancelled Max."

"The whole tour?"

"Well... I'd like that. But so far only Denmark and Sweden."

"Get me out of here." Max tries to sit up.

Ally pushes him back down. "No."

Max flops back onto the pillow and clamps his mouth shut. "Piss off."

"Max—"

Max jerks his face away from her and stares at the wall. Moments later he hears Ally close the door as she leaves.

He holds his breath trying to fight the pain away, but the dam breaks and he sobs. His nose blocks and his eyes leak like a broken tap. He curls himself into a ball and let's himself howl.

33

TOM

Tom throws back his whisky and plonks the glass down on the bar. The barman looks over at him. Tom clicks his fingers and points to his glass.

In a glass is okay. Not straight from the bottle... Keep telling yourself that.

The barman pours another and sits it in front of Tom. He picks the glass up and downs the nip. It burns down his throat and warmth spreads from his gut to the rest of his body. *Just this one last time.*

He cracks his neck and relaxes his shoulders.

"Another for him. And I'll have the same." Ally's voice fills his ears.

Tom looks to his left as Ally plants herself on the stool next to him. "Thanks." Tom turns on his stool to face her. "He awake?"

"Yes." Ally picks up the drink the barman slid in front of her and throws it back. She slams the glass onto the bar and nods for another. "He's in the safest place, right now."

"They can't keep him in there forever."

"No. They can't." She purses her mouth and looks at Tom. "You saved his life."

Tom watches her a moment before gulping his own whisky.

"And the tour has been cancelled." She sips her new drink.

"The whole thing?"

"Yes. I told him it was only Denmark and Sweden for now. But... I cancelled the lot."

Tom inhales and holds it a moment. "He'll go spare."

"I don't want to think about it right now. I need to not think about him for a few hours. I'm exhausted."

"I don't blame you."

She looks up at his face and her eyes rest on the cut over his left eye. She reaches across and runs a thumb over it. "So, are you ever going to tell me what happened?"

"Long story. But let's just say a stiletto to the forehead isn't ideal."

"A stiletto?" Ally picks up her new drink and grins. "I hope it was a Louboutin."

Tom laughs. An uninhibited, free laugh and it feels... amazing.

"Can't say I checked. But I do hope so. If it was a dodgy knock off, I'll feel cheated."

Ally snorts and motions for another drink. She turns to Tom. "You know, it'd be cheaper and easier to get a bottle." She raises an eyebrow. "We deserve it."

Tom chews on his lip and fixes his eyes on Ally's. The whisky fogs his brain, and he shrugs. "Why not." He turns to the barman. "Bottle of Stauning." He glances at Ally.

Ally leans towards the barman. "To go."

To go.

TOM FOLLOWS ALLY INTO HER HOTEL ROOM. SHE SWIRLS A HAND IN the air. "I'd have scattered rose petals everywhere, but I wasn't expecting company." She giggles, kicking her shoes off.

Tom chuckles as he pulls two glasses off the mini bar, cracks open the bottle and sits on the floor at the foot of the bed, leaning against it. He pours into the glasses and holds one out for Ally.

She plonks beside him, and they clink glasses.

"Well, Max performed as though he didn't have a care in the world the other night." Ally sips her drink.

"I must say that's the first pop concert I've ever been to." Tom gulps and pours another.

"And?" Ally grins.

Tom jerks a brow and grins. "Not quite my thing."

Ally throws her head back and laughs and Tom tries to ignore the soft skin on her neck.

Whisky and loneliness are a bad combination.

Tom blows a breath out and stares straight ahead at the TV. He swirls the whisky in his glass a moment before swallowing it.

"Tom?"

Tom turns his head and Ally is right in front of his face. He swallows. "Yep?" *Shit.*

Ally lunges forward and pushes her mouth against his. He falls back onto the floor as she pushes him down. He grips the comforter on the bed and attempts to pull himself up.

Ally sits up and stares into his eyes. "You married?"

"Ah, no…"

"Serious relationship?"

"It's... complicated?" *Cliche, but true…*

"This doesn't have to mean anything," Ally whispers, undoing his top couple of buttons and sliding her hand across his chest.

His skin tingles and his eyes close a moment, remembering the last time someone ran *her* hand over his chest. He remembers *her* breath as it brushed his face. *But… she isn't coming back.*

Tom opens his eyes and Ally is watching him, biting her bottom lip. Her hand is still inside his shirt and the other is resting on his belt.

"Pretend I'm her, Tom. I really don't care."

Tom takes a couple of breaths to process what Ally said. *But you're not her.*

The whisky swirls through his bloodstream and Ally undoes the rest of his shirt. Her fingers patter across his skin and she lowers her mouth back to his. All hope of resisting disappears, and he wraps an arm around her back, rolling her onto the floor.

They tear at each other's clothing, until it's strewn all over the room.

Tom grips onto Ally's hips as she wraps her legs around him. He closes his eyes and pictures Isabella beneath him.

Ally slides her legs off him and pushes him down to the floor. He holds his breath as Ally snakes her mouth across his chest and down his body.

TOM OPENS ONE EYE AND CHECKS THE SCREEN OF HIS PHONE. *3:05am.* He shakes his head and glances at Ally, asleep next to him. His head pounds and he pinches the bridge of his nose.

This is bad. Very bad.

Tom slides to the edge of the bed and stands up. He pulls his clothes on and opens the room door, wincing as the soft click is like a gun shot through the darkness. He glances over at Ally through the light from the hall, hugging a pillow against her, sound asleep. He lets out a breath and walks out of the room.

Moments later he is in his own room and he throws himself onto the bed and flicks the TV on. He gulps water and wills the pain in his head to dissipate.

Max's face lights up the TV screen and words in Danish are rolling across the bottom. Tom doesn't need to be fluent to know what the story is about. He feels a pang of guilt in his chest.

I said I'd take care of it. But instead I sleep with your sister.

"I'm a fucking hero," he mutters, scrunching his face up.

TOM GULPS FROM THE MUG OF BLACK COFFEE AND SIGHS. GRIPPING A hand to his head he claws through his hair, willing the pounding to stop. *One day on the wagon and I topple face first off it.* He scans the hotel restaurant, thankful it's practically empty.

The phone on the table rings. Private number.

Fine Kat, Let's play.

He swipes the phone up and pushes it to his ear. "What do you want?"

The caller is silent for a moment.

"I know it's been a while, but a hello is a good start." Her voice is fuzzy, as though a million miles away.

Tom's heart jumps into his throat and he sits up straight in the chair. "Iz?"

"Hey."

He grips the phone tighter and exhales.

This timing is like something out of a B grade movie.

"Sorry to call out of the blue. Are you on a job?"

Her voice was honey in his ears. "In a manner of speaking. But… don't apologise for calling me." He pushes his hand into his chest to curb the thumping. "Don't ever apologise."

He hears her breath down the phone, and it does nothing to slow his heart. "It's so nice to hear your voice."

"God Iz, you have no idea." Tom closes his eyes. He rests his face against the screen of the phone, as though it brings him closer to her.

"Are you okay?"

Tom blows a breath out and rubs his eyes. "I'm fine."

"You're not fine."

"I'm hungover," Tom admits.

"Tom…"

"How's your father?"

"Amazing."

Tom smiles to himself. "Good to hear."

"I think about you every day."

Tom squeezes his eyes shut and thinks about the fact Isabella was the only one he thought about the previous evening. The entire time. *God, I'm a bastard.*

"Tom?"

"Sorry, what did you say?"

"I miss you."

Tom's breath hitches and he pushes the phone against his ear harder. "I miss *you*."

"I sent you a letter."

"You did. I haven't opened it yet."

Isabella laughs. "Why not? Are you afraid it'll bite?"

"No, I … I didn't want to read that you weren't coming back."

"You think I'm not coming back?"

Tom's heart stands to attention and he sits up. "How could I expect you to?"

"I know that you don't. But that doesn't mean I won't." Tom hears a small sniffle and knows her eyes are full of tears. "I should go. I …um... "

"So, it's not forever?" Tom whispers.

"I hope not. Forever is a really long time."

The line goes dead and Tom rests the phone against his forehead a moment before dropping it on the table.

James slides into the chair across from him and slaps his coffee on the table. He fixes his eyes on Tom. "I thought Isabella Wirth was dead?"

Tom's heart stops beating.

Fuck.

34

JAMES

James stares hard into Tom's eyes and enjoys watching the colour drain from his face. His heart drumrolls through his chest.

Tom leans back in his chair and scrunches the tablecloth in his fist.

James drops his eyes to Tom's hand and grins. "Interesting."

"How long were you standing behind me?" Tom's voice is barely above a whisper, his fist remains clenched.

"Well, I was about to sit down when your phone rang. So… I waited."

"The whole time, then."

"Yep." James fiddles with the salt and pepper shakers. "How is she?"

Tom sucks in his cheeks, staring at James. "Who?"

James smirks. "I heard the whole conversation, Tom."

"Is that right?"

"So, time to share." James leans forward on the table, drumming his fingers making the cutlery rattle.

"You know a lot more than you should already." Tom slams his hand down on top of James' and pulls him across the table, so they are nose to nose. "Who wants to know?" Tom hisses in James' face.

James stares back into Tom's eyes and gathers every ounce of resolve. *Choose. He saved your life.*

"My Uncle."

Tom releases James and he falls back into his chair.

"*Why* does he want to know?"

"He was mates with Jack. He thinks this Isabella girl killed him. And you helped."

"And what are you getting out of this?"

James pours water from the jug on the table and drinks, eyeing Tom.

"I'm waiting," Tom snarls.

James drops his eyes to the starched tablecloth. He runs a hand over his throat and recalls the rope being lifted off him.

In the same moment his Uncle's voice echoes through his head.

I would have let you hang.

"I'm facing jail time. Drugs. Misconduct." He shrugs. "Uncle Pete gave me a proposition, and I said yes." He takes another gulp of water. "Not that he gave me a choice."

"He's blackmailing you?"

"Yep."

Tom folds his arms.

James ventures into the jungle. "You're in love with her."

"She's de—"

"Cut the bullshit, Tom. I heard you."

Tom lifts his chin and peers at James. "What do you want?"

"Want?"

"To keep your mouth shut."

James interlaces his fingers behind his head and leans his chair back so it's balancing on two legs. *Let me have some fun first.* "I want to hear you say it, Tom."

Tom glares at James and turns his lip up. "Isabella is alive."

James plonks his chair back down on all its legs. "Look how easy that was."

"I'll never say it again."

You've squirmed long enough. "And neither will I."

Tom tilts his head. "What?"

"My Uncle would have let me hang. You didn't. He's family. You hate me." James shrugs. "Take it as an act of gratitude."

"I don't hate you."

James flicks his eyes up to Tom and grins. "You say *I'm* a terrible liar."

"I don't hate you," Tom repeats. "You're a royal pain in my arse. But I don't hate you."

"I've spent too long trying to fit into the square hole my family tried to shove me in."

"Where would you prefer to be shoved?"

James shrugs. "I wish I'd been born to a different family. A different life. One where I got to make the decisions about my future."

"What future do you want?"

James bites on his lip and roams his eyes around the near empty restaurant. "I'm quite liking this gig, to be honest." He looks at Tom, who hasn't moved a muscle.

James stands up. He presses Uncle Pete's number and waits.

"James."

"Yeah… Tom won't budge." James stares straight at Tom. "She's dead. And I'm done. Best be preparing your court martial." He hangs up and tosses the phone at Tom. "Oh, and I'd like a decent phone."

Tom catches it, still watching James.

James saunters from the restaurant smiling to himself.

That felt good.

35

TOM

Tom taps James' stone age phone on the table. *What the fuck just happened?* He picks up his coffee and takes a gulp, realising it's gone cold. He forces the liquid down his throat and grimaces.

His mind drifts back to Isabella. Her voice. *What was she doing?* She called. That's dangerous. He closes his eyes, resting his head in his hands. If he concentrates hard enough, he can smell her shampoo… *I'm pathetic.*

"Morning."

Tom's eyes pop open and his heart jumps. Ally sits across from him. *Oh, God this is awkward.*

He smiles. "H… hi." He clears his throat.

Ally grins. "I would love to have watched your walk of shame this morning." She raises her coffee cup to her mouth, still grinning.

"Walk of sha… ahh. No. I had to... go?" He winces.

Ally pouts her lips like a duck, a smile lacing the corners. "Go where?"

"To my…" *My room. Just say my room.*

Ally laughs and puts her cup down. "Relax, Tom. I'm teasing you."

"I'm relaxed." Tom's voice rasps and he swallows.

"Yeah… yeah I can tell." Ally leans forward. "I was drunk and horny. Thanks for being a trooper." She winks.

Excuse moi? "Wait... what?"

"What?"

Tom leans on the table and smiles. "Did you… use me?" He feigns horror, slapping his hand to his chest.

"One hundred percent."

Tom's eyes widen. "And to think I felt guilty for sneaking out at three am."

"Oh God, no. I was relieved when I woke up and you weren't there. Awkward morning after conversation?" She shivers. "No, thanks."

Tom's mouth is half open and he stares at Ally. "I… honestly don't know how to feel." *Less guilty. I feel less guilty.*

Marginally.

"You're not the first, and you won't be the last." She clicks her tongue. "But thanks. You were one of the best."

What the hell? Tom clamps his mouth shut and raises an eyebrow at Ally.

Ally leans forward. "Tell me, did you picture *her* the whole time?"

Tom lets the breath he held escape. "Yes."

Ally nods once. "You're welcome."

Tom frowns and watches as she sips more coffee.

I just wanted a quiet cup of coffee. Tom pinches the bridge of his nose.

"Okay, so... we're back to normal?" Ally waits.

"Yeah... yes. Normal."

"Excellent. I don't suppose you'll go visit Max?"

The sudden change of track unsettles Tom. "Visit him?" His throat squeezes. "I don't really like hospitals much."

"Me neither. But he's refusing to talk to anyone. And I thought..."

Tom rolls his eyes.

Jesus.

TOM CLIMBS THE STEPS INTO RIGSHOSPITALET. A SHIVER RUNS through him as he remembers the last time he was in a hospital. He woke up there with a tube hanging out of his lung. *Not great.*

His phone rings and he's grateful he has an excuse to not go inside yet. He reads the screen. *Judith.*

Here we go.

"Martha."

"Get back to London. Immediately."

"And a very good morning to you, too."

"I'm in no mood, Tom."

"You sound tense." He sits on a step and leans his elbows on his knees.

"A jet will be waiting for you and James this evening at the same airfield you flew into. Nineteen hundred. Be on it."

The phone goes dead and Tom keeps it against his ear, staring out at the street.

"Fantastic."

He stands and drops the phone in his pocket.

Tom wrinkles his nose at the odour inside the hospital lobby. Bleach and sanitiser. He shows his identification, and the reception girl checks he is on the visitor list for Max Morgan.

"*Værelse fem en fire.*" The girl smiles at Tom and points to the lift.

Tom raises both eyebrows and holds both hands up.

She giggles and her cheeks deepen in colour. "Room five one four. Up in elevator." She points again.

Tom nods. "*Behage,*" he winks at her and she looks down at her keyboard, pink spots appearing on each cheek.

Bless her.

As Tom gets in the lift, he punches a message into his phone.

We are on a plane tonight. Pack your bags.

Seconds later James' phone vibrates in Tom's pocket.

Oh, yeah. That's inconvenient.

He wanders down the hospital corridor to Max's door. He leans on the door frame and observes Max staring out the window.

"It's not quite the penthouse."

Max jumps and turns to Tom. "Buttercup." His voice is weak and scratchy.

Tom walks into the room and straddles the chair next to the bed, resting his arms along the top rung of the backrest. He watches Max and says nothing.

"Did Ally send you?"

"She did."

Max nods and picks at the blankets.

Tom watches him for a moment. "She's worried about you."

Max rolls his eyes but doesn't look up at Tom. "She worries about everything," he mumbles.

"With good cause, Max."

Max smiles at Tom. "She told me you gave me mouth to mouth."

"I did."

Max's lips turn up at each end. "So, your mouth was…" he gestures to his own mouth and raises an eyebrow.

"Yes. Numerous times."

Max blows a breath out and leans forward. "Well, you see I have no recollection of that. So maybe you could reenact—"

"Nope." Tom shakes his head.

Max tutts. "Worth a shot."

"It would have been weird if you didn't."

Max chuckles and leans back into his pillow.

Tom runs his thumb across his top lip. *No point delaying it.* "Max, James and I are leaving tonight."

Max clutches the blankets. "Leaving?"

"Yes. Back to London." Tom waits as Max glances at his lap with a furrowed brow. "So, you're going to have to talk to Ally."

Max scoffs. "She wants to put me in rehab."

"Rightly so."

"I don't *need* rehab."

MARTHA STOOD AT THE WINDOW, HER BACK TO TOM AS HE LAY IN A *hospital bed.*

"There's a rehab place down in—"

"I'm not going to rehab," Tom snaps.

"Tom—"

"No!" Tom barks. "I don't need rehab..."

"I SAID THAT ONCE." TOM FIXES HIS EYES ON MAX'S.

"And?"

"And… maybe I should have gone."

"Why?"

"Because it would have helped me." Tom takes a breath. "Maybe, I wouldn't still be relying on a bottle of whisky to help me sleep or calm me down."

"Right." Max shifts his eyes back to the window. "I'd only be taking up space for someone who deserves it."

"Ally needs you, Max."

As though on cue, Tom's phone vibrates, and he peers at a text from Ally.

She's outside.

Tom slides his phone back into his pocket and looks at Max.

Max shakes his head and sniffles, still looking out the window. "I'm useless."

"You keep believing that and it's all you'll ever be."

Max slowly brings his face around to Tom. "How philosophical of you."

Tom shrugs. "What if I told you I learnt something from you?"

"From me?" he whispers.

"I learnt that I don't want to be like you."

Blunt. Tom holds his breath and waits for Max's reaction.

"Well... good for you, Buttercup." He smiles but his eyes don't light up. *"I* don't even want to be like me."

"Once you start liking yourself, everything will be different."

"How do you know?"

"My Mum told me once." Tom stands up. "And she never lied to me."

"Well, thanks. I guess." Max looks up at Tom.

"Thank you too, Max." Tom nods at him once before walking out the door, closing it behind him.

36

MAX

M ax stares up at the ceiling to stop himself watching Tom's backside as he leaves the room. *It's like a peach.*

He hears Ally's voice in the corridor. She's speaking in a hushed tone, but he can make it out.

"And?"

"And" Tom's voice isn't hushed. "He'll speak to you. Give him a minute."

"What do you think he'll say when I tell him?"

Max's ears prick. *Tell me what?*

"I suggest you don't. He won't like it and he'll freak out."

"Well, they said the psych ward was full, so that buys me a few more days." Ally's voice is louder now.

Psych ward? What the hell?

Max's heart speeds up and he sits upright. "No fucking way," he whispers to himself. He gets out of bed and creeps to the door to listen through the crack.

Tom's chuckle travels into Max's room. "He's still going to go nuts. I'd love to stay and help… really…"

"Ha. Liar."

Max hears a small slap as though someone whacked someone else's arm.

First, Tom's leaving, and now… psych ward? Fuck. This.

"He needs help," Ally continues.

"I agree. But *he* won't agree. And you know it."

"Well, they won't let him out until he's assessed so…"

Try and fucking stop me.

Max creeps back to his bed and jumps in. He faces away from the door and pretends to be asleep. A few seconds later he hears Ally's voice next to him.

"Are you awake?" she whispers.

Yes.

"Max?" Ally puts her hand on his shoulder and sighs. He concentrates on breathing evenly until he hears her leave the room.

Max stays put a few more minutes before sitting up and swinging his legs over the side of the bed.

Game on.

He tiptoes to the door and peeks out at the empty hall. He darts back to the cupboard next to his bed and pulls out the bag full of clothes Ally had left him. Moments later, dressed in cargo pants and a hoodie, he stashes the bag back in the cupboard. Sticking his wallet and phone in his pocket, he leaves the room.

He walks down the hall with purpose, pulling his hoodie up over his head and face.

"He's sleeping," Max hears Ally's voice around the next corner. He opens the nearest door and slips in. It's a disabled toilet.

He holds the door with enough of a sliver to watch Ally and a nurse heading towards his room.

Adrenaline spikes through his blood. He runs from his hiding place and into the open lift.

Go time.

The lift seems to take eons, but in reality, it is probably about ten seconds. On the ground floor he walks past the reception desk, careful not to make eye contact with anyone. He gets out the doors and makes a beeline for a lone cab he spots parked next to the ambulance bay. His breathing thunders through his ears and every tiny noise behind him makes him jump.

He opens the back door of the cab and slides in. "Drive. Go."

The driver holds up both hands in confusion. "Where you go?"

"Anywhere that's away from here." Max makes a shooing motion with his hand. "C'mon, let's go. Go!" He glances out the back window as the cab pulls away from the kerb.

Nothing.

Max turns back in his seat and closes his eyes. His heartbeat hums and he takes some deep breathes to try and slow it down.

He slouches in the back of the cab as it weaves through traffic, glancing down at the clothes Ally had brought him.

The girl has no fashion sense.

His phone rings. He turns it on silent and ignores his sister's call.

He gazes out the window as the city darts past. The cab driver keeps glancing in the rear-view mirror at him. He pulls his hood tighter around his head and face.

I must look homeless.

"Drive," Max mumbles.

"You have destination?"

"Nope. ..." Max motions in circles with his hand. "Drive wherever you want."

The cab driver's eyebrows settle in a squiggly line and he shrugs.

Max pulls his phone out and— against his better judgement — checks social media.

'He's still amazing.'

'How the fuck did I not pick that?'

'It was so obvious in hindsight.'

'He's the same glorious man he was before.'

Max rolls his eyes and keeps flicking his thumb at the screen. He makes the mistake of going into his direct messages.

'You are a disgrace. I am unfollowing you and I can't believe I ever thought you were cool.' Max recognises the name.

God, she's only fourteen. He scrunches his eyes closed and drops the phone on the seat next to him.

"You famous one?" The cab driver interrupts Max's silent struggle.

He opens his eyes. "Pardon?"

"You here for singing?"

"Yeah..."

"My daughter. She love you." The cab driver nods his head, smiling.

Max's chin jerks up. "Used to love me?"

"No, no… she at show. Love you."

Max's chest expands a little and he sits upright. "Where is your daughter?"

The cab driver checks his watch. "On bus, home from school."

"How old is she?"

"She sixteen." The cab driver slows to a stop at a red light and swivels in his seat. "Can I take photo for her?"

Max smiles. "What's your name?"

"Fred."

"And… how far away do you live, Fred?"

MAX SITS IN THE KITCHEN OF A TWO BEDROOM FLAT. THERE'S NOT A lot of furniture — only essentials. Fred brings cake and tea to the table.

"Any moment," Fred smiles. "You very kind man."

Max sips the tea as the door opens. He looks up as a girl dumps her school bag. Max holds his breath.

"*Far! Hvorfor er du—*" Her eyes drift to Max. "*Åh herregud!*" Her hand flies to her mouth and she stumbles back against the closed door.

Max stands.

"Laura," Fred says. He motions her towards them.

She creeps towards Max as though he may disintegrate. Max smiles and her hand slaps against her chest.

"Max Morgan?"

"Nice to meet you, Laura."

"You are in my home?"

"Looks like it. You speak English?"

"Yes. I learn at school." She looks at Fred. "I am teaching Father. Slowly." She smiles at her father and Max feels the warmth between them. She looks back to Max. "How are you in my home? Can I hug you?" She covers her mouth with her hand again. "I mean…"

Max holds his arms out either side of him. "Of course."

Laura skips to him and hugs him. Max feels the tightness of her arms and the tremble in her body.

"You are standing in my kitchen." Laura moves back and stares at him with wide eyes.

"Yes. Maybe you will have cake and tea with me?" Max gestures to the empty seat next to him.

Laura stands with her mouth agape, staring at Max. She slides into a chair with her eyes stuck on his face. "Are you okay?"

Max bites his lip. "Why wouldn't I be?"

"I saw on the television. You went to hospital."

Max nods. *Of course.* "Yes. I was… unwell."

"Your concerts have been cancelled."

"Yes."

"What is wrong?" Laura nibbles on a small cake.

Max sips more tea and considers her a moment. He glances at Fred who is smiling like The Joker. *God love him.*

"Tell me Laura, who do you live here with?"

"It is myself and my father." She puts the cake down and runs her fingers around the edge of the plate. "My mother died two years ago," she added softly.

Max's stomach dropped. "I'm sorry."

She looks up at him through the hair hanging over her face. "Thank you." She smiles. "You helped me through that time."

"I did?"

Laura nods. "Your music. When I was sad. I would listen."

Max puts both hands flat on the table and takes a breath. *God, I treat my fans like dirt.* "That means a lot to me," he whispers.

"You hurt yourself," Laura states. There is no question in her tone. Her eyes rest on his wrist.

Max looks back up at her and swallows. "Yes."

"Why?"

He gives a lopsided smile. "I don't like myself very much."

Laura gasps. "But you make so many people happy."

Ironic, isn't it.

"Maybe before." He shrugs and traces the checks on the table-cloth with his finger.

"No. Always."

"How did you feel when the stories came out this week?"

"How did I feel?" She frowns and lifts one end of her top lip. "I felt bad."

Max nods.

"For you," she finishes.

Max flicks his eyes up to her. "For me?"

"Yes. So many people said things. Cruel, mean things."

"And you?" Max raises a brow.

"I love you." Her cheeks glow pink. "You made me feel happiness and hope when I thought my world ended." She shakes her head and drops her eyes to the floor.

I gave you hope?

"And anyway," she continues. "Who cares who you love?" She grins. "You will still sing, yes?"

Max stands up and gazes out the window. He turns back to see Fred reach across and hold his daughter's hand on the table. *They only have each other.*

"Maybe, when I am feeling better. Yes." Max smiles.

Laura nods. "The world needs your music. I need your music."

Max walks to her and hugs her. "And I really needed to hear that," he whispers to her.

His phone vibrates against his leg and he stands up, pulling it from his pocket. He sees Ally's name. *Fine.*

"Ally," he holds his breath and waits.

"Where are you? Are you okay? What the hell?"

He kicks a toe into the floor and smiles to himself. *Ally's way of reaching across the table and holding my hand.*

"I'm fine."

37

JAMES

James sits on his bed, head in his hands. He presses his fingers into his temples and concentrates on breathing.

Jail. Well, shit.

Someone pounds on his door and he jerks his head up. His pulse spikes and he wipes the white powder from under his nose. He lopes to the door and yanks it open, gripping the edge of the door to keep balance.

"Oh, hey." James sniffs a breath in and shoves his hands in his pockets.

Tom narrows his eyes. "You high?"

"Yep." James wanders back into the room.

"So, you *are* having a breakdown. Excellent."

"I'm not. I'm ... anxious." He sits on the bed and his knee jitters.

Tom watches him a moment longer before pulling out a smartphone and tossing it to him. "Phone."

James catches it. "Thanks."

Tom squints at James. "What gives?"

James shrugs. "I'm fucked. I'm going to jail. Do you know what they do to rich kids in jail?" His breathing intensifies. "*Military* rich kids?"

"I wouldn't know. Not being one myself. Or having been to jail." Tom leans against the wall with one shoulder, folding his arms. "I came to tell you that we're flying out of Denmark tonight. Nineteen hundred. Pack your bags." Tom drops his arms and turns towards the door. "Oh, and no more coke."

James pulse pushes its way into his throat and hammers against his neck. "Wait! We're going back to London?" *Fuck.* "Tonight?"

Tom turns back to him. "Where else would we go? Tahiti?"

James leans over his knees and gulps in large breaths. The room spins. "I can't breathe. I can't." He feels a hand on his shoulder.

"James. Breathe." Tom's voice is calm and assuring. "Coke and anxiety aren't a good mix."

James nods and gasps in air. "I know," he manages. "I ..." He cocoons his nose and mouth in his hands and tries to slow his breathing down.

God, this is humiliating.

"I didn't want to waste it." He forces a laugh and Tom chuckles next to him.

"Don't worry about London. I'll handle it."

"How? We're talking about the fucking King of the Royal Navy, Tom." James sits upright and looks at Tom. "And no offence, but he isn't *your* biggest fan." James smirks.

Tom raises both palms and shrugs. "Who is?"

"Martha?"

"Yes Martha. Who can pull strings." Tom stands up. "Be ready to leave at eighteen thirty."

James' new phone rings in his hands and he glances down at it. "Shit."

Tom holds his hand out. "Give it."

"No way. Are you mental? You'll only make him angrier."

"Who me?" Tom rolls his eyes and wiggles his fingers with his palm out.

James places the phone in Tom's open palm and winces.

"Admiral Moore. How wonderful of you to check in." Tom grins at James before spinning and walking to the window. "James? Oh, he's… high."

James pushes a squeaky gasp out. *Oh, God.*

He watches as Tom holds the phone a couple of centimetres from his ear and peers down at the street below. Seconds later he brings it back to his ear. "You sound upset."

James watches as Tom wanders around the room. He dusts off a lampshade, inspects a pen holder on the desk and opens the mini bar to grab some water. *How does he stay so calm?*

"That's quite a lot of fucks in your rant considering you ended with… I don't give a fuck," Tom remarks.

James closes his eyes and tries to stop his breathing from running away with him. *Holy hell.*

"Oh look, there's another one."

"Oh, God," James groans.

Tom glances at James. "You know what, Admiral? Let's have a little chit chat when we get back, yeah? Words can be *so* miscon-strued over the phone."

He pauses and grins at James.

"Right, you are then, tata." He ends the call and tosses the phone back to James. "He gets angry, doesn't he?"

James stares at Tom with his mouth hanging open. "What did... fucking hell, Tom!"

"Relax. We have a two-hour plane ride for you to get angsty and upset. Enjoy the coke while it lasts."

James leaps from the bed and grabs Tom by the shirtfront. Tom glances down at his hand and back to his face. "So, it runs in the family then?"

James dips his head against his arm as he clings to Tom's shirt. "No. But... fuck." He spins and throws himself face first into his pillow.

"Dramatic." Tom quips.

James groans into his pillow and hears Tom's phone go off.

"Grant," Tom pauses. "Ally, what phone are you..."

James rolls over and peers at Tom.

"Okay, slow down... where are—"

Tom looks at the ceiling and blows a breath out. "Stay there. I'm on my way." Tom taps his phone against his forehead and squeezes his eyes shut.

"Bad news?" James asks.

"Tell me, James," Tom jiggles his jaw. "Do you believe in past lives?"

"Past lives?"

"Yes. Because I'm starting to think karma is a bitch."

James sits up and scrubs a hand through his hair. "What the fuck are you on about?" *My brain can't cope with this right now.*

"It's like someone has decided that I'm here to wade through everyone else's shit… and be expected not to get my clothes dirty. You know?" Tom tilts his head.

"Okay. No offence Tom but you're being kind of weird."

Tom spins and stalks to the door. "Oh, and don't bother packing. We aren't going anywhere."

38

TOM

"Where are you? I'll come get..." Ally cranes her neck forward and squints as she listens on her phone. "You'll get a cab? Where are you?... Hello?" She pulls the phone away from her ear and stares at the screen.

Tom glances at her from his spot on Max's hospital bed watching the tiny television screen. "What's the deal?"

"He's... having tea..."

"Having tea?" Tom wrinkles his forehead. "I hope there's biscuits as well."

"What?"

"Well, tea is so bland. You need something sweet. You know?" He tilts his head and grins at Ally.

She screws her face up and shakes her head. "Tom, I'm in no mood for weird British jokes."

Tom's face goes serious. "Oh, it's no joke. Tea is *blergh*." Tom screws his nose up.

A small smile creeps along Ally's lips. She rolls her eyes to the ceiling.

Desired effect. Tom jumps down from the bed and puts his hand on her shoulder. "He said he's fine. Let's go to the hotel so we're there when he gets back. Yes?"

Ally slides her eyes to Tom's face. "Okay," she whispers.

Tom nods and steers her to the door.

"I may need a drink tonight," Ally says as they walk down the corridor of the hospital.

Dangerous.

Tom purses his lips to stop his grin escaping. "I'm back on the wagon." *And I miss Iz. A lot. And she's coming back.*

"The wagon?"

"Yes. That rickety piece of shit I keep falling off."

"You're an alcoholic?" Ally stops and faces him.

Tom's stomach drops. *Alcoholic. Alcoholic.* "I'm... It's not good for me."

"Because you're an alcoholic?" Ally stares straight at Tom and it makes his skin prickle.

Tom stares back at her. "Yes."

Ally steps into Tom and walks her fingers up his chest. "You are a very interesting human, Tom."

Tom looks down at her hand on his chest and swallows. "Um, thank you?"

Ally grins and walks to the lift. "You're welcome."

THEY GET INTO THE CAR WAITING FOR THEM AND ALLY TURNS to Tom.

"Okay, question and answer time."

Tom huffs and folds his arm. "What is it with you and your brother? Can't I be mysterious?"

Ally laughs and slumps back into her seat. "Nah, we like to know all the things." She bites her lip and squints. "Tell me. Where is *she?*"

"Who?"

"The one you're head over heels in love with."

"I'm not… head over…" Tom shakes his head.

"Is that right."

Nope. "Yes, that's right."

"Has anyone ever told you you're a terrible liar?"

"Yes." Tom looks at Ally to find her smirking with a raised brow.

"You don't imagine another woman if you aren't in love with her."

Tom winces inwardly and looks out the window again.

"So, where is she?"

"Haven't you got other questions that are burning a hole in your brain?" Tom holds both palms up and shrugs. "Like, where do I get my clothing from? Or, who cuts my hair?"

"Nope. This is far more intriguing."

Tom sighs and rubs his face.

"So, again… why aren't you with her?"

Tom clears his throat and runs a finger around the collar of his shirt. "It's complicated."

"You said that last night. I thought you were being polite."

"No… it really is… complicated." *With her pretending to be dead and all.* "She lives abroad and it won't work."

"Lives abroad where?"

Belgium. "Texas." *Texas? What?*

"So, you should move on?"

"Probably."

"Will you see her again?"

Not soon enough. "I don't know."

Ally jerks. "You don't know?"

Tom slaps both hands down on his knees. "I'm done now." He eyes Ally and she slinks back in her seat.

"Of course." She smiles. "Sorry."

"It's fine," Tom mumbles.

Ally pauses. "So, I don't suppose you still have that jet leaving this evening?"

"Yes."

"Do you think Max and I could be on it too?" Ally clasps her hands in front of her. "I need to get him out of here."

Tom chews on his bottom lip, staring back at her. "Fine," He nods. *Why the fuck not?*

Tom glances out the front window as they arrive at the hotel. A cab pulls up at the kerb and Max casually steps out of it. Tom gestures towards them. "Speaking of…"

Ally follows his gaze and gasps, leaping out of the car. She hurtles towards her brother who is already in an embrace with the cab driver.

Tom frowns and smiles to himself at the same time. *Max hates people.*

Tom climbs out of the car as Ally grabs Max and hugs him, taking the opportunity to slip past and into the hotel. He gets into the lobby and leans against the wall.

Time to sort James out.

He pulls his phone out and presses Martha's number.

"Tom."

"Martha."

"Don't even think about making an excuse not to be on that plane tonight."

"Look at you being all angry. Are you shaking your finger, too?"

Martha huffs into the receiver and Tom grins.

"What can I do for you, Tom?"

"Admiral Peter Moore."

"What about him?"

"I need you to do some digging."

"Digging?"

Tom wanders around the lobby aimlessly while he talks. "I remember before he took the top job there were rumours."

"So?"

"So... I need you to find out if they were true and if there's evidence."

"Why on earth—"

"Can you just look?"

"What steaming pile of cow dung has James stepped in?"

Tom imagines Martha's face and chuckles. "Well, Uncle Peter wants to arrest him and throw him in jail. And as much as I find him an irritating little twerp… I hate the brass more. So…"

"Being placed with me was supposed to negate this whole jail business."

"Yes well, it seems he didn't quite get what Uncle Peter was after…"

"Which was?"

"Evidence Isabella is alive and that we killed Jack."

"But you didn't… I see."

"So, I'll leave that with you then?" Tom raises his eyebrows.

"I'll get back to you." She hangs up.

Six hours later, Tom buckles himself into the plane seat and gazes out the window.

A hand on his arm makes his head turn. Max perches on the seat next to him.

"Don't worry I'm not sitting here the whole trip. I wanted to say thanks again."

"What for?"

"Making me see I was being a dickhead. And that I need…" he looks at Ally who is standing near the door of the plane grinning at James. "Rehab," he whispers.

Tom sits straighter in his chair. "You're going to rehab?"

"I told Ally I'd consider it. But not back home. I can't do that."

"So where?"

"I hear the English countryside is nice." He shrugs.

Tom nods. "It is." He thinks of Avebury and smiles to himself.

"So, yeah…" Max stares intently at Tom.

Tom shoots him a definite warning look and folds his arms over his chest.

Max laughs and shuffles off the seat. "I think I'm going to sleep for a while."

He nods towards the rear of the plane.

"Excellent choice."

"If you want to snuggle… you know where to find me."

Tom smirks. "And there it is."

Max laughs again. "Like you said earlier… it'd be weird if I didn't." Max wanders off to the rear of the plane.

Seconds later James is in the seat vacated by Max. "Tom."

Closing his eyes and taking a steady breath in, Tom tries to keep the tension out of his shoulders. He opens his eyes and rests them on James' anxious face. "James."

"Did you speak with Martha?" James quirks a brow and sucks air through his grit teeth.

"It's under control." Tom rubs his eyes with a forefinger and thumb. "You need to relax."

"That's easy for you to say," James chews on his bottom lip while jiggling his jaw back and forth. "You aren't going to be hauled off to jail."

"And neither are you."

"Bu—"

Tom swivels in his seat and grabs both of James' shoulders. "Lesson Six. Trust me."

"But—"

"Lesson six." Tom repeats louder.

James nods his head. "Okay, okay." He stands and nods towards the back of the plane. "I might go have a kip up the back."

"Good plan. Max is looking for someone to snuggle with if you're feeling lonely."

"Ha ha." James stumbles up the middle of the cabin.

Tom grins to himself and slides down in his chair, leaning his head against the headrest.

"Tom."

For the love of...

Tom turns and sees Ally strapping herself into the seat next to him. *There are four other empty seats on this plane. Four.*

Tom exhales a breath. "Ally."

"Don't stress. I'm not about to ask you to join the-mile-high club." She smirks.

"I'm already a member." Tom deadpans.

"I'm not," she whispers, winking.

Tom waits a beat. "What can I do for you, Ally?"

"Stamp my card?"

Tom says nothing.

Ally rolls her eyes. "Still on the wagon, then?" She grabs a bottle of water and wiggles it in front of him.

"So far." He grabs the water and cracks the lid. "Thanks."

"Close to the edge?"

"You know, considering your brother is going into rehab, you aren't being overly supportive of my plight." He gulps a mouthful of water and raises his eyebrows.

Ally gazes at him a moment before shaking her head. "You're right. I'm being selfish." She leans on the arms rest and sucks her bottom lip in. "But you really were great. Your Texan girlfriend doesn't know what she's missing."

Tom's gut tumbles at the mention of *her* and he takes another mouthful of water to disguise his discomfort. "Did you need something specifically?"

"I'm sorry," Ally says quietly. "I'm socially awkward. Too much time travelling with Max." She slams herself back in her seat and huffs out a sigh.

"I see."

This is going to be a long flight.

39

JAMES

The plane taxis along the rural landing strip after landing. James clutches at the arm rest until his fingers ache.

"You really don't like flying do you, Gumnut?" Max stretches on the opposite seat and pulls his knees up to his chest, feet on the leather.

"I'm ..."

"You're?"

"I'm freaking the fuck out," he mumbles roaming his eyes around the cabin.

"About?"

"I'm in some trouble."

Max leans forward and wiggles his fingers. "Oh, I love me some trouble."

"Well, my Uncle is gonna throw me in jail."

"Why?"

"Because I didn't get him what he wanted." James shakes his head and dips it into his hands. He runs his hands through his hair and scratches his head violently.

"Steady on, Gumnut. You'll give yourself a patchy do." Max leans forward. "Listen, I'm going into rehab, for fuck's sake. That's *practically* jail." Max shrugs. "So, you know… I get it."

James peers up at Max. "That's nothing like jail and I really *don't* think you get it."

"Look at that, Mum. The kids are arguing again." Tom leans on the back of Max's chair. Ally is next to him.

James leaps from his seat. "Where are we going? Back to the warehouse? Or somewhere else? Your flat even?"

James' eyes are dry, and he blinks a couple of times. His breathing comes out in spurts as he waits for Tom to answer.

"My flat?" Tom snorts. "Not likely."

Max peers out his window. "You know, this is the first time in forever that I haven't had a bunch of people waiting for me to get off a plane," he muses. He leans forward against the window and frowns. "Though, it does look like we have a welcoming party of some sort."

James scurries across to Max's seat and looks out. His stomach contorts and he clutches at it, squeezing. "Oh, fuck." He flops into the seat and keeps squeezing his gut.

Admiral Peter Moore is standing next to an official car with two other men in uniform complete with berets, next to him. *He brought the MP's.*

Tom bends down to look out the window behind Max's seat. "Ahhh… he's not even giving me time to prepare."

"Prepare?" James' voice comes out as a squeak.

Tom stands up and grins. "Nevermind. It's fun to make it up as you go along."

James blinks a few more times and stares at Tom. "You… what?"

The stewardess opens the door and Tom whirls around. "This should be fun." He jerks his head towards the door, looking at James. "Shall we?"

James leans back in his seat and folds his arms. "No, we shall not. I'm not getting off this plane."

"Get the fuck off the plane," Tom's voice slides into James ear as he leans down over him.

James refuses to look at him, instead staring straight ahead at the wall as though he is a petulant child. "Nope."

Ally's voice breezes into the tense moment. "Max and I might … we'll see you outside."

James hears scuffling as the pair disembark.

Tom remains looming over James as he folds his arms tighter across his chest. "Tell me, James. How long do you plan to stay on the plane?" Tom's voice is conversational now and he sits in the seat Max vacated seconds before.

"Until he gives up and leaves." James thrusts his head towards the outside of the plane.

"Which we both know won't happen."

James shrugs and chews on his tongue.

Tom leans forward. "You aren't leaving this airstrip with him."

James barks out a laugh. "What do you think you can do to stop him, Tom?" James twists in his seat. "He's the First Sea Lord of the fucking Royal Navy."

"Exactly."

"Exac…" James twists his face in irritation. "Exactly?"

Tom nods. "Exactly." He stands up. "C'mon, let's get out of here."

"I said no."

"Has anyone ever told you, you carry on like a spoilt brat?"

James slides his eyes up to Tom who is scowling at him from the plane door.

"James. If you are not off that plane in exactly ten seconds I'm coming on board." Uncle Pete's voice shouts from the tarmac through a bullhorn.

James rolls his eyes. "He brought a bullhorn?"

Tom peers out the doors and gives a little wave. "He needs to learn to project."

"To what?"

"Project. You know… speak from the diaphragm." Tom breathes in a deep breath and pushes his hands into his body under his rib cage.

James stands up and lets out a snort "Has anyone ever told you that you know heaps of useless shit?" James stands in front of Tom, trying to eyeball him but knowing his fear is evident.

Grinning, Tom gestures James down the steps. "After you."

James stands at the door to the plane and squares his shoulders. "Fine," he huffs and marches down the steps.

James walks towards his Uncle. The nausea builds in his gut until the acidic burn reaches the back of his throat. He sees the hard face that looks remarkably like his father. *I hate you.*

"Admiral," James mumbles.

"MP's." Admiral Moore keeps his eyes on James as the military police approach him. James drops his bag on the ground and keeps his hands open.

"Whoa, whoa... one second." Tom's voice cuts over the marching of the MP's boots.

"Your help isn't required, Grant. Back off," Uncle Pete growls.

James feels a hand wrap around his elbow and Tom pulls him back to stand next to him. "I disagree, Admiral. I think James could do with my help as a matter of fact."

James chances a glance at Tom, who is grinning at his Uncle and appears completely relaxed. *Of course, he is.*

"The thing is Admiral, I thought we could have a little chat about... your extremely important position within the Royal Navy. And what having a tearaway nephew in jail could do to your image. But... if that isn't enough, maybe we can talk about how you came upon your current position in the first place?" Tom raises his eyebrows.

James holds his breath and looks back at his Uncle. *What the...?*

Uncle Pete clamps his mouth shut and glares at Tom.

"It seems blackmail is one of your favourite... shall we say... tools of the trade?" Tom points his finger to the sky. "Oh, and bribery. Sorry. Forgot the big one."

Uncle Pete's shoulders jerk ever so slightly. He clears his throat.

"Step down." He motions to the MP's who march back to their position behind him. "Where do you suggest we talk, Grant?"

James coughs and leans forward over his knee. "Wait a minute…" He stands and peers at Tom. "What the hell is going on?"

Tom flicks his eyes to James. "Did I, or did I not say I would handle it?"

"You did."

"I did." Tom slaps James on the back as though old college friends. "And what James, was lesson six?"

James breathes out a long breath. "Trust you?"

"Exactly."

Tom rubs his hands together and makes a show of shivering. "It's rather windy out here. And we have some friends we need to drop off."

He throws his head towards Ally and Max who are standing next to the car that was left for them.

"What say, we meet at the warehouse in three hours?" Tom raises his eyebrows and waits. "Or is that way past your bedtime, Admiral?"

James closes his eyes. *You did not just say that.*

"Fine." Uncle Pete grunts, stepping into his car, slamming the door. It peels away seconds later.

James watches the car a moment before turning to Tom. "What happened?"

"Have you ever played chess, James?"

"Yes…"

"Checkmate."

James follows as Tom jogs to the car. "Wait, what?"

Tom turns as he throws his bag into the boot. "He's fucked. And he knows it."

"He's fucked?"

"Royally."

40

MAX

"We're sharing a room tonight, Max, and I'm not hearing another word about it." Ally huffs.

Max rolls his eyes and plonks his head against the window as Tom and James get in the car. "Whatever," he mumbles.

"Are you sulking again, Max?"

Max glances up and sees Tom's green eyes staring through the rear-view mirror at him. Before Max can open his mouth the car jerks forward as Tom drives.

"I'm not sulking." Max scratches his head. "Ally thinks she needs to sleep in my room."

"Because if I don't you might have an episode."

"I'm fine!" Max explodes. "I told you."

"You say a lot of things," Ally mutters.

Tom shushes the pair of them. "Okay kids, enough bickering. Where are you staying?"

"The Savoy," Max orders. "And this time I want the Royal Suite."

Tom chuckles. "There's the Max we all know."

Ally slaps her phone against her ear. "Yes, I'd like to make a booking…"

✿

AN HOUR LATER MAX WATCHES AS TOM AND JAMES PULL AWAY FROM the hotel. *I'm gonna miss that suit.* Max lets out a long breath.

He turns to watch Ally dragging her suitcase into the lobby and skips after her.

God, it feels weird when there's no fans waiting. Max looks around at the empty surrounds and his shoulders slump. He follows Ally into the almost deserted lobby as his stomach grumbles. He slaps a hand over it and ignores the reception girls who have stopped gossiping to stare at him.

He tugs at Ally's arm. "Hey, I'm hungry."

"Fine, we'll get some room service in a bit."

"No, I wanna go out." *I want dumplings.*

Ally huffs out a loud sigh and signs the paperwork in front of her. The receptionist gives her a keycard and she spins around. "Max, no. That's ridiculous."

"I don't care. Let's go to Chinatown. It's only ten thirty."

Ally grabs Max's arm and steers him away from the front desk.

"Are you mental? What? You're just gonna walk around Chinatown?"

"I'll wear my hat and wig. No one will know it's me."

Ally scrunches her eyes shut. "I'm so tired, Max. We can order in if you want something else."

"No! I wanna go see stuff." Max pauses and tilts his head. "C'mon Al, you and me. We can hang." He winks. "Like we used to. Before the madness."

"Like you said, it's ten thirty. What exactly do you want to see?"

Max shrugs. "Things. Lights. Whatever. Just, not the inside of *another* hotel room." He clasps his hands under his chin. "Please?"

Ally drops her head and her shoulder slump forward. "Fine," she mutters.

Max jumps onto his tiptoes and claps his hands together. "Yay! Okay, let me find my hat." He bends over his suitcase and rummages through it. He spots his disguise clothes and yanks them out.

"Max, calm down… you're throwing things everywhere." Ally scoops up the discarded items from his suitcase and shoves them back in.

Max wraps his arms around Ally's neck and pecks her on the cheek as she bends down. "What would I do without you, Al?"

"Honestly? No idea."

"C'mon let's go! They can take our bags up for us." Max skips towards the doors. He turns to watch Ally speaking with the reception before she wanders over to him. *She really doesn't want to. Bless her.*

"I'll grab a cab," she mumbles walking out the door.

"It's only a short walk," Max grabs her hand. "Let's get some fresh air."

Ally huffs into the night air as Max drags her along.

※

THEY WANDER DOWN THE MIDDLE OF CHINATOWN. MAX LOOKS UP AT the bright red lanterns strewn over their heads. "Isn't it gorgeous," he whispers. "I want these at home." He glances at Ally who has her arms wrapped around herself, looking around constantly. "Relax Al. No one knows it's me."

"Yeah… I feel…"

"Feel what?" Max skips ahead and looks up at the colourful gate in front of him. "And one of these! It would be nice near the pool…" He turns but can't spot Ally. "Al?" He whips his head around. "Ally?" he says louder.

"Yeah," her voice creeps up behind him. "I'm right here. Around the pool? Really?" She peers up at the arch.

Max shrugs. "It's so colourful." He looks back at her. She still hugs her arms around herself. "Anyway, you feel what?"

"Huh?"

"You said you felt something?"

"Oh, yeah… no. It's nothing. I guess I'm paranoid that someone is going to see you."

Max scoffs and points to his blonde wig and baseball cap. "In this?"

Ally laughs. "Max, it's honestly not that good of a disguise, you know." She flips her phone out and starts typing into it.

He grins at his sister, enjoying the rare moment of hanging out with her. No fans, no concerts.

Her.

He smiles to himself before looking around and pointing to a restaurant. "That one. It looks yummy." He runs over to the front doors and reads the menu pinned up outside. "And they have dumplings!" He turns around triumphant, to hurry Ally up. But she isn't there.

Max glances around the street. "Ally?" He rolls his eyes and exhales loudly. "Ally! I'm hungry!" His eyes dart around the street, expecting her to be window shopping. *She's always window shopping.*

He wanders back to the middle of the pedestrianised street. His head whips back and forth.

Where are you?

He pulls his phone out and calls her number. He stalks down the street, looking at every single person's face he comes across. Her number rings out. He presses it again. *What's going on?* His heart speeds up and his breathing struggles under the weight building on his chest. Her number rings out again.

He stops in the middle of the street.

"Ally!" His breathing comes out in short bursts and his head has nothing inside it. He spins on the spot. "Ally!" He claws at his chest, pulling his clothing away to give himself relief from the anvil now sitting on his chest.

Where the fuck are you?

41

TOM

Tom dumps his suitcase and keys on an empty desk in the warehouse and wanders to the kitchenette. He pulls open the fridge and finds a sad banana and a plastic container with a limp salad inside. *Well, shit.* He slams the fridge closed and flicks the coffee machine on. His pocket vibrates and he pulls his phone out.

He glances at James who is sitting on one of the couches near Martha's office, staring into the distance.

"You look dazed, James," Tom remarks as he opens a text from Ally.

If you fall off that rickety piece of shit, you know where to find me.

Tom winces and slips his phone back into his pocket.

"I'm about to be bent over that desk," James points to an empty desk. "And royally fucked."

Martha's door opens before Tom can say anything. "Ah, gentlemen. You made it."

Tom leans against the tiny worktop in the kitchenette and grins. "Missed us?"

"Hardly." Martha purses her lips. "So, it seems you have some sticky goop to wade out of, James?"

Martha gestures the pair into her office with a flick of her head.

Still grinning, Tom pushes himself off the worktop and follows her in. He plonks down on the lumpy sofa.

"Moore will be here in about half an hour," Tom states, leaning back. "And you really need a new sofa." He wiggles his backside into the cushions and grimaces.

"Noted," Martha chips.

James shuffles in and perches next to Tom, on the edge of the sofa with his back straight.

Tom slaps his shoulder. "Relax. You look like a two by four is shoved up your bum."

"That's because there is!" James hisses at Tom.

Tom rolls his eyes. "Lesson six." He leans back and closes his eyes. "Hey, if you have nervous energy to burn off, that coffee machine should be ready." Tom opens one eye and peers at James.

James blows air out of his mouth making his lips vibrate. "Fine." He stands and stalks out of the office.

"Kat's in London." Martha sits on the coffee table and watches Tom.

He sits up and stares at her. "How do you know?"

"I've had a track on her since Denmark. She arrived back here a day ago. After your little encounter, no doubt."

"I see." Tom leans forward and plants his eyes on the floor. He steeples his index fingers under his nose.

"I don't think she's here to visit the Crown Jewels or see Buckingham Palace."

Tom flicks his eyes up to Martha. "I would agree."

She nods. "Let's deal with this James situation first." She stands up and grabs a folder off her desk. She thrusts it at Tom. "Don't say I never do anything for you."

He grabs the folder and opens it to find receipts for hotels, and photographs of Admiral Peter Moore in some compromising positions with a number of different women.

"You really are a genius," he whispers, flicking through the photographs.

"Yes. Turns out dodgy private investigators are keen to chat when the price is right."

"Indeed." Tom pulls out print outs of emails. "What kind of moron is he? He put all his threats and blackmail in writing?"

"In fairness, he deleted them and thought they had disappeared forever."

"Until you came along…" Tom shakes his head. *She never ceases to amaze me.*

James runs back into the office, slopping coffee over the sides of two mugs. "He's here. He's at the door." James is out of breath. He practically drops the mugs onto the coffee table.

Tom peers at the coffee slopped everywhere. "Did you remember the sugar?" He picks up a mug and sips. "*Blergh*. Nope."

James is practically dancing from one foot to the other.

Tom raises his eyebrows. "Well, are you going to go let him in?"

"Me?" James squeaks.

God, you are a weak piece of shit. Tom stands and cracks his neck. "Allow me." Tom saunters to the doors and yanks them open. "Look at you. Sharp." Tom reaches across and dusts the ribbon bar on the Admiral's jacket. "So important."

"You touch me again; I'll rip your arm off." Moore hisses.

Tom snorts. "Okay, Pete." Stepping back, he gestures Moore inside.

"You have no respect for anyone do you, Grant?"

"Actually, I respect a great number of people. Just not the pieces of shit that don't deserve it." He winks and notes the colour in Moore's face deepen.

"Let's get this over with," Moore grunts. "I have two MP's outside waiting to haul that sorry excuse of a nephew to jail, where he belongs." He stomps towards Martha's office as Tom leisurely strolls behind him.

"I should have asked Martha to get a cake," Tom muses.

Tom rocked back on his heels and waited for Commander Ford to open the door to the warehouse.

Tom raised an eyebrow. "You're telling me that a super-secret,

nameless intelligence agency runs out of this piece of shit building?"
He looked up at the doorway as he walked through it.

"Watch your mouth, sailor."

*Tom eyes Commander Jack Ford, wearing civvies, looking more
like an eccentric uncle than a high-ranking Naval officer.*

"Yeah, right."

*Ford whirled around and poked a finger into Tom's chest. "You
should be thanking your lucky stars you're even being considered for
such a position. Because you sure as hell aren't going anywhere in
the Royal Navy."*

"You think I want to?"

*"Clearly not. Your discipline leaves a lot to be desired. But as
much as I hate to admit it, you have skills. Skills that can be useful
here. You certainly seem to be able to disappear easily enough when
you don't want to be found."*

*Tom chewed the inside of his mouth and stared back at his soon to
be former Commanding officer.*

*The office door in front of them opened and a small woman stood
in the frame. She widened her eyes a moment before composing
herself. "Tom."*

Tom stared at the women, and for once had no words.

"Tom, this is Martha."

"I know who she is," Tom whispered.

Martha pursed her lips and stared at Tom.

"You know each other?" Ford frowned.

"Yeah. Recruitment branch." Tom meets Martha's eyes.

"Yes, I was there for a couple of years. I remember signing you up, Tom. You lasted twelve years, then?"

"Yeah..."

"And now you're here?" She raised an eyebrow, and a smile crossed her face.

"Looks like it."

Martha looked up at Ford. "Thank you, Commander. I'll take it from here." She opened an arm towards her office, ushering Tom inside.

Ford peered at Tom one last time. "And stay away from my daughter. Claire is too good for you."

Tom peered over his shoulder and smirked as Ford turned on his heel and marched out.

Once he heard the door click, Tom spun around to face Martha. "You just disappeared. No warning. Nothing."

"As far as the outside world is concerned. This agency doesn't exist, Tom." She placed a hand on his arm and gestured him to the sofa. "I'm sorry I couldn't tell you before."

"But you could have called me. Sent me a fucking telegram. Something!"

"I didn't think you needed me anymore?"

"Yeah well... I don't..." Tom swallowed.

"Still..."

Tom sat down. "No one knows, right?" he asked.

"About our history? No." Martha sat beside him. "And that's how it will remain."

Tom nodded, staring at the table in front of him. "There's no cake." He gave Martha a sidelong glance and a half smile.

Martha stood and patted Tom's shoulder before she walked towards the kitchenette. "There's always cake."

Tom walks into the office behind Admiral Moore. James jumps off the lumpy sofa and stands at attention. Tom's eyebrows crease as he watches James tremble. *Calm the fuck down, James.*

"Former Sub-Lieutenant James Moore," Admiral Moore barks.

"Sir."

"You're under arrest for—"

"Admiral Moore," Martha's voice fills the room.

Moore peers at her as though noticing she is there for the first time. "Ms Cole," Moore hisses. "*If* you don't mind."

"I do mind, actually." Martha points to the chair in front of her desk. "Sit."

"I beg your pardon?"

Martha walks around her desk to stand toe to toe with him. "I said, sit." She points to the chair again.

Moore squints at Martha and she holds his stare.

Tom smiles and picks up the folder off the coffee table. He whips out one of the photographs and holds it out. "I suggest you do what she says."

Moore's eyes slide down to the photograph and Tom watches his Adam's apple bobble as he swallows. His eyes flick back to Martha's and she tilts her head, still pointing at the chair.

Moore sits.

"Excellent." Martha leans against her desk and folds her arms. "Now, tell me Admiral. What exactly were you hoping to gain from James being paired with Tom?" She raises both brows and waits.

Moore glances at Tom who walks and stands next to Martha. "I wanted information," he mumbles.

Tom leans forward with a finger behind his ear, "Sorry, could you speak up?"

Tom hears a whimper from the couch and James shakes his head slowly, breathing into his cupped hands.

Man up, for God's sake.

"I said, I wanted information." Moore pinches the bridge of his nose.

"What information?" Martha looks directly at him.

"Jack Ford was a good friend." Moore juts his chin towards Tom. "He and that Russian killer murdered him. I wanted answers."

Tom pushes his lips into a thin line and eyes the Admiral.

"I *know* they're responsible and I *know* she's still alive."

Martha chuckles. "You know nothing, Admiral."

Tom's phone vibrates and he checks it. *Max's number.* He grunts and shoves it back in his pocket.

"I know I'm right." Moore mutters. "And if James was any sort of man, he would have got me what I needed." He shoots a look at his nephew, who is still breathing into his cupped hands. "But it appears he is weak as water. So, now he can face what's coming to him."

"We both know that isn't going to happen," Tom opens the folder and gives it to Moore. "You wined and dined your way into this job.

Fancy dinners, prostitutes. I guess money *can* buy power?" He nods at the folder. "It's all there. Do have a look. We can wait."

Moore closes the folder and slaps it on the desk.

"Oh, that's yours." Tom picks the folder up and throws it into Moore's chest. Photographs and documents slide out and litter the floor. "We have copies. So, no problem." Tom grins.

Moore's breath becomes louder as he clamps his mouth shut and exhales through his nose.

"So," Martha walks back around her desk and sits down. "You will drop all pending charges against James Moore. You are also going to forget trying to probe what happened in Paris. A Russian assassin by the name of Katerina Ivanoff killed Jack. Isabella Wirth is dead." Martha folds her hands on the table. "That's all you need to know." She looks at Tom. "Anything else, Mr Grant?"

"Yeah, if you ever mention the name Alexei Petrov again. I'll be doing more than dusting your ribbon bar." Tom leans forward, glaring into Moore's sweaty face. "Understood?"

"Are you threatening me?"

Tom grins. "Abso-fucken-lutely."

Moore stands and smooths his jacket. "I think we're done here."

Tom's phone vibrates again. He ignores it and gestures Moore towards the door. "Do come again. Maybe next time there will be cake."

Martha slaps a hand to her forehead. "I knew I forgot something."

Moore spins on his heel and marches out the door.

James gasps from the couch. "Oh, my God," he stands and scurries across the room. "I can't believe what just happened."

He slumps into the chair his uncle vacated.

"How did you…" He puffs air out of his mouth like a blowfish.

"Never ask her how she does it." Tom shakes his head. "It's best not to know."

He pulls his phone out and sees a missed call from Max. He frowns at the screen.

He presses call, puts the phone to his ear and walks out to the main floor.

"Tom! I can't find her! She's literally disappeared into thin air!" Max's breaths come hard and fast down the phone line. His voice is higher than usual and there's noise behind him, as though he is in the street

"Okay, Max. Breathe. Who's disappeared? And where are you?"

"Ally! She's gone. One minute she was right next to me, and then next she's nowhere." Max draws in a loud breath. *"Nowhere."*

"Okay, I'm sure she's not far. Stop breathing like that, you'll pass out."

"But she isn't! I've looked everywhere."

"Where are you?"

"Chinatown."

Tom rolls his eyes. *Of course, you are.*

"Okay …" *For fuck's sake.* Tom massages his forehead. "Stay there, I'll be ten minutes." He ends the call. "Fuck me!"

"Problem?" Martha's voice is behind him.

"Who fucking knows," Tom mutters. He slides his phone into his pocket only for it to go off again with a text. Tom lets out a loud, irritated huff and looks at the screen. A text from Ally sits there, waiting to be opened.

She's disappeared because she wants a fucking booty call. He opens the text and sees a photograph.

Ally stands holding a bunch of roses. She has a cut across her right cheek, blood drips down her face, mixing with a stream of tears.

Tom's breath hitches in his throat and he coughs. Icicles clog his veins. He bends over the desk in front of him, drops the phone and claws his hands through his hair.

42

MAX

Max stands in the middle of the street, hugging his arms around himself. He shivers but he can't be sure it's because of the cold or the fact he can't find Ally.

I should keep searching. But Tom said to stay put.

Max's eyes fill with tears and he squeezes them shut, hoping they don't fall down his cheeks. His breathing is sharp and uneven, and his chest hurts from the effort of holding in his emotions. He crouches down to the ground and rocks gently back and forth. A hand touches his shoulder, and he jerks his head up. An elderly man smiles.

"I'm fine," Max croaks. "I'm..." he walks to the edge of the street and leans against a shopfront; the old man follows.

Please leave me alone.

The man nods at Max, who holds his hand up. "Thank you, I'm fine."

A hand closes around Max's elbow.

"Get in the car," Tom's voice hisses in his ear.

His heart leaps and he grabs hold of Tom's shirt with both hands. "What's going on?"

"I'll explain in the car. Get in." Tom nods towards his car, that is haphazardly parked on the other side of some bollards designed to keep vehicles out of the pedestrianised street.

"But I—"

"Max, get the fuck in the car," Tom jerks him towards the car and practically throws him into the back seat.

Max's blood pressure ignites, and he claws himself up and sticks his head between the two front seats as Tom gets in.

"What the *fuck* is going on, Tom? You don't get to throw me—"

"Ally's been kidnapped." Tom ignores Max for a moment as he noses the car out into the never-ending flow of traffic. He spots his opportunity, floors the accelerator, and sends Max tumbling backwards.

"What?" Max claws at his chest, his breathing takes off again. He pulls himself back to a sitting position in between the two front seats. "Tom! What do you mean kidnapped?" His voice squeaks and he clears his throat. "Who would want to—"

"A fucking crazy bitch." Tom slams the brakes on and punches his fist into the horn.

Max falls forward against the centre console, knocking the wind out of his lungs.

A couple, more interested in each other than the road, scurry off to the pavement.

"Fuck's sake," Tom mutters under his breath. He swings the car around a corner and speeds up.

Max climbs through the front seats into the passenger side and buckles in. "Tom. Tell me what's going on." Max's voice shakes in time with the tremble in his body. "Why would anyone want to kidnap her? Is it because of me?" His eyes sting and he coughs out a sob. "Me?"

"It's because of me." Tom slams the brakes on outside The Savoy. "Get inside." Tom nods towards the lobby.

"No!"

Tom peers at Max. "Get inside, Max."

"Not until you tell me what the fuck is going on?"

Tom reaches across and grabs Max's shirt at the throat, he yanks him forward so their noses are practically touching. "Get inside. And we can sort this shit out." Tom's eyes are hard but Max senses fear in them.

It makes his own insides squirm like a million spiders have been let loose in his gut.

"Tom, I feel sick."

Upstairs, Tom paces in front of where Max perches on the sofa in the Royal Suite.

"What's…" Max waits.

Tom sits on the table in front of Max and clasps his hands

together over his knees. "Max, Ally's being used to get to me. And I'm sorry. I'll get her back to you. I promise."

"Wait," Max's heart is out of control. "What? To get to you?"

"Yes." Tom's phone rings and he slams it to his ear. "Do you have a location?" He stands and paces again.

Seeing Tom so *not* in control sends prickles running all over Max's skin. He starts scratching at his wrist.

"Well, she'll turn it back on. Keep trying!" Tom stops and squeezes his forehead with his thumb and forefinger. "Sorry," he mutters into the phone. "I know."

He tosses his phone onto the coffee table and sits on the adjacent sofa.

"You… you don't know where she is?" Max digs a finger into his cut.

"Not right now," Tom's voice is raspy and dry. He grabs a bottle of water off the table and gulps it. "But we will."

Tom's eyes lift to Max and he tuts. Reaching over, he swats Max's hand away from his wrist. "Stop it."

"Can you please explain why my sister is not here?" Max whispers. He tries to keep his breathing even but loses the battle.

Tom rubs his face and looks at Max. "She's being used as bait. To get me to find her."

"Why?"

"Because," Tom looks at the ceiling. "Because." Tom stands up and lets out an aggravated groan. "Kat wants to kill me."

"Kat?"

"She's a…" Tom looks at Max. "Stop doing that!"

Max looks down, not having realised he was scratching at his wrist again. Blood covers his bandage and fingers. He leans forward over his knees and hugs himself. He sucks in a shaky breath and closes his eyes a moment. When he opens them, he sees Tom at the window staring out, tapping his finger to his lips.

"Tom?"

Tom turns and looks at Max. He raises his eyebrows, but his eyes are exhausted.

"Will you bring her back to me?" Max's voice is brittle and soft.

"Yes."

43

TOM

Tom scrunches his eyes shut. *Why did I say yes?*

Because no isn't an option.

"I can't lose her," Max whispers. He is rocking back and forth on the sofa. For the first time since meeting Max, Tom feels sorry for the rich, damaged pop star.

Tom walks over and sits across from him. "I'll find her. I promise. And I'm sorry."

Max stares at the coffee table and nods, not looking at Tom "Yeah, I know. I trust you."

At those words Tom's chest caves in.

Jesus.

His phone pierces the silence in the room and he grabs it. Ally's name lights up the screen.

"Hello?"

"Tom?"

Tom's heart squeezes. "Ally!" He looks at Max who clutches the sofa either side of his legs; his eyes stuck on Tom's face.

Ally says no more.

"Ally?" Tom shifts his eyes from Max. *It's too much.*

"Hello, Tom. How nice to hear your voice."

Tom's throat goes dry. "Tell me where you are, and I'll come to you. Unarmed."

Kat cackles down the phone. "But you know how much I like to play."

Tom closes his eyes. "Don't hurt her," he whispers.

"Too late," Kat whispers back. "Here…"

Seconds later a howling scream shoots down the line, accompanied with sobs and sniffles.

Tom's knees wobble. "Kat! Stop!" He grips the chair in front of him. He heaves in a breath. "What the fuck are you doing?"

"I like to brand my handy work."

Flashes of Isabella's scars interrupt Tom's train of thought. Nausea creeps up the back of his throat and he swallows it down past the golf ball blocking its path.

The phone goes dead.

Tom glances at the clock on the wall.

Not enough time.

He calls Martha's number. Max's lips tremble and dropping his eyes to Max's knees, he sees they are just as bad.

"Tom, I couldn't get it. The phone's off again."

"She's playing games."

"Keep rolling the dice." Martha hangs up.

Tom sits down again. "Why don't you go to sleep, Max?"

Max gapes at Tom with wild eyes. "Are you fucking insane? Sleep?"

"You can't function on no sleep."

"Well, lucky I have a pill for that."

"No. No drugs. Sleep."

The phone rings again.

Ally.

"Yes?" Tom sits forward in the chair.

"Tom, find me," Ally's voice is strained. She sobs through her words. "I don't know what I did. She won't tell me." Ally coughs before Tom hears her vomit.

Tom closes his eyes. "Ally?"

Ally coughs again. "She said it's your fault, I—"

Tom sits upright. "Ally?"

"Oh Tom, you should know better than to think I would let you chat too much."

Tom eyes the clock and waits.

"You are not going to speak? Beg me to let her go?"

Tom's nostrils flare. "Would it make a difference?"

"Let's play a game, Tom."

"What are the rules?"

"It's simple. Left, or right?"

"Excuse me?" Tom's gut clenches.

"Pick one."

Tom breathes an even breath through his nose. "I will not."

"Last chance or I pick for you."

"Kat. Stop."

Tom refuses to look at Max.

"Five, four, three—"

"Stop!"

"Two… last chance?"

"Kat—"

Tom hears a gunshot followed by squeal and blood curdling howls. He jumps off the sofa. "Kat, you *crazy fucking whore*. Stop!" He grips the phone tighter against his ear. Sweat trickles down his back.

Max leaps off the sofa and grabs Tom's shirt front. He clings to it. Tom doesn't bother to pry him off. He stands and looks at the clock.

Gotcha.

"See you soon," Kat whispers.

The line goes dead.

Tom lowers the phone and closes his hand over Max's and gently pulls them away. "Sit down." He nods to the sofa.

"But, what…"

"I need to make a call. And then I'll go get her. Sit down." It takes everything Tom has to keep his voice even and soft. He closes his eyes for a moment and imagines the green fields behind his child-hood home, and the clouds wisping above him. *Breathe.*

Max walks backwards, falling onto the sofa.

Tom waits, knowing his phone is about to ring. It lights up and he answers before it makes a sound. "Did you get her?"

"I'm sending coordinates now. But Tom, you know this is a trap."

"Yes."

"Don't get yourself killed."

Her tone is gentle. *Pleading.* And it sends a shot through his chest. He tugs at his shirt over his heart and stands up.

"I won't."

⁊

TOM FLICKS THE HANDBRAKE ON OUTSIDE AN OLD INDUSTRIAL PARK. He sits with both hands resting on the steering wheel and looks at the brick buildings that line the street in front of him.

She could be anywhere.

He steps out of the car and surveys the warehouses. His phone goes off and he sees Ally's name.

"I'm here." He runs his eyes back and forth as he walks forward, amongst the brick and steel buildings.

"I see." Kat chuckles. "You handsome thing."

Tom swallows and peers at the windows facing him.

"Ally is happy to hear that you made it. Is that right, my dear?"

Tom hears quiet whimpers and his chest hammers.

"I asked you question."

A scream pierces the phone line, but also the night air. Tom's senses heighten. *She's close.* He walks faster, peering through windows and trying doors.

"Oohh, almost," Kat taunts.

"Leave her be, Kat. I'm here. Come get me." He jiggles a door, and it swings open. His pulse quickens and he creeps down a dark hallway to what looks like a bunch of storage units.

"Oh, Tom." Kat sighs. "One hallway too soon. I am so sorry I cannot stay to greet you."

Tom grips the phone tighter as Ally's screams echo through the building he stands in.

Until they stop.

Tom clutches his gut and sprints down the hall, outside. He shoves the phone in his pocket and kicks open the door to the next hallway along.

A breeze hits him in the face as he sees the door at the other end is wide open.

He stalks down the hall on shaky legs, slamming his fist into doors as he passes them, until right at the end, one swings inward.

It's dark and Tom fumbles for a light switch, finally clicking it on. He chokes in a breath of air and falls forward onto his hands and knees, clawing his fingers into the concrete floor.

Blood slowly crawls across the pale concrete floor towards him, as though beckoning him to come closer. Ally's lifeless body slumps against the back wall. Her head lolls forward against her chest but Tom can see where the blood seeps from.

He closes his eyes and shakes his head, "Fuck," he squeaks to himself. He takes a couple of breaths before crawling across to her. He ignores the stench of vomit and urine.

You poor girl.

He pulls her into him and lifts her face. Her eyes are glazed but fear is etched within them. Her mouth gapes as blood trickles from the corners. But the blood congealing from the gash in her neck is unmatched. Her body is warm, and the blood seeping into Tom's shirt is hot against his skin.

Tom runs a hand over her face, noting the cuts to both cheeks, deep and vicious. It's only then he lets his eyes fall to her legs, noting her left leg obliterated from the knee. Kat's evil cackles replays in his mind. *Pick one.*

He drops his face onto the top of her head, resting his forehead against her soft hair. He feels the scream welling up in his gut, he sputters and holds his breath in an effort to stop himself but it's no use.

A scream so guttural and primal he can't be sure it comes from him reverberates around the walls of the small room. He stops and holds his breath again, biting his bottom lip so that he tastes his own blood.

The silence is deafening.

44

TOM

Tom stumbles into the warehouse.

Martha rushes out of her office and grabs him on both arms. "Are you alright?"

Tom slowly brings his eyes to meet her and shakes his head. "No," he husks. "I am not."

He collapses into a desk chair and sprawls his upper body across the desk. Squeezing his eyes shut, he sees Ally. Dead on the floor. Covered in blood and cuts. Her knee shot out. He sees the cleaners coming to take her away to make her look somewhat presentable before Max finds out.

"She didn't deserve that," his voice floats out from under his arms. He sits up, squinting against the light. "I need to tell Max."

Dread bubbles in the deepest pit of his body.

Tom grimaces at the thought of telling Max his sister is dead.

Dead. Because of me. He looks at Martha who has pulled a chair across and sits next to him. Her hand is on his back.

"I've sent a car to bring him here."

A pang hits Tom in the chest.

"Okay," he whispers, staring across the room at the kitchenette. The thought of food makes his stomach somersault. He swallows the ache in his throat and stands up. "I should clean up." He walks towards the locker room at the rear of the warehouse.

"Tom?"

He turns and looks at Martha.

"This isn't your fault."

Those words hit Tom somewhere between the eyes and he blinks. Anger roars up the back of his throat and he can't swallow it down.

"What?" He creeps back to where Martha sits. "Not my fault did you say?"

Martha stands. She holds a hand up. "I know you're upset but—"

"Upset?" Tom spits. "Upset?

Martha stares at Tom and purses her lips. "We need to be tactical and find Kat."

"Oh. Oh, find Kat, you say?" Tom clenches his fists at his sides and squints at Martha. "What a fucking great idea. Why hadn't I thought of that? You're really on the ball Martha. It's not like Ally is dead because of me. Because she had the misfortune to cross paths with *me.*"

He jabs his fingers into his chest and heaves a breath in. "You're absolutely right. How on *earth* is it my fault?" He stops advancing when he is right in front of Martha, who hasn't flinched.

"Tom," she rests her hand on his arm and he bats it away.

"No. You do your *fucking job* and find that bitch before she hurts someone else. Tell me, why the *fuck* is she one step ahead? All the time?" He holds his breath for a second. "Why?"

Martha blinks once. "Go and shower. Max will be here soon."

Tom's phone rings and he stares at Martha.

"Are you going to answer your phone Tom?"

He pulls it out and looks at the screen. Ally's name flashes and it churns Tom's already shredded stomach. He raises the phone to his ear.

"What?" he whispers.

"I thought I should check on you."

"How kind."

"Indeed."

"How is this going to end, Kat?"

"Oh, I have very big plans for you. You are going to love it."

"I'm sure," Tom rasps.

"You killed my sister, Tom. You need to feel true pain. Natasha was my family."

"So was Isabella."

"You mean Irina. And yes, she was… until she betrayed me." Kat tuts. "Anyway, no matter. She is dead."

Tom's knees buckled and he stumbled forward. He scrambled across the ground to Isabella.

She lay motionless, face down.

Nausea spread through his body; acid burned the back of his throat.

He scooped Isabella into his lap, the front of her jumper soaked with dark, thick blood. He pressed a hand against her chest, blood seeped through his fingers.

The bulk of her clothing stopped him from feeling the body he had come to know and want.

TOM SHAKES HIS HEAD ONCE AND PULLS IN A BREATH. THE MEMORY of that night still makes his chest constrict. *The bulk of her clothing... was a bullet proof fucking vest.*

He pulls his shirt away from his chest in a fist and grits his teeth. "You're next, Kat."

Kat cackles.

"Oh Tom, you are so dramatic. See you soon."

Tom lowers the phone from his ear and stares at the blank screen a moment. He slides his eyes to Martha who has her stare fixed on him.

He squeezes the phone in his hand before hurling it across the room. It hits a desk partition and smashes on the floor. Tom observes the broken pieces a moment and gulps in deep breaths.

"I'll need a new phone," he mutters before stalking to the locker room.

Tom slams into the locker room and bends over the sink. He splashes cold water on his face before glaring at himself in the mirror. He slams his palms into the mirror and shuts his eyes.

Ally's blue eyes stare back at him behind his closed lids. They interchange with Claire's lifeless blue eyes staring at him with the same blank gaze.

TOM ADVANCED ON NATASHA, PUMPING ROUND AFTER ROUND INTO HER *chest. Her body slammed backwards into the wall and slid to the floor. He kept shooting. He shot until all fifteen rounds were in her chest. Then he dropped his pistol and crumbled to the floor.*

TOM TURNS TO FACE A ROW OF LOCKERS ON THE WALL BEHIND HIM. Emotion hits him in the face, and he clenches his jaw.

Trying to regulate his breaths he paces the tiny room, back and forth. Back and forth. His knuckles graze along one of the lockers. He bends forward and lets out a gasp of pain from deep in his lungs before slamming his fist into a locker. He stands and slams it again. He leans forward with both hands against the cool steel of the locker, but it does nothing to cool his anger.

He brings his arm back and slams the locker again, his other hand follows until he's punching and kicking at the locker. He rips it away from the wall and pushes it to the ground. He kicks and stomps it until he has nothing left.

Nothing.

He slumps on a wooden bench at the side of the room and leans against the wall. He heaves in breath after breath, trying to slow everything down.

Clawing at his blood-soaked shirt, he rips it off and throws it on the floor.

A knock at the door shatters his sudden peace.

He turns his head. "What?"

"Max is here."

45

MAX

"Please, sit down Max." The tiny woman gestures to a sofa at the side of her office.

It looks lumpy.

Max sits and claws at his knees. "Is Tom here?"

The woman smiles. "Yes. He won't be a moment. I'm Martha Cole."

Max nods and sweeps his eyes peruse the office.

What a huge desk for such a tiny woman.

"So, who are you exactly?" Max tilts his chin up at her.

Martha sits on a chair opposite Max. "I'm in charge."

This makes the corners of Max's mouth turn up. "You?"

She laughs. "Yes. I know." She nods as the door to her office swings open.

Max swivels his head and sees Tom standing in the doorway, chewing on his lip.

He's alone. Why is he alone?

Max springs from where he sits and scurries to Tom, stopping in front of him. "Where is she?" He wrings his hands in front of him and runs his eyes up and down Tom's body as he stares back. "Is she okay?"

Tom nods towards the lumpy sofa. "Sit down, Max."

His voice is quiet. Too quiet.

Panic bubbles to the surface and Max grasps at the base of his own throat. "Tom?" His gut churns and whirls as though on a spin cycle. "Where's my sister?"

"Sit down and I can explain."

"Explain?" Max squeaks. "Explain what?" He walks backwards towards the sofa as Tom follows. He sits and leans over his knees, hugging them.

"... paramedics."

Max catches the end of Tom whispering to Martha.

A bundle of TNT explodes in Max's gut and he leaps off the sofa again. "Paramedics? What do we need paramedics for? Is she hurt? Where is she?" His breathing comes out in short bursts and his chest struggles to keep up.

Martha leaves the office, shutting the door behind her.

Tom sits on the coffee table, gesturing for Max to sit in front of him. "She isn't here, Max."

Max lowers himself onto the sofa and hugs his arms around himself. "Then... where?" His eyes drop to Tom's hands that are clasped together, elbows resting on his knees. "What happened to your knuckles?"

Tom glances at his hands and shrugs. "Punched a locker."

"A locker?" Max jerks a lip up and scratches at his wrist. "What's going on, Tom?"

Tom raises his eyes to meet Max's and stares at him a moment.

Silence envelopes both of them and blood pumps through Max's ears.

Tom swallows before taking in a breath. "I couldn't..." he stops and clears his throat. "I couldn't..." Tom drops his face into his hands and digs his fingers into his forehead.

"You... you couldn't what?" Max trembles and gasps breaths in. His head empties and he clutches the edges of the sofa cushion to remain upright. "Couldn't?"

Tom slides his hands off his face and grabs Max's shoulders. He looks him in the eyes. "I couldn't save her, Max. I'm sorry." Tom's eyes stay on Max's. "She's gone," Tom whispers.

Max heaves in a breath and it grates against his throat. He clutches his stomach. "She's... no." Max shakes his head. "No, she's... I need her." He jerks his face up to Tom, who still grips Max's shoulders. His face is blank. "I need her, Tom!" He gasps in more air, but it makes his chest hurt. "You promised to bring her... back..."

His eyes are hot, and tears slide down his face.

Tom closes his eyes and drops his face again.

"No! Tom!" Max jumps up from the sofa. "Don't you fucking dare. Look at me!"

Tom's eyes travel up to where Max stands over him.

"You *promised,*" Max whimpers. He thrusts a hand out, slapping

Tom's shoulder. His other hand follows. He slaps him again as the adrenaline and pain course through his body. He curls his hands into fists and keeps hitting.

Tom stands and lets Max pummel his chest.

"You said you'd bring her back!" Max wails, his fists attacking Tom, who doesn't move. "Say something!" Max brings both hands back and pushes.

Tom rocks back on his heels. "There's nothing I can say. I failed you."

Max drags his arm across his nose and mouth. "So what? You're just gonna stand there and let me hit you?" His face is soaked with tears and his nose runs.

"Does it help?"

Max crouches down on his haunches and lets out a wail. "No!" he shouts. "Nooo!" He slumps onto the coffee table and bumps his forehead against it. He lifts his head and bumps it again, harder. He lets out another wail before lifting his head again, but this time Tom grabs him and sits him back on the sofa.

"Max. Stop."

Max raises his face to the ceiling and screams. He grasps his wrist and digs his nails in. He tears them along his cut.

Tom's hand comes over the top but Max jerks free and pushes his fingers in harder. His breathing is erratic, making his head woozy. He coughs and splutters, trying to pull in more oxygen.

"Max, you're going to pass out." Tom pushes him back against the sofa cushions and holds him there. He gently pries Max's hand off the cut. "Please don't hurt yourself," Tom whispers.

Max opens his eyes and gazes at Tom. A moment of calm settles over him and the dizziness stops. "I can't be without her," Max croaks. "I'll hurt myself." He hiccups and drops his head back against the sofa cushion. "She stops me from hurting myself."

"I know."

Max lolls his head towards Tom. "Is this real?"

Tom nods. "Yes, Max."

A new brand of pain erupts in Max's gut and travels up his throat. He collapses forward over his knees and vomits on the floor. Acid burns his tongue and tears sting his eyes. " I... can't..."

He draws in a loud wheezing breath. He crumbles off the couch to the floor and rolls himself into the foetal position. The hard concrete floor is cool against his cheek and he closes his eyes. The acrid smell of his own vomit invades his nostrils, and it makes him heave again.

"Max—"

"Don't speak to me." Max crawls onto all fours and fixes his eyes on a spot on the floor. He jerks his head up and before Tom can grab him, he smashes his face into the concrete floor.

"Fuck," Tom pulls him off the floor and wraps his arms around him from behind, holding him so he can't move. The pain slices through his head, releasing the unbearable weight sitting on him for a moment. Max slumps against Tom.

Blood drips down his face and into his mouth.

"Martha!" Tom's voice roars.

Max closes his eyes, and his knees give way.

He feels Tom's arms support him as he crumbles to the floor.

Max hears voices and footsteps. Something sharp is jabbed into his arm.

"Tom," he mumbles.

He opens his eyes to find himself on a gurney, staring at the ceiling. Everything is fuzzy and soft around the edges.

"Max." Tom's face comes into view over him.

Max blinks once and tries to focus on Tom's green eyes. *His eyes are so green.*

As he is wheeled from the office, he closes his eyes, the movement making him nauseous.

Maybe I'll wake up and it's a dream. Just a dream.

46

TOM

Tom throws his keys on the kitchen worktop and collapses onto his sofa. He checks the time on the new phone Martha gave him. *Fucking five a.m.*

He leans forward and massages his temples, blowing a slow breath of air out. He lets himself fall sideways onto the sofa and closes his eyes.

Ally's eyes gaze at him from her bloodied face.

Nope.

He sits up again and eyes the cupboard above the fridge. *It's only half a bottle. Won't even touch the sides.*

"Still..." he mumbles to himself and stands up. He makes it to the edge of the kitchen before shaking his head and leaning over the worktop. He scrunches his face up and rubs both hands through his hair.

Max's hands shoot out and wrap around his thirsty throat.

Tom pulls the bottle down from the cupboard and yanks the lid off. The aroma travels into his nostrils and he holds his breath. He sees Max in a hospital bed, an IV hanging from his arm. He tips the bottle upside down and watches the amber liquid disappear down the plughole. Once empty, he drops it into the sink. It lays on its side, mimicking the bottle next to Max's pool.

"Bed."

BUZZING SOUNDS THROUGH THE SILENCE. TOM HOLDS THE PILLOW over his head and rolls over. More buzzing follows. Throwing the pillow to the side he opens one eye and sees sunshine peeking through the venetian blinds on his window.

"Fuck off," Tom whispers to himself.

Another buzz.

Tom groans and slides out of bed. Throwing a t-shirt and tracks on, he stumbles to the door and slams a fist against the call button.

"What?" he grumbles.

"Open up." James' voice crackles through the speaker.

Tom plonks his head against the wall and grits his teeth.

Are you fucking kidding me? Sighing deeply, he presses the entry button and opens his door an inch, before retreating to the sofa. Leaning his head back and closing his eyes, he starts to nod off again.

"Coffee?"

Tom's eyes pop open and he blinks to focus on the takeaway cup being held under his nose.

He struggles into an upright position and takes the cup. "Thanks," he mumbles, taking a sip. "You remembered the sugar."

"I fear your wrath," James smirks into his own coffee.

Tom rolls his eyes. "What time is it?"

"Ten thirty." James taps the sides of his cup with both index fingers.

Tom blinks his sandpaper eyes slowly and nods. "I'm assuming you've spoken with Martha?" Tom mumbles.

"Yeah. Fuck. She called me after Max was hauled away. Told me what happened."

"Right. So, you know Kat's on the loose."

"Yes. So, what now?"

Tom furrows his brow at James. "Well, I had planned to sleep all day. Until you showed up."

"Okay," James nods, staring at Tom.

"What do you want James?"

"I wanted to say thanks."

Tom puts the coffee down and squeezes his forehead. "There's no need," he husks.

"No, but. There is."

Tom sighs and gestures for James to continue.

"My whole life, I've been the spare heir that was useless at everything. Everything *they* wanted me to do, anyway." James dips his eyes to the floor and shrugs. "No one ever had my back, and no one fought for me."

"You poor little rich kid," Tom grunts.

"Exactly," James nods. "Entitled little punk."

Tom can't help but be surprised at the admission. "And now?"

"And now... I can see that there's shit going on I never even stopped to think about before. Like, Max. Fuck. He has everything. But he tried to off himself. And cuts himself."

Tom tries to ignore the vision of Max slamming his face into the floor, but it stays front and centre, replaying over and over again. He clutches his gut and shifts on the sofa. He swipes up the coffee and gulps, so he doesn't have to say anything.

"Anyway," James bites his lip. "I want to stay at the agency."

Tom frowns. "I don't think I'm the one to ask."

"No, but... can you vouch for me at least?"

"James. You're a pain in the arse."

"Yes."

"And not overly reliable."

"No."

"And you go to water when you're scared."

"I do."

"And frankly, I don't like you much."

"That's fair." James raises his eyebrows and gives a half grin. "So... that's a yes?"

"If I talk to Martha later, maybe I'll mention it."

James claps his hands once. "Yes! Great. Thanks." He sips his coffee again. "Oh, but don't bet on talking to her today. She's not around."

Tom's ears prick. "What do you mean? She's always around."

"Yeah well, she's not at the warehouse and her phone is off."

"Her phone's off?" Tom jumps up. "Her phone's never off."

James shrugs. "Maybe she needs a rest after everything. She's pretty old."

"So, no one has heard from her since I saw her?"

"Seems that way. I went into the warehouse earlier to see her and she wasn't there. That fat reception lady told me she wasn't in."

"Penny."

"Yes! She was whinging about having to clean up spew or something."

"She's always complaining," Tom grumbles. He grabs his phone and tries to call Martha. Her phone is off.

Tom's lungs squeeze and he stalks to the bathroom. "I'm showering and then we find Martha."

"What do you mean find her?"

TOM STALKS INTO THE WAREHOUSE AND PENNY LEAPS FROM HER DESK at the front.

"Hey Tom! Haven't seen you in so long." Her cheeks deepen in colour and James snorts behind him. She waddles around the desk and stands in front of Tom and James. "What's up?"

Tom peers around the warehouse. There are at least five other people wandering about.

Ugh. People.

Tom lands his eyes back on Penny. "Where's Martha?"

"No idea. She wasn't here this morning when I got in." She

reaches back to her desk and picks up a piece of paper. "She left this to ask me to get her office cleaned."

Tom plucks the note from her chubby fingers.

I'd like the vomit and blood on my office floor removed.

Tom frowns and rubs a hand across his chest. Max's broken face flashes through his mind's eye. He scrunches the paper up and tosses it on the desk.

He marches to her office door and opens it. *Neat as a pin.* Pulling his phone out he calls her number again. This time it rings.

"Nathan."

Tom's stomach plunges to the floor at the mention of his covert name. *Shit.* "Judith."

The line goes dead.

Tom stares at the screen and hits redial. The phone is off again. He flops into the chair next to Martha's desk.

"What is it?" James asks, leaning against the desk with his arms folded.

"She called me Nathan."

"Why?"

"Because she's in trouble." Tom looks at James. "I have to find her."

"Who's Nathan?"

"Me.

47

TOM

Tom runs out to the main floor and glances at the desks. His eyes rest on Malcolm. *Middle age Malcolm.* He darts to the desk and grabs his arm.

Malcolm snaps his head up and fumbles with his phone he had been intently watching. "Oh, h... hey Tom." His eyes travel down to the grip Tom has on his arm. "Can I help you with something?" He pulls his glasses off and throws them on the desk.

"Yes," Tom yanks him out of his chair and drags him into Martha's office. Tom points to Martha's chair.

"Sit."

Malcolm's eyes stretch to round circles. "In Martha's chair? No... I'll —"

"Sit the fuck down."

Malcolm sits.

Tom gestures to the computer set up behind Martha's desk. "Can you work that thing?"

Malcolm rolls his eyes, "What sort of question is that? Of course, I can—"

"Great. Fire it up."

"But… that's…"

"Martha's. Yes, I know. I need you to trace her phone."

Malcolm's eyebrows leap to the top of his head. "What? Are you crazy?"

"Nope." Tom gives James a sidelong glance.

"Are you going to say anything?"

"Oh, ah… yes. Fire it up." James nods and Tom grunts.

"Lesson seven, sound like you know what you're talking about. Even if you don't," he hisses.

James nods again and gives Tom a tight-lipped smile.

Tom turns back to Malcolm. "Well?"

Malcolm types in a command and turns to Tom. "Her phone is off."

"Yes. I am aware." Tom grabs a chair and straddles it. "But can you tell me where it was last time it was turned on?"

Malcolm leans forward and squints at the screen, "Umm…"

Tom jerks his head at the door. "James, go get his goddamn glasses."

James scurries from the room and Malcolm turns to Tom. "What's going on?"

"I don't know where she is," Tom mumbles.

"Maybe she's on a date," Malcolm chuckles.

Tom slams his palm down on the desk and Malcolm jumps clear off the chair.

"Do I look like I'm laughing, Malcolm?"

"Ah, no. Sorry I —"

James runs into the office and thrusts Malcolm's glasses at him. He gives Tom a triumphant grin.

"Relax James, you didn't solve conflict in the Middle East. You retrieved eyewear." Tom turns back to Malcolm who is typing and reading the screen.

"So, the last tower she pinged off was along the Thames. I can try and triangulate..."

"On the river?" Tom wrinkles his forehead up.

"Well, not on the river literally. Close by."

"Well, yes thank you Malcolm. I didn't think she was floating on her back enjoying the sunshine." Tom huffs and points at the computer screen. "What's that bit flashing for?"

Malcolm adjusts his glasses and reads. "It's back on."

Tom swipes his phone out and presses Martha's number. It rings.

"Tom." Kat's drawl slams into Tom's ear.

He clenches his jaw, flaring his nostrils. No words come to him.

"Are you going to speak? After all, you called me."

"I called Martha." Tom clicks his fingers at Malcolm. "Trace it," he mouths.

"Yes, I shall put her on for you."

Tom watches Malcolm and chews on the inside of his cheek.

"Tom."

Tom grips the back of the chair. "Martha. Are you hurt?"

"No—"

"And that is all you get. Must not stay on line too long."

The call ends.

"Shit," Tom mumbles.

Malcolm shakes his head. "Nope. Couldn't get it."

Tom's teeth grind together, and he feels as though he may chip a molar. A loud knock fills the room and Tom turns to the office door. He glances at James.

"Ah, yep. Right." James paces to the door and pulls it open.

"Hey, hey!" Penny shrills.

James moves to the side and Tom sees Penny holding a long stem rose with a white card hanging off it.

"This came for you, Tom. Dropping the ladies' knickers again, huh?" She winks and waddles to him, holding out the rose.

Tom takes the rose from her and stares at it, pressing his lips into a straight line. He tears the card off the flower and reads it.

Home is where the heart is.

"My flat." Tom looks at James. "She's in my fucking flat."

TOM LEAPS UP THE STAIRS TO HIS TOP FLOOR UNIT, TAKING THE STEPS two at a time. James scurries up behind him. A tabby cat sits in the middle of the hall licking its tail. Tom scoops the cat up and shoves it in James' arms.

"It belongs in that flat," he nods at Lorna's door and paces to his own.

"You want me to…"

Tom stops outside his door and puts his ear against it. *Nothing.*

"Tea? Oh, no I can't right now but maybe another—"

"James!" *Fuck's sake.*

James bounds across to Tom. "Sorry, she was a sweet old lady. She had a tea cake and—"

Tom whips his face around and glares fireballs into James' face.

James clears his throat. "Anyway, work to be done…"

Tom slides his key into the lock, and it clicks. Edging the door open he peeks around the corner.

The flat appears empty.

"They aren't here?" James whispers.

Tom holds up a hand to shut James up. Sweeping his eyes back and forth from the lounge to the kitchen, Tom creeps towards his bedroom. His eyes run over his unmade bed and the bathroom door that's ajar.

They aren't here.

Tom turns and smacks straight into James. "Jesus Christ."

"Sorry I was —"

"Lesson eight. Don't ever touch me." Tom raises his eyebrows and stalks past him back to the middle of the lounge.

"What if I need to rescue you?"

Tom snorts. "That will be the day I give up on life, James."

"Harsh." James plops down in an armchair. "Now what?"

Tom paces in front of the television. "But this *is* home," he mumbles to himself.

"What about your mum and dad's house? Would she go after them?"

Tom halts and frowns out the window at the skyline.

"Does she know where your parents live?" James persists.

Tom turns and watches him playing with a random coaster on the coffee table, spinning it around on its corner.

Islington.

Tom's phone vibrates and he pulls it out.

"Tell me Tom, did you go to your flat?"

"Seems so."

Kat chuckles. "I must say, you were quite the cutie pie when you were younger. I do love a man in uniform."

Tom thinks of the one photograph Martha framed of the pair of them. It's on her mantel piece. *Her mantlepiece.* He darts to the kitchen and grabs the keys to his bike. *It's faster.*

"Know this. When I get there. You are dead. You're *fucking* dead, Kat."

He shoves the phone into his pocket and grabs his helmet.

James jumps up. "Where are we going?"

"*We* are going nowhere. *I* am going to Islington."

"What's in Islington?"

"Home."

48

JAMES

James stares after Tom as he disappears from the flat.

"Um… Right. So, I'll…" James sucks on his bottom lip and looks around the flat.

The grey sofa, bare walls. One desk without a chair.

You could buy a fake plant or something.

James hears the unmistakable rumble of a motorbike starting and scurries into the kitchen. He peers through the window to the resident parking below and sees Tom shoot out of the car park on a shiny black Harley. *Of course, he has a Harley.*

Something churns in James' gut. Defiance? Anger? Not jealousy.

Maybe a tiny bit of jealousy.

"I'm not some useless git," he mumbles and stalks into the hallway, pulling the door closed behind him.

He runs down to the front doors.

Taking the bus here earlier was a bad choice.

He gets outside, hails a cab and throws himself into the backseat, directing the driver to the warehouse.

"C'mon, c'mon," he mumbles as the cab weaves through heavy traffic.

⁂

JAMES RUNS INTO THE WAREHOUSE, EXPECTING TO SEE PENNY BEHIND the front desk. Her chair is empty.

Shit.

He barrels onto the main floor. Malcolm is at his desk peering at his phone.

James scurries to him. "Hey! Um, I need your help." James bites his lip and hops from one foot to the other.

Malcolm ignores him and continues watching a black and white puppy chasing his tail before falling into a pool. Malcolm wheezes out a chuckle.

"Hey!" James swats the phone out of his hand.

"What the hell?" Malcolm glares up at James. "You aren't Tom, you know. Pipe down."

James isn't sure what possesses him, but he grabs Malcolm at the collar and yanks him out of his chair, which is impressive considering Malcolm's immense girth.

"You are going to fucking help me, Malcolm." James realises he can't hold Malcolm up much longer given his weight and drops him back down.

Malcolm reclines in his chair, rubbing at his neck. "If I help you will you bugger off?"

"Yes."

Malcolm lets out a mucousy sigh and heaves himself out of his chair. He holds both palms up and stares at James.

"C'mon hotshot. What do you want?"

James grimaces at Malcolm's uncouth existence and shoves him towards Martha's office.

Once inside James closes the door and leans against it. "Where does Martha live?"

Malcolm frowns. "I don't know. Islington or Hackney somewhere? Why?"

James pushes Malcom towards Martha's computer and nods towards the chair. "Look her address up."

Malcolm's eyes jump to the top of his head. "Are you crazy? That comes with the penalty of death! No one knows where Martha lives."

"I'm fairly sure Tom knows."

"Yeah, well… that's different."

James tilts his head. "Meaning?"

"I don't know." Malcolm lowers himself into Martha's chair. "She trusts him the most." He shrugs.

"Right, well. I need her address. Now."

"I told you it's a—"

"Offence punishable by death, yeah you said. I'll take the fall." James gestures to the keyboard. "Get typing."

Malcolm sighs another wet breath and James stomach churns.

You're gross.

Malcolm types and peers at the screen. He points at the screen and rolls backwards in the chair as James leans over the keyboard.

James chews on his lip and memorises the address. "Right. I need a car."

"And?" Malcolm struggles to his feet.

"And... you need to find me one."

Malcolm glares at James. "I don't think I like you, New Kid."

"I don't like you either. Weirdo." James grabs Malcolm's collar again and pulls him closer. "But I still need a car."

Malcolm stares James down for a second before rolling his eyes. "Penny!" He shouts in James' face before turning and shuffling out of the office. "Penny?"

"Mal." Penny appears in front of the pair of them. Her hands are clasped in front of her. "What's up, fellas?" Her cheery smile and rosy cheeks irritate James, but he can't work out why.

Malcolm jerks his head back at James. "This idiot needs a car."

"Right. Sure. Come with me," she finishes with a weird giggle that sends James' nerves on edge. She goes to her desk and looks at a keytel next to her drawers.

James has sweat pushing out of every pore in his body. "Can we hurry this up?"

Penny plucks a set of keys and dangles them in front of James' face. "Here you go. It's parked out the back."

James snatches the keys and runs towards the back doors.

"Oh, you'll need to fill in the diary! And keep a receipt if you get fuel..." Penny's voice fades as the steel doors shut behind him.

James stands in the back carpark and sees no less than fifteen cars all parked up, waiting to be driven.

How am I supposed to…

James clicks the key and a mini lights up in the third row of spaces. James scoffs, marching towards it. "A mini. I'll look like Mr Bean," he mutters folding himself up into the car.

Seconds later he tears out of the carpark and heads towards Islington.

49

TOM

Tom rumbles his bike to a stop at the top of the street, not wanting to alert Kat to his arrival.

He pulls his helmet off and stares down at the bend where Martha's house sits.

His eyes slide three houses down from the corner and rest on the dilapidated house he lived in for two years. It's still a run-down shack with peeling paint and a broken front door.

You think they'd fix it.

Remembering why he's there he climbs off the bike, and jogs down the street. Rounding the bend, Martha's house comes into view and his heart jolts into action. The blinds are all down.

Tom sweeps his hand across his back feeling his pistol slotted into his waistband. He mentally recounts where the knife drawer is in the kitchen and the spare stash of weapons Martha had always kept in the top cupboard in the hall.

She never knew I found them.

He creeps around to the back of the house and jumps the fence. All the back windows are also blocked out with blinds. He looks around the back garden. Neat as a pin except for a rusted red bicycle leaning against the house. Tom blinks as a warmth spreads through his chest.

"Happy Birthday." Martha smiled at him and ushered him into the lounge.

Tom saw a shiny red bicycle standing in the middle of the room with a blue bow on the handlebars. He stopped walking and stepped backwards into Martha, his backpack still on his shoulders.

"It's not every day you turn fourteen." She slid his bag off his back and gave him a gentle nudge forward. "Go have a look."

"But...: He turned around and gazed at her face. They were the exact same height now. "That's mine?"

"Yes, Tom. It certainly isn't mine." She laughed.

"But. I don't get presents. Ever."

"Well, now you do."

He crept to the bike and ran his hand over the seat. He blinked back tears that annoyingly blurred his eyes. "Sorry," he mumbled.

He wiped the back of his arm across his eyes.

"What for?"

"Boys don't cry."

"Of course, they do."

Tom shook his head and dinged the bell on the handlebars. "You shouldn't have got me anything."

"Why not?"

"Because I'll be taken away again soon anyway."

Martha grabbed both of Tom's shoulders and turned him to face her. "That's not going to happen Tom. I said I would look after you. I keep my word."

Tom sniffled and looked back at the bike to avoid Martha's eyes. "Can I ride it?"

Martha stood up and smiled. "Of course."

Tom blows a quiet breath out of his mouth and drags his eyes away from the rusted bicycle. He climbs the three back steps and tries the doorknob. The door swings open and he peeks around it, into the kitchen.

The house is silent.

Tom walks in and moves to the cutlery drawers. He opens the second one.

"I would not, if I were you."

Kat's voice stabs him in the back of the neck. Prickles run down his spine.

He turns to find Kat standing in the doorway to the utility room. She aims her trademark Beretta at him. He leans against the worktop, gripping it with both hands.

Kat smirks and struts into the kitchen. "I must say Tom, realising who Martha is to you was quite the revelation."

"Where is she?"

"Resting. It has been quite ordeal for mature lady." Tom closes his eyes and tries to keep his breathing even. "But if you wish to see her."

Tom opens his eyes and watches as Kat nods towards the lounge. He walks to the door and sees Martha. A noise like a squeak or moan escapes his mouth before he can stop himself and his knees weaken. He grabs the doorframe to steady himself.

Martha is tied to one of the dining chairs. Her wrists are behind her back. One foot is in a steel bowl of water. The other remains on the floorboards. Her head is lolled on her shoulder and she appears to be asleep.

"You cut her hair?" Tom croaks.

He observes Martha's grey locks strewn across the floor of the lounge. Her hair, once a smart bob, now a cropped mess.

"Ah, yes. A reminder of who is boss." Kat whispers: her mouth is against Tom's neck and the Beretta is pushed into his back.

Tom grimaces as her warm breath hits his skin. Her hand slides under his shirt and pulls the pistol from his waistband. She throws it down the hallway.

Tom's eyes drop to the floor around Martha's feet. Extension cords lie, plugged into four live sockets and frayed at the ends.

"What the fuck are you doing, Kat?"

Kat shoves him forward. "Sit." She points to a dining chair, in the middle of the room; it's back to Martha.

She moves to the window and opens the blinds.

"Now that you have arrived, we can have some sunshine."

Tom sits on the chair as Martha stirs with the sudden light hitting her face. He clenches his fists on his knees and turns to watch her. She jerks her head up, blinking her eyes a couple of times.

She squints at Tom. "You're here," her voice is strained and raspy.

"Of course, I'm here."

"She'll kill you," her voice is louder now, angry.

Tom purses his lips and stares at Martha.

"As you can see Tom, I have Martha in lovely circuit." Kat stoops to Martha's feet and gathers the frayed cords, tied together with a thin rope. She holds the bundle above the bowl of water. "I drop this rope and she gets quite the shock." Kat throws her head back and laughs.

Tom slides his eyes around the room. It's exactly as he remembers. Except for the macabre vision of Martha forming an electrical circuit in front of the fireplace. He's within two arms lengths of her, but still so far away.

Kat stands and points her Beretta at Martha. She loops the rope around the wrist of the hand holding the gun and sweeps across the room to stand in front of Tom. "One wrong move Tom and I shoot her through heart. Or I drop the slack of this rope and... sizzle. Now, tell me." She swings one leg over Tom's knees and straddles his lap, her face inches from his. "What do we know about my skill with a gun?"

Tom stares straight back into her freezing cold eyes. "You never miss."

Kat lets a smile creep along her red lips. "Very good." She shifts herself forward and her nose brushes his.

Repulsion edges towards the back of Tom's tongue and he swallows the lump in his throat. His eyes move to the Beretta still trained on Martha and the rope holding the frayed wires only inches above the water.

"See if you are quick enough, Tom," Kat whispers. "I dare you." She pushes down hard into his groin and runs her tongue along his top lip.

She stares into his eyes and he glares back without blinking. Kat pouts and looks down at his lap. "No reaction, Tom?"

Tom wipes the back of his hand across his mouth. "Hand lotion and a box of tissues is more of a turn on than you." He presses his lips together and leans back against the chair, squeezing his hands into fists.

Kat cackles and grabs the top of the chair back, over Tom's shoulder and pushes her chest against his. Her red blouse gapes open down her cleavage. Her gun remains trained on Martha. "I don't like to be insulted, Tom."

"That's unfortunate."

She nuzzles her face into his neck, her hand moves from the chair and closes around his throat, enough that it's a struggle to breath freely. *She drops her arm and Martha's dead. Fuck.*

Tom closes his eyes and concentrates on staying neutral.

You won't win.

"What if I push here," Kat's grip tightens against the glands in his neck. Tom squirms slightly and Kat grins. She loosens her grip. Their eyes meet again, and Tom sharpens his glare.

Kat moves her face to the side and presses her lips against his ear. "We both know how this will end. I am going to shoot you through heart. I was hoping to have little fun with you first. But you seem adamantly opposed to idea."

She slides her hand down his neck, resting it against his chest.

Tom catches movement over Kat's shoulder. He flicks his eyes to the window while her face is against his neck. James peeks around the corner of the frame. Kat's lips trail down his neck to his shoulder.

He swallows to hide the nausea.

Tom narrows his eyes and jerks his head towards Martha. James follows his gesture. Tom sees his eyes widen as he notices the frayed wires and bowl of water. He flicks his head, left or right to Tom.

He's asking where the power box is.

Tom darts his eyes to the left and James disappears.

"What happens next, Tom?" Kat sits up, blocking the view of the window.

I buy a few minutes.

"Maybe I was a touch hasty," Tom brings his gaze back to hers and slides his hands up onto her hips.

Kat's nose twitches and a grin spreads along her lips. "Decided to have little fun before you die?" Her mouth rests against his.

Ugh.

"I'm a mere male, Kat," he mumbles against her lips.

"You think Mummy wants to watch?" Her breath blankets his mouth, her free hand slides to the top of his trousers.

"She's not my Mum."

Hurry up James, you useless git.

The tell-tale sound of every electrical appliance in the house powering down echoes through the room.

50

TOM

Tom grips Kat's hips tight and shoves her backwards. She lands with a thud on her backside. The cords fall into the water, dead and useless. Martha winces regardless.

Can't blame her.

Kat shrieks as the Beretta slides across the floor, stopping at Martha's chair. She scrambles to her feet and bolts to the back door.

Tom's eyes land on Martha, but she's having none of it.

"Get the bitch!"

Tom spins and runs into the back garden.

Kat is at the fence, halfway over. She stops to wink at Tom and blows him a kiss. He flies down the steps and across the garden. She waits until he reaches the fence to drop over the side. He grabs the back of her shirt and he hears a ripping sound as she drops onto the ground.

Tom scales the fence.

Kat runs down the alley between the back-to-back houses. She's fast and weaves through the fences effortlessly as though knowing which way to go in a maze. She stops at the corner of a house and runs a hand down her neck to the ripped front of her blouse.

She gives Tom another wink and glides her tongue along her teeth before turning and running.

At least she's wearing bright red.

He streaks after her and notices James appear at the other end. Kat stops and looks back to Tom and then James before crouching and springing over another fence. She disappears over it with ease and sprints away.

"Go around the front," Tom shouts at James.

James takes off towards the front of the row of houses and Tom leaps over the same fence, following Kat.

Tom's blood whooshes through his ears as his pulse pumps clear out of his neck. He lands in a small back garden littered with old bikes and auto parts. He dodges the mess and scrambles down the side of the house to the front. He jumps the gate and gets to the street.

James is in the middle of the road around twenty feet away bent over his knees, heaving in air.

"James!" Tom runs to him and James points at a row of local shops.

"She... went inside... there." He pants. "I think."

"You think?" Tom shouts. "Go back and help Martha."

"What? But —"

"Go!"

Tom runs to the butcher shop without waiting for James to argue. He drops his shoulder, charges at the front door and slams it open as the lock breaks.

He hears clapping.

Kat stands behind the serving counter, leaning against the glass case used to display meat. Plastic sprigs of parsley and pretend grass is scattered around the empty trays.

Wednesday afternoon. It's always shut on Wednesdays.

Tom bends forward with his hands on his knees and pulls in oxygen. "You... stopped running."

"Because I am not afraid of you, Tom."

Tom stands and watches her as she stares back with no expression. Her cold hollow eyes unnerve him. "You should be."

Kat smiles and tilts her head. "How many times have you let me get away from you?"

Tom swallows and refuses to acknowledge the question.

"Even when I killed your lover. You did not try to catch me." Kat takes a couple of steps forward and Tom clenches his fists, standing his ground. "You were too busy crying over her useless, dead body."

A muscle above Tom's eye twitches and his teeth grit. He walks a wide circle around Kat, and she mimics him.

"Do you still think about her body, Tom?"

Tom squints at Kat as he continues to walk the opposite circle to her.

"Do you remember her legs wrapped around you? Her sweet breath against your face?"

"Fuck you, Kat."

Kat smiles, running her tongue along her teeth. "Maybe you would not need the lotion and tissues if she was still with you, no?"

Tom lunges at Kat driving her backwards against the display case. He looms over her, grabs her jaw and squeezes.

She gasps and digs her fingernails into his arms before jerking her knee up and hitting making contact with Tom's crotch. The air wooshes from his lungs as he doubles over, and pain shoots up into his gut.

Mother of...

Kat scrambles out from underneath him and through to the back of the shop.

Tom takes a moment to breathe before standing upright. He swallows the nausea from the hit and slams through the flappy door. He marches into the area where carcasses are chopped up.

How fitting.

A row of meat hooks dangles off along one side of the room, some holding full pig carcasses. Kat weaves beneath them, grabbing empty hooks as though on equipment in a playground. Tom stands at the opposite wall, watching her. She grins as she wiggles each hook.

She's looking for a weapon.

A loud ting echoes around the tiled walls and a large hook bounces to the middle of the room. Tom lurches forward at the same time Kat pounces. She gets her hands to it first but Tom's wrap around hers and he squeezes. They fall to the floor and struggle against each other. Tom manages to slam Kat onto her back, and he climbs on top of her. Pinning her to the ground. He pulls her arms above her head, both of them still gripping the meat hook.

Tom's eyes flick around the worktops and he spots a gleam underneath a pile of wooden chopping blocks.

Kat squirms beneath Tom and he sits down harder on her hips.

"Oh Tom, we always seem to end up here," Kat pants.

"Must be fate," he hisses, digging his fingers into hers so she releases the hook. "Let it go, Kat. This is over. For you."

Kat spits in Tom's face and his eyes involuntarily close for a second, but it's long enough for Kat to thrust her hips up and push him off balance. She scurries out from under him as he wipes his eyes and scrambles after her. He grabs her ankle, and she jerks her knee up and kicks out, slamming her foot into the middle of his chest.

Tom gasps for air as his lungs empty. He sees Kat standing at the other end of the steel bench. She jiggles the meat hook against her leg. She runs at him and plunges the meat hook down toward his face.

Tom rolls away and it hits the floor.

Kat lets out a howl of rage and advances on him again.

He kicks both feet out and connects with her knees.

She hits the tiles. Hard.

Tom pulls himself up from the floor and leans over the steel bench, trying to get air back into his lungs.

Kat stands up on the other side, her eyes narrowed. "Now, I am done with your games, Tom. Admit you have lost and let us finish this nonsense."

Tom notices the stack of chopping blocks and the same gleam of a knife blade he saw moments ago. He slides his hand towards the knife handle and covers it. He runs his eyes over the rest of the work-tops. No other knives have been left out. *Perfect.*

"I'll never concede to you, Kat." Tom grimaces. "It's like you don't even know me. I'm offended."

Kat smirks. "I know you, Tom. Better than you think."

He wraps his fingers around the handle and slowly slides the knife out while holding Kat's glare.

"I know that losing Irina crushed you. I was so proud of my work. You took leave for months after." Kat pouts. "Poor baby."

Tom slips the knife into his waistband and steps out from behind the chopping blocks. "I took a holiday, Kat. It's what normal people do. You should try it, though… You aren't walking out of here, so…"

Kat giggles and winks at Tom. "You are so optimistic, Tom." She holds up the meat hook. "You see this? I plan to rip your throat out with it, before I hang your dead carcass from another." She nods at the row of hooks.

"I'm flattered you'll go to so much effort for me."

"It is no trouble. It will be worth it."

"No doubt." Tom circles Kat again, making her oppose him until he has her lined up. He stops moving and holds both hands out at his sides, palms up. "So, here I am. Come get me."

Kat drifts her eyes up and down his body. As though a volt hits her, she lurches forward and runs at him.

Tom waits until the absolute last second as the hook is about to plunge into his throat before jabbing her arm away. The meat hook flies from her hand and slides across the floor. Her scream is laced with fury.

He yanks his knife out and drives Kat backwards into the wall with his forearm across her chest.

Her body slams against the stainless-steel sheeting. Air huffs out of her mouth and her wide eyes are fixed on Tom's face.

Tom yanks her down to the floor where she sprawls with her legs out in front of her. He straddles her lap, pinning her back against the wall. Holding the knife to her throat, he waits.

Kat's eyes falter for a second before hardening again. "Tom," she whispers. "You are so clever."

"I like to think so."

Kat's eyes drop to Tom's hand holding the knife against her skin. "Are you going to slice my throat?"

Tom lowers the knife. "Nope."

Kat's head tilts to the side. "Too much blood for you?"

"No." Tom pushes his face into hers, their noses touching. "Too quick and easy for you."

Kat smiles. "I am not afraid of death, Tom. I have been looking it in eye my whole life."

Tom wraps a hand around Kat's throat and tilts her face up. "It makes sense we ended up in a butcher shop. Wouldn't you say Kat?" He restrains himself from squeezing all the air out of her right then.

No, I have something better for you.

"Why so, Tom?" her voice fights against his fingers.

"Well you *are* an animal. It seems only fitting."

Kat smirks. She attempts to squirm out from under Tom but can't move.

Tom raises his knife and holds it against Kat's cheek. "You fucked with my family, Kat. That's a big no-no."

"I thought she was not your mother?"

"As good as." He presses the blade into her skin and carves a 3 into her cheek. She squeals and jerks her head away.

Tom grabs her face and twists it back towards him. He fights the bile wanting to rise, back down to his gut.

"You came into my home and stained it. That's unacceptable." He pushes the blade into her cheek again and carves a 5.

Kat's breathing becomes a pant and sweat beads above her brow.

"And you killed Ally. She had nothing to do with you and me. That was evil and twisted. Not that I expect anything less from you."

He squeezes her throat again and carves a 9 into the same cheek. Kat whimpers this time, and Tom grins at her. The knife blade is patterned with streaks of thick red, mimicking the blood on her face.

"You look so pretty." He releases the hand around her throat and watches her.

"Get it over with Tom. I am done with you."

"All in good time. There are a few things you should know."

Kat's chest heaves and Tom feels her trembling beneath him.

"I do not care to hear anything you have to say."

"Oh, I think you'll like this one." Tom adjusts his knees, so she is pinned painfully against the wall. "You were right about one thing, Kat. Irina Petrov is indeed dead." He narrows his eyes and stares into hers.

"Good... riddance," Kat spits between trembles.

Tom smiles. "But, you see," he trails the blade down Kat's chest and holds it beneath the middle of her ribcage.

"Isabella Wirth, on the other hand…"

Kat's eyes widen.

Tom moves so his mouth is against her ear. "She lives," he whispers before plunging the blade up into her heart.

Kat gurgles and wheezes. Tom stands up and watches her slump forward, the knife still stuck in her chest. He observes the life leave her body, as she jerks and wheezes, fighting against the inevitable.

Tom sits on the cold floor and next to Kat's lifeless body. He pulls his phone out and calls Martha.

"Tom! Where are you?"

"I'm at Peter O'Reilly's butcher shop."

"And?"

"And Kat's dead on the floor. I'll need a clean-up."

"A clean… She's dead? Dead, dead?"

Tom reaches across and yanks her face up. Her eyes gaze through him. "Yep. Dead." He drops her head back to the floor with a clunk.

"I'll wait for the crew to arrive, and if you put the kettle on, I wouldn't mind a brew."

He ends the call and sits against the wall. He glances down at Kat's dead body.

"What shall we chat about?"

51

TOM

Tom walks up the front path to the house that, until today, he hadn't visited in seventeen years. The same path he trudged along walking in from school, and when he hid in the shrub against the house.

He notices his Harley parked in the front garden. He frowns at it as he walks past. He glances down at his blood smeared clothing.

I'm always covered in blood.

Stomping up the front steps he pushes open the front door, knowing Martha would have unlocked it for him— the way she used to when she expected him home in the afternoons.

He peeks into the lounge; it's back in its usual neat order. James is drinking tea and shoving cake in his mouth.

There's always cake.

James looks up and notices Tom. He stands up as Tom walks in and throws himself on the sofa.

"Why are you standing up? I'm not the Queen." He leans over and grabs a slice of cake.

"I don't know." James sits and picks up his teacup again. "How was it? You alright?"

"Why are you drinking out of a teacup?" Tom raises an eyebrow.

"Um, isn't that what you drink tea out of?"

"No."

At that moment Martha appears and hands Tom a mug of hot tea. She sits next to him on the sofa. "What happened?"

Tom gulps some of the scalding liquid and it sears down his throat. "Kat's dead," he rasps out. "And that tea is too hot."

Martha's lips purse in her trademark cat's bum and she waits.

Tom sighs. "I stabbed her through the heart. And make sure you don't tell old man O'Reilly next time you're buying a pork roast. He'll have a stroke." Tom grabs another piece of cake. "To be honest I can't believe he's still alive."

"His son runs it these days. I'm assuming it's spick and span again?"

Tom nods. "You'd never know we were there."

James clears his throat. "So, remember how you said that if I ever rescued you…" He grins and slurps his tea.

Tom grimaces. "Don't think I'm not questioning my whole existence to this point, James."

"But I did good right?"

Tom looks at James.

Throw the kid a bone.

"Martha, James would like to stay with the agency." Tom blows on his tea and sips.

Martha turns her body slightly and peers at James. "Is that right, James?"

James puts his teacup down and misses the saucer. He recovers the teacup before it spills. "Ah, yeah. I mean… Yes. I would."

Martha crosses her arms over her chest and continues to peer at James. Tom grins into his tea.

"And what are your thoughts on this, Tom?" Martha tilts her head.

Tom keeps sipping his tea and eyes James. *He's squirmed enough.* Tom puts his mug down. "I suppose he's useful."

"From you, that's a compliment." James pops the last corner of cake in his mouth.

"Don't push it," Tom grumbles.

"Right, so… now that I'm part of the team and all…"

Tom's eyes slide to James and he widens them, waiting.

"What's the deal with you two?" James leans back in his chair sipping from the tiny teacup.

"First of all, get a goddamned mug, you look ridiculous." Tom jerks his head towards the kitchen. Tom grabs the teapot and pours more tea.

James stands. "Says he, who is pouring tea out of a pot with a tea cosy on it."

"Are you insulting my tea cosy, James?" Martha asks, her face stony.

"Ah, no. No, I am not... insulting your..." James bites his bottom lip.

Tom snorts as James scurries past him and out to the kitchen. "Give him a break. You're worse than me," Tom whispers.

"Where do you think you learnt it?"

She gives him a wry grin as James walks back in with a mug and picks up the teapot.

Martha tuts. "Not that mug, that's my special mug."

"Oh umm... sorry I..."

Tom rolls his eyes. "Sit the fuck down, James."

Martha chuckles.

Tom looks at her and observes her hair chopped and sticking up all over the place, and it sends a chill through him. *The bitch cut her fucking hair off.* "I've never seen you without your hair perfect."

Martha runs a hand up through her violated hair. "No, I suppose you haven't." She sips her tea and says nothing more.

"So?" James' voice cuts into Tom's reverie. "What's the deal?"

Tom glances at Martha.

Martha clears her throat. "Tom came to live with me when he was thirteen."

James' eyebrows rise to his hairline. "Really?"

"Really." Martha pauses to eat a bite of cake. "Now, James." She chews and swallows. "You must understand that *no-one* outside of this room knows our history. And if you intend to stay working for me. You'll never breathe a word of it to anyone." She sips her tea and stares at him. "Do you understand?"

James stares at Martha, his mouth agape. He slowly moves his eyes to Tom. "Are you guys related?"

"Nope." Tom shakes his head.

"So how…"

"I lived up the road in a house with my foster parents. The father used to hit me. Martha got me out." Tom shrugs. "I was just a kid so…"

"And you listened to me complaining about my privileged upbringing?"

"Don't think I didn't want to snot you, James."

"Fair. What happened to your parents?"

"My Mum died, and I never knew my Dad." Tom gulps tea to stop talking. "No more questions."

James' eyes travel to the mantlepiece where there are a number of photographs displayed, but only one of them features Tom.

Tom follows his gaze. "The day of my passing out parade with the Royal Navy."

"Wow," James whispers. "This is… wow."

Toms scoffs at James. "It's not that exciting."

"And," Martha chimes in. "I only told you because you are sitting in my lounge and you kind of saved my life."

James whips his head back to Martha. "Kind of?" he squeaks.

"Okay, you did." Martha nods and gives him a rare smile. "And I appreciate it."

Tom smirks. "That's the best you'll get out of her. I'd take it if I were you."

James puts his mug down and stands up. "I should go. I... this feels..."

"Weird," Tom finishes for him, also standing up.

"No, it's," James tilts his head. "Wow."

Tom gestures him to the front door and as they walk out Tom grabs James shoulder. "James?"

"Yes?"

"How did my motorbike get there?" He nods towards where his Harley is parked.

"Oh, I moved it for you."

Tom's grip on James' shoulder tightens. "You rode my bike?"

James skin pales. "Oh. Ah, yes. Just down the road. Nowhere else... I thought it would be helpful..."

Tom steps forward and squints in James' face. "If there is one tiny, scratch on that bike..." Tom stops and purses his lips. "I'll shoot you."

James lets out a loud breath. "It's... I didn't. Um..."

Tom continues to stare James down. "And if this," Tom gestures to the house and himself. "Get out, *Martha* will shoot you."

James nods, gawking at Tom. He goes to open his mouth and Tom cuts him off. "And if you say wow one more time..."

James blinks and nods. "I won't say anything."

Tom watches James walk out the front gate and disappear up the road.

Well, shit.

He walks back into the lounge and Martha is still sitting, sipping her tea. She looks up at Tom as he wanders in, reclaiming his spot next to her.

"I knew you'd come," she murmurs.

Tom picks his tea up and takes a gulp. "What happened?"

Martha sits her cup down and places her hands in her lap. "She got into my car as I was leaving the warehouse this morning. After you left." Martha shrugs. "She turned my phone off and told me to drive home."

"How did she know about us?"

"She didn't. Not until we got here, and she saw the photograph," Martha nods towards the mantle. "She asked me why on earth I would have a photograph of the pair of us. I refused to answer so she cut my hair." Martha scratched at her cropped hair.

"Then she tied you to a chair?"

Martha nods. "Yes. And found your old bedroom and tore it apart."

"But it's a spare room now."

"Well, yes but I had kept…" She looks up at Tom.

Tom's brows furrow. "Kept what?" He stands and walks down the hall.

His old bedroom is strewn with paper and books. He bends down and picks up an old school report with his name on it.

"You kept this stuff?"

Martha stands in the doorway and nods. "I thought you may want it one day."

Tom sits on the end of the bed and reads, "Becomes distracted when he's bored. Has an issue with authority." Tom scoffs and glances at Martha. "No idea…" He throws the report back into one of the boxes.

"Go shower. I have spare clothes here for you."

"I should go…" Tom stands up.

Martha steps into the room. "Or maybe you could stay and rest tonight? I don't really want you going home to an empty flat."

"I'm fine."

Martha narrows her eyes and folds her arms across her chest.

Tom sighs and looks at the ceiling. "I won't drink anything. I'm on the wagon."

"While I appreciate that you think you won't drink, I'm concerned that it may be too much for you."

"It won't be," Tom mumbles.

Standing in his childhood bedroom in front of the only guardian that ever gave a crap about him, he suddenly loses the urge to argue.

"I have something you want. But I'll only give it to you if you promise to stay and sleep."

Tom's eyes pop open and he smirks at Martha. "You're bribing me now?"

"I am."

Tom slumps onto the bed and drops his chin into his hands. "What is it?"

Martha pulls her phone out and types something.

A moment later Tom's phone vibrates. He pulls it out of his pocket and reads the message. "A number?"

"Isabella's number."

Tom's heart throws itself against his ribcage. "You've had it this whole time?"

"Yes. But I knew if I gave it to you, you wouldn't be able to help but call her. And it was dangerous."

"No, I…" He looks at Martha. "You're right."

Martha nods. "I usually am." She steps back into the hallway. "Go shower, there's clothes in that chest of drawers." She points to the drawers in the corner of the room.

"How do you even know my size these days?"

"Who do you think orders your suits?" She gives him a tight smile and disappears down the hall.

52

TOM

"Tom?"

Her voice loosens all the knots in his shoulders, and he squeezes his eyes shut, pressing the phone harder against his ear. "Hey Iz."

"Are you alright? God, what's happened?"

Tom laughs.

"Why are you laughing? Have you hit your head? What's going on?"

Tom laughs harder and he realises he is enjoying hearing her voice.

"Tom! Are you drunk?"

Tom shortens up.

It's a fair question. "No. I'm not. And I'm fine."

"Did you call to laugh?" The smile in her voice travels over the phone.

"No. Though, your concern is touching."

Tom hears her breathe out. "I've worried about you every day since you left. Don't hold it against me."

Tom's chest aches at the thought she worried about him for the past six months. "Kat's dead, Iz." Tom hears nothing on the other end of the line. "Iz?"

"H... how?"

"Stabbed through the heart on the floor of a butcher's shop. Surrounded by pig carcasses. It was classy."

"Oh God," Iz whispers. "You? Was it you?"

"Yes."

"Did she hurt you?"

"Well… she *did* try to rip my throat out with a meat hook."

"With a… Tom, stop. I'll have a heart attack."

Tom laughs again. "I'm fine."

"But…?"

"But," *I have literally come home with my tail between my legs, about to have a fucking break down.* Tom clears his throat. "How's your father?"

"He's… good."

"But?"

"But… nothing. Can I come to London?"

Tom closes his eyes and leans against the sofa back. "Please do."

Can you be here yesterday?

"I'll tie up some loose ends here and be there as soon as I can."

Tom's eyes open and he leans forward. "Loose ends?"

"Yeah … Papa and…"

"What's going on, Iz?"

"Papa isn't… well."

Tom pulse quivers and he sits forward on the sofa. "What?"

"I need to stay with him until he's better."

His heart nose dives. "Of course. Do you need—"

"No. He needs me. Here. For now."

Tom swallows and chides himself for being selfish. "Are you okay?"

"Yes. Don't worry about me, Tom. I'll be with you as soon as I can. I promise. Prepare yourself." Her smirk is tangible and Tom smiles despite his disappointment.

"Prepare myself?"

"Yes. Do I need to spell it out?"

"No. Unless you want to."

"Maybe I'll leave it to your imagination."

Tom grins into the phone. "I have a very active imagination."

Isabella pauses. "I love you, Tom," she whispers.

Tom lets out a breath. "I love you."

"Bye." Her voice cracks and she sniffles.

Tom chuckles and rolls his eyes. "I've heard you cry before, Iz." He tosses the phone on the table and leans over his knees, massaging his temples with his fingers.

Disappointment bubbles through his veins and he shakes his head. *Don't be a selfish bastard.*

"How is she?" Martha's voice cuts through the silence.

She's still a fucking long way away. Tom sits up. "Fine."

Martha sits on the armchair. "And you?"

Tom flicks his eyes to Martha's face and says nothing.

She nods and crosses her ankles. "I thought as much."

"There's nothing to *think as much* about, Martha. I'm fine. I'll head home tomorrow."

"Please don't." She clears her throat as if stopping herself from saying any more.

Tom peers at her as she smooths out an imaginary wrinkle in her skirt. "Why?"

"Because there's a crash on its way and I'd prefer it if you were not alone in your flat when it comes."

"Do you think I'm mentally unwell?" Tom sees Max's face hitting the floor again and blinks, holding his eyes closed a moment.

"No, but you've been through a hell of a lot in not only the last six months, but since Claire died and I... am partially responsible."

"Martha. I'm thirty-six now. Not thirteen."

"And I'm still your..." She purses her lips.

Tom raises his eyebrows. "My?"

"Boss."

Tom grins. "Yes, you are." He takes a long sniff of air. "And as my... boss, are you cooking a roast?"

"Yes. Is it still your favourite?"

"Is there crackling?"

"Of course."

"Apple sauce?"

"Homemade."

"Then, yes it's my favourite." He gives her a small smile.

Tom lies in the single bed and stares at the ceiling. All the familiar sounds of the house going to sleep for the night bring him comfort. He pulls the covers up and checks the time on his phone. *22:59. I've been staring at the ceiling for half an hour.* He hears the creaks of the hallway as Martha wanders to her bedroom.

"Knock knock?" The bedroom door was already open. Tom turned towards it from facing the wall. Martha walked in holding a mug. She sat on the end of the bed.

Tom sat up and pushed himself against the bedhead.

"I thought this might help you sleep." She held the mug out and Tom peered inside.

"Milk?"

"Warm milk. First night in a new house might feel a bit strange, so I thought this would help."

"Warm milk?" He took the mug and looked at the contents.

"Yes. You've never had warm milk before?"

Tom shook his head. He sipped and felt comfort spread down his throat and into his belly.

"Never?"

Tom looked up at the woman who had opened her house to him. "My Mum didn't really eat animal stuff. So, neither did I."

"And what about up the road?"

Tom shrugged. "They didn't pay much attention to me. They only took me for the payments."

Martha put her hand over her mouth and furrowed her brows. "I'm sorry that happened to you, Tom."

Tom nodded and took another sip of milk.

"Maybe tomorrow we can go get you some new clothes?"

"Maybe..." He put the mug on the table beside the bed and scrunched himself against the headboard again.

Martha smiled and stood. She patted his arm. "Sleep well. I'm down the hall if you need me." She turned at the door. "Do you want me to close this?"

Tom nodded. Once the door was closed, he picked the mug up again and drank.

TOM ROLLS TOWARDS THE WALL AND CLOSES HIS EYES. *THIS BED'S too fucking small.*

"YOU MAY AS WELL HAVE KILLED HER YOURSELF." MAX SCREAMS at Tom before smacking his face into the floor.

Tom sits on the floor next to Ally's dead body, trying to patch the cuts and stop the blood from her neck.

Max continues to slam his face into the floor, over and over.

"Me too, Tom. You may as well have killed me too." Claire's soft voice is behind him. He turns to see her standing with blood running down the front of her dress from the gaping wound in her neck.

Max's face smacks the floor.

Tom scrambles to stand and pulls Claire against him. Her blood covers his shirt as she crumples to the floor at his feet.

Max's face hits the floor.

A gunshot sounds from nowhere and Tom looks over Claire's dead body and sees Isabella fall to the ground. She reaches out, trying to crawl to him.

"I can't get to you," she wheezes.

Max's skull cracks.

A meat hook flies through the air and jabs him in the neck. He is yanked forwards, breath whooshes out of the open wound in his throat.

Kat's face is in front of him and she's laughing.

Max is dead on the floor.

TOM SITS UP AND GASPS FOR AIR. HE REACHES ACROSS FOR ISABELLA and smacks his hand into the wall. *Fuck.* He scrambles out of bed and looks around the moonlit room.

No one here.

"But they were…" he whispers, wiping the back of his forearm across his mouth and sweaty face.

He claws at his throat and checks the time on his phone. *01:23.*

Thirst climbs up to the back of his tongue and he stumbles out of the bedroom towards the kitchen.

He punches the kitchen light switch and opens the cupboards above the fridge. Jars of flour and oats greet him. He pulls them out and reaches to the very back of the cupboard.

Nothing.

His head snaps to the pantry and he yanks open the doors. He throws bread and biscuits to the floor. A box of cereal spills everywhere and he grunts to himself. Jars of herbs and spices clatter together as he pushes them aside. A jar of some kind of pasta falls to the floor and smashes.

"Fuck."

"Tom?"

Tom spins around and sees Martha in her dressing gown standing at the door.

"Don't you even have cooking sherry for fuck's sake?" He slides to the floor amongst the glass and pasta, struggling to slow his breathing. The thirst persists and he swallows, trying to ignore it.

Martha grabs a broom and sweeps the mess into a pile.

Tom claws his fingers through his hair and tries to stop the tremble overtaking his body.

Martha sits on the floor beside him. "And here comes the crash."

Tom hides behind his hands and holds his breath. "I'm fine."

"Yes, Tom. I know."

53

TOM

Tom peels his eyes open and finds himself lying face down on the sofa. One arm is hugging a pillow to his face, the other hangs down to the floor.

A blanket has been draped over him at some point.

She waited until I fell asleep.

Tom winces and sits up. He scratches a hand through his hair and looks around the lounge. A glance at the pendulum clock on the wall tells Tom it's already ten thirty. He throws the comforter off him and stands up.

"Martha?" he calls through a yawn and stretch.

He wanders into the kitchen and sees an empty toast rack, loaf of bread and jar of marmalade sitting in the middle of the table.

On closer inspection a note is propped up against the sugar bowl.

Getting this mess on my head fixed. Eat. I'm serious. Eat.

Tom scoffs and throws bread into the toaster. He peers into the backyard while it cooks and spots his old red bike. *It really is rusty.*

🐟

TOM LOOKS UP AS THE FRONT DOOR OPENS. HE DROPS THE STEEL wool.

"You look like Judi Dench."

"Didn't she play the Queen once?"

Tom shrugs. "Maybe one of them."

He picks the steel wool up again and continues to rub it along the chrome of the bicycle.

"Tom, are you cleaning your bike in my lounge?"

"Yep." He points to the sheet. "I put a sheet down."

"So, I see. One of my good sheets, no less."

Tom frowns. "Good? Martha, it's mauve."

"And expensive." She puts her bag down on the coffee table.

Tom eyes the bag as he continues to scrub. "Did you take a pistol to the hairdresser?"

"Two of them."

He grins and plops the steel wool into a bucket of water.

"Did you eat?" She raises her eyebrows.

"Yes."

"You never told me… Is Isabella coming back to London?"

Tom's chest caves and he fishes the steel wool out of the bucket. He squeezes it as though it's a stress ball and bites his bottom lip. "Not right away." His voice comes out husky and he swallows.

"Why not?"

Tom exhales and shakes his head. He starts on the handlebars. "Because her father isn't well."

Don't.

"Oh, I see."

Tom concentrates on the rust and avoids meeting Martha's eyes. He feels them burning through his face.

"And are you okay with that, Tom?"

"Have to be."

"But—"

"Hey," Tom throws the steel wool into the bucket and looks up. "Do you remember that time you wouldn't stop asking about the kids at school teasing me because of my Mum?"

"Yes, you threw a jug of orange juice against the wall and broke a vase."

"And then...?"

"And then you ran out of the house, jumped on that bike." She nods at the bicycle. "And didn't come home for four hours."

"So, let's maybe drop all the questions."

"You need to talk about—"

"I don't need to talk about anything, Martha. And let's not forget I now have a bigger bike that can take me further away than this rusty toy." He flicks his eyes up to hers. "And this time you can't ground me for a week."

"Do you not recall this morning? You were clawing through the pantry looking for cooking sherry? I'm surprised you didn't neck the vanilla essence sitting on the middle shelf."

"Still can't ground me," Tom mumbles trying to wipe the orange rust dust from his hands.

"I can put you on desk duty again." She folds her arms.

"You wouldn't."

"Try me."

Tom stills and presses his lips into a thin line. "What do you want to talk about?"

"Well," Martha sits. "Maybe I talk, and you listen."

Tom hauls himself off the floor and sits across from Martha.

He gives her a pointed look.

"You go to the meetings," Martha holds her hand up as Tom heaves in a breath and plonks his head back against the wall. "And you will participate."

"It's not my—"

"Not your thing. Yes, you said. But I don't give a fuck, Tom."

Tom lifts his head and glares at Martha.

Did you just say fuck?

"What is Isabella going to think if she comes back and you're a pickled mess having nightmares?"

"I'm not a pickled… I'm not having nightmares."

"So, you woke up sweating through your clothes and thirsty for no reason?"

Tom shrugs and looks out the window, past Martha.

"Thank your lucky stars I'm not making you see a shrink."

Tom sits up as though a hot poker hits him in the back. "I am *not* seeing a shrink. I don't need to see a shrink."

"Then go to the meetings." Martha crosses her arms and leans forward, staring Tom in the eye.

"Okay Martha," Tom intertwines his fingers and rests them against his mouth. "Have you ever been to one of those meetings? First of all, it's in a church hall. I feel judged the second I walk in there. Second, they talk about feelings and cry. A lot." He leans back and holds his hands out with a shrug. *Case closed.*

Martha blinks once. "And?"

Tom huffs and rolls his eyes to the ceiling. "And... I'm fine."

"You can't con me, Tom. And you know it." She stands up. "Now, if you're staying for dinner, I need some meat. Maybe you can pay Mr O'Reilly a visit for me." She strides into the kitchen and Tom hears her flick the kettle on.

TOM WALKS INTO O'REILLY'S BUTCHER SHOP.

This time the lights are on and meat packs the display case. It glows its weird red colour under the special lights. A chill rests inside his veins and it has nothing to do with the refrigeration in the shop.

"Well, well." A crackly voice floats out from behind the register.

Tom looks up into the wrinkly old face of O'Reilly himself. "Hey, look at you. Still alive." Tom leans on the case, resting his chin on his arms. "Martha said Michael runs this place now."

"He does, but I like to come in some days." O'Reilly pulls himself up from his chair and leans on the countertop holding his hand out. "Plus, the front door was stuck. Had to get a locksmith."

Tom grins and shakes his hand. *Sorry about the lock and killing a maniac out the back yesterday.*

"Is Martha okay, son?" O'Reilly jerks a brow.

Tom frowns. "Yes? Why wouldn't she be?"

"Because you're here. You haven't been back in years."

Tom's gut tumbles as he thinks about that fact. "No, I guess I haven't."

O'Reilly observes Tom, making him feel like a bug under a microscope.

"Yes, so… I need some…" Tom glances at the meat display. "Lamb chops."

"Martha doesn't like lamb."

"I know."

"Are you being a cheeky brat?" O'Reilly smirks at Tom through his wrinkles.

Tom grins. "Me? Never."

O'Reilly bags up the lamb and hands it to Tom. "You look tired."

Tom takes the package and snorts. "So, do you." He slides money across the counter.

O'Reilly pushes a button on the register and the draw opens. He throws the note in and smiles, settling back into his chair. "Say hi to Martha for me. And tell her I warned you about the chops."

"Yeah, yeah," Tom walks out into the sunlight.

The chill that ran up and down his bones the whole time he was inside the shop disappears.

Ten minutes later he walks into the kitchen and dumps the meat onto the table. Martha wanders over and inspects it.

"I don't like lamb."

Tom gives her an over exaggerated wince. "My bad."

He goes to walk away, and Martha grabs his arm.

"Clean up that mess in the lounge. And then go have a sleep. You're exhausted."

"At what point are you going to stop telling me what to do?" Tom crosses his arms over his chest, peering at her. "Anyway, shouldn't you be at work?"

"I took a few days," Martha sits at the table, sipping her mug of tea.

Tom plonks on a chair opposite her. "*You* took a few days? You never take a few days."

"I think current circumstances warrant it." She eyes Tom before lifting her mug to her mouth. She swallows her tea and shrugs. "Besides, we have no active jobs at the moment. And you're…"

Tom tilts his head. "I'm?"

"You need a break."

"And a babysitter, apparently." Tom grimaces and picks at the tablecloth.

Martha leans across the table and waits for Tom to meet her eyes.

"You know you turn into an insolent child in this house?"

Tom nods. "Yep." He stands. "Might go have that nap. Looking forward to the lamb." He jerks both eyebrows up once and grins. "Nighty night."

"Tom! The bicycle!"

"Yeah… I'll do it later."

He grins to himself as he hears Martha mutter something under her breath.

She loves it.

54

TOM

Tom's alarm goes off but he's already shrugging his jacket on. He picks up the phone. *04:45am*. He creeps down the dark hallway, avoiding the creaky floorboard halfway down. He reaches the kitchen and grabs the piece of paper Martha had written on yesterday. Picking up a pen he writes.

I've gone home. I'm fine. Don't stress. I'll eat.

He drops the pen and looks around the kitchen one more time. He doesn't want to admit to himself that being here for two days allowed him to find a calm. A calm he certainly wouldn't have found in the flat.

That would be admitting Martha was right. Can't have that.

He rolls his bike onto the street, so he isn't starting it up under Martha's window and slides his helmet on. He rolls down the hill a bit and turns on the ignition, taking off down the road. He glances in his mirror as the house disappears from view.

Maybe I won't take so long to come back next time.

The cold morning air whips around his bare neck and it's oddly cleansing. He points the bike in the direction of Avebury and opens the throttle.

TOM ARRIVES AT HIS CHILDHOOD TOWN AND FLICKS HIS KICKSTAND down. He checks the time on the bike.

07:08.

He sees a couple of bright yellow dandelions jostling softly in the morning air. He picks them and walks on. Moments later he stands in front of his mother's headstone and lays the dandelions on top. Rocking down onto his backside he sighs out the tension in his shoulders.

"Sorry I only brought weeds. No time for anything fancy." He smiles to himself as he remembers his mother's defence of dandelions.

"People think they are mere weeds Thomas, but they are very special and very useful. Never underestimate a dandelion."

"They still aren't fancy," he whispers. "I'll get something fancier for Iz."

He lies back, watching the clouds sweeping across the sky and pulls his jacket tighter around him. "You'd like her, Mum."

Closing his eyes, he remembers being nine and his mother fixing his huge nine year old problems.

. . .

"*But Mrs Mason didn't even explain it properly. I hate school and I hate being told what to do.*" Tom kicked a chair before scratching both hands through his hair, letting out an aggravated huff.

"Now Thomas, sit down." His mother patted the sofa next to her. He stomped over and flung himself onto the soft cushions. "What do we do when we're confused or upset?"

Tom folded his arms and scowled.

"Do we kick chairs and huff and puff? Or do we sit and take deep breaths and calm down?"

Tom folded his arms tighter around himself and rolled his eyes. "You take deep breaths and make weird noises. I huff and puff. And kick chairs."

"Chant, my sunshine." She ruffled his hair.

"What?"

"I chant. It's not weird noises."

"Well, it sounds weird," he mumbled.

She grabbed his hand and pulled him off the sofa. "Come, let me give you something to help when you're upset."

He let her lead him to the special box she kept at the foot of her bed. She opened it and pulled out a rock that looked like glass and held it out to him.

He took it and turned it over in his hand. "What is it? Doesn't look like medicine."

"Oh, but it's better than medicine. It's clear quartz."

Tom rolled his eyes. "Another weird rock."

"It will help clear your mind. And take away pain and negativity."

She closed his fingers around it. "It's yours now."

She kissed his hand.

"But how can it do all that?"

"Faith, sweetheart."

TOM LIES BACK AND WATCHES THE CLOUDS. "NO DINOSAURS TODAY." He stretches his legs out and relaxes under the morning rays of sunshine. His eyes close and he waits for peace to wash over him.

He can't be sure how long he nodded off for, but he wakes, sits up and brushes some dirt off his mother's headstone.

"Thanks for the chat," he whispers.

He rides back into the village and wanders the early morning streets. He bides time until the store he wants to visit opens and sits at a rustic cafe. He drinks organic coffee and chews on a muffin made with sweet potato. *Blergh.*

He pushes the plate with the half-eaten muffin away and looks across at the store his mother always dragged him into.

A woman finally opens its door and flips the open sign over. She wears a long turquoise skirt and lacy long sleeve top. Exactly something his own mother would have worn. He smiles and stands up.

He ducks under the low door frame and into the tranquil, incense scented surrounds. A strange warmth spreads from his gut to his chest and through his bloodstream. His breathing evens out and he cracks his neck side to side.

Tension melts away as he wanders about looking at colourful pictures of angels and bowls of bright coloured rocks.

"Hello," a soft voice floats through the air behind him.

He turns and sees the turquoise skirted woman standing with her hands clasped in front of her. A gentle smile touches her lips.

"Uh, hi." Tom feels completely alien in front of her, in his boots and leather jacket, in the middle of this tranquil space.

"I'm looking for…" his eyes dart around the store.

"Something calming?"

He snaps his head around to her again. *How did you know that?* He becomes aware that he has both hands clenched in fists and is chewing on his lip. He releases his fists and wiggles his fingers.

He clears his throat. "Quartz?" He jerks his top lip up at one corner.

She smiles and leads him to the back of the store. She waves an open arm across bowls and bowls of coloured crystals.

Tom leans forward, frowning and reads from the cards sticking out of each bowl. *Clear Quartz.* He grabs the biggest one he can see and tosses it in the air, catching it again.

"It's not a juggling ball," the woman laughs.

"Ah, no. Sorry."

She walks to the register as Tom follows.

"Are you after some clarity? Positive vibes?"

"What?" He plonks the crystal on the counter and the woman gestures to it. "Oh, no. That's a load of mumbo jumbo." He sucks on his bottom lip as she gasps, pushing her hand to her chest. "No offence."

He grabs a ten pound note out and hands it to her. She takes it without saying anything and gives him his change. "I'll wrap it for you."

"No, it's fine." He picks it up and shoves it in his pocket.

"Don't forget to cleanse it," she urges as though it may explode if he doesn't.

"Yeah, right." Tom's brows settle into a wiggly line. "Cleanse it. I'll... do that."

I'll actually toss it in my drawer next to the black one. "Thanks." He turns and paces out of the store.

He knows the rock in his pocket is simply that —a rock. But it feels as though his mother is with him again, for a minute and it makes the ride back to reality easier.

HE OPENS THE DOOR TO HIS FLAT AND GLANCES AROUND.

A soft mew travels up from the floor and he looks down to see the tabby cat weaving around his ankles. He sighs and picks her up.

Across the hall he knocks and waits. Lorna peeks out through the gap allowed by the chain.

"Tom," she crackles.

She pushes the door closed and the chain jangles. She opens it again and holds her wrinkly hands out. Tom plonks the cat into them.

"We have to stop meeting this way Lorna." He winks and turns back to his flat.

"Where's the fun in that?"

Tom grins as he hears her door click shut.

He slumps onto his sofa and pulls his quartz out. He turns it over in his hand before tossing it onto the table.

Avebury does weird things to me.

His phone vibrates and he looks at the ceiling. "C'mon!"

He yanks it out and sees Isabella's name. His frustration vanishes and he fumbles the phone, pressing answer.

"Iz."

"You lied to me."

"What?"

"You aren't okay."

Tom rubs his eyes and sits back into the sofa cushions. "You've been speaking to Martha."

"Yes. Where are you?"

"In my flat. Wishing you were here."

"I wish I was too," she whispers.

"I really am fine, Iz. Don't let Martha scare you. She's peeved I took off before she woke up probably."

"Took off? From where?"

Tom remembers Iz has no idea he spent time with Martha as a kid.

Now isn't the time.

"Her office. But I'm fine. Please don't worry. Look after your father so I can see you."

"She sleeps in her office?"

"It's Martha. She does loads of weird stuff." He eyes the quartz on the table.

Not that I can talk.

"Will you go to the meetings?"

"She told you that?" Tom grits his teeth.

"Yes, but only because she knew I'd tell you to go."

"Iz. I really don't—"

"Tom! Do you, or do you not want me in your flat wrapped around you?"

"Well… yes."

"Then go to the meetings."

"That's blackmail of the highest order." *But I'm willing to concede.*

"Will it make you go?"

He leans forward and smiles. "When you say wrapped around me…"

"I thought you had an active imagination?"

"I can…"

"Fine, then imagine away. But… only if you go to a meeting."

"I feel like a child who is being bribed to use the potty for a new toy."

"Well, if you want to play, you'll do as you're told."

Tom huffs a loud sigh down the phone line.

"You know I'll be there as soon as I can be," she whispers.

"I know. Look after your father. I miss you."

"I miss you. Bye." The line goes dead.

Tom stares at his phone.

She never lets me say goodbye.

He leans over and picks the quartz up and holds it up to the light coming through the window. He wanders to his desk and opens the small draw containing the black rock. And Isabella's letter.

He drops the quartz next to the black obsidian and plucks the letter out. He settles back onto the sofa and turns the envelope over in his hands.

She's coming back.

The notion that he can see her again makes the letter not so difficult to read. He rips it open and pulls out a postcard. On the front is a photograph of the sculpture they both observed in The Louvre. *Cupid Revived by Psyche.*

He looks at the two lovers a moment before flipping it over.

Revived x

55

TOM

Isabella presses her mouth to his, pushing her chest against him. Her legs are wrapped around his waist.

She pulls away, her hot breath hits his neck, and he tangles his fingers through her hair.

"God, I missed you," she whispers against the dip in his throat.

Tom drops his head back against the headboard as she trails her mouth down his chest...

Tom draws in a loud breath as his eyes snap open. He has the sofa cushion gripped in his fist. He releases it and rolls onto his back, slowing his breathing.

At least it wasn't a nightmare.

"Active imagination indeed," he mutters to himself.

He glances to the window and sees dusky light. *How long did I doze for?*

A CHECK NEXT TO HIM REMINDS HIM HE'S ALONE. HE KNEW IT BUT it's still disappointing.

It felt so real.

Flicking on the television the evening news lights up. Max's face fills the screen and Tom leans forward, turning the volume up a few notches.

"... Landed back in Sydney where he faced a press conference looking fragile and tired."

Max shakes his head as a reporter asks a question, shoving a microphone in his face.

"No. It was a… tragic accident."

He looks directly down the barrel of the camera and takes a deep breath.

Tom's insides squirm. Max is staring directly at him.

"I'll be going into rehabilitation after her funeral. I'm telling you this because it's important to realise when it's all too much. I didn't let myself be helped and it nearly cost me my life, by my own hand. Now, my sister is no longer here, and I can't bring her back. But maybe I can help myself. So, to all my fans. I'll see you soon, and please look after yourself and take the help you need. Thank you."

He drops his head and moves away from the camera.

Well, fuck.

Tom blows a slow breath out leaning forward over his knees. He cups his nose and mouth in his hands. Guilt sloshes around in his gut as images of Ally, bloodied and tortured flash in front of him. He closes his eyes and pulls air back into his lungs.

The postcard from Isabella is on the coffee table. He picks it up and puts it in his pocket. Checking the time, he grunts and rolls his eyes to the ceiling.

Fine. If it'll stop the nagging.

He grabs his bike jacket and stomps out the door.

WALKING INTO THE CHURCH HALL, THE WEIGHT OF FAILURE SETTLES itself heavily on Tom's shoulders.

I don't need to be here.

He sees Amanda at the front setting chairs up in a circle. He turns and paces back outside before she spots him there. Walking around the open, grassy area next to the hall with his hands on his hips, he sucks deep breaths in through his nose.

A glance at his watch tells him he is still early enough to leave before anyone else turns up. Tom eyes his bike parked next to the faded sign at the front of the hall. His fingers twitch and fiddle with his keys in his pocket.

Iz's words swirl around in his head. *"Well, if you want to play, you'll do as you're told."*

He rolls his eyes to the sky and shakes his shoulders out. The thought of seeing her again spurs him to walk back into the hall.

Amanda glances up as he stands in the doorway, biting his bottom lip. She smiles and walks towards him. *Ah, fuck.*

"Hi."

Tom nods once, "Hi."

He jiggles the keys in his pocket.

Amanda's eyes drop to his pocket and back to his face. "It's normal to feel nervous."

"I'm not… nervous. I'm …" He looks at the chair he always sits on, next to the boring biscuits. He clears his throat but doesn't continue.

"No, of course."

Tom can feel Amanda's eyes on him as he looks everywhere but at her. He lets out a slow breath and resumes biting his lip.

"Have a seat." She gestures to his normal choice of chair.

He flicks his eyes to her a moment and sits.

Amanda pulls a chair over and sits in front of him, crossing her legs and placing her hands in her lap. She looks at him and says nothing.

Tom raises his eyebrows and tilts his head. "What?"

"There's still ten minutes before anyone arrives, if you'd like a chat."

Tom smiles. "And what would you like to chat about Amanda? The weather?"

Amanda grins. "If you'd like."

Tom pokes the inside of his mouth with his tongue and shakes his head, dropping his eyes to the floor.

"Why are you here… *Tom*, isn't it?"

He sits up straighter and looks Amanda in the eye. "Because the women in my life won't stop pestering me."

"Women? Plural? How nice for you." She grins.

"No, I mean my… boss and… my... significant person."

She'd stab me for that.

"She must love that title." It's Amanda's turn to poke her tongue into the inside of her cheek.

Tom chuckles despite feeling like he's being dissected. "She'd whack me in the back of the head in fairness."

No, she'd stab me.

"I bet." Amanda leans forward and waits until Tom's eyes meet hers. "Correct me if I'm wrong. But you like to be in control, don't you? And when you feel like you're losing that control you freak out. Yes?"

Tom looks around the room and at the doors before looking back at Amanda, whose eyes haven't left his face. "I have to be in control. It's my job."

"I'm going to let you in on a little secret, Tom." Amanda leans forward. "Here, you aren't at work. You aren't at home and you aren't with your… significant person. You're ... just Tom."

But I'm never just Tom.

He leans back and folds his arms across his chest. "Thanks for the heads up."

Amanda stands and slides the chair back next to the table of biscuits. "Fourth time lucky then," she nods towards the circle of chairs.

Tom watches her walk back to the front of the room before a girl appears next to him, reaching for a biscuit. *Well, if it isn't Ms Step Number Eight.*

Tom flicks his eyes away and looks out the window.

Please don't talk to me. Please don't talk to me.

Tom's leg bounces and he clenches his fists inside the pockets of his jacket.

"Hello," her voice hits him in the ear.

Shit.

Tom gives her a tight smile as she leans against the table and nibbles the corner of her biscuit.

"I'm Myra."

"I know." Tom nods.

Her eyes widen. "You…?"

"Step eight." He glances at her tiny purse over her shoulder. "Did you bring tissues this week?"

God, I'm a bastard.

She pats her purse and shakes her head. "No. But, I've tumbled down the ladder since then." She sits in the chair Amanda vacated.

Tom winces.

"Sorry," he grumbles. "I'm…" Tom shrugs.

"I get it." Myra smiles and grabs another biscuit. "I was the same."

"The same as what?"

"I sat in that same chair for at least seven sessions before I joined the circle." She nods at Tom and stands up. "So, you know… the circle doesn't hurt." She winks and wanders to the front of the room.

Tom scoffs to himself. *I never thought it hurt…*

Tom grabs a biscuit and stands. He bites into it and forces his feet to walk towards the chairs.

Four people besides Amanda and Myra are sitting in the circle. One other woman and three men. They all give him nods and smiles as he pulls a chair slightly back from the rest of the circle and sits.

Amanda raises both palms in welcome. "Good evening everyone. I'm Amanda and I'm an alcoholic. I'm also chairperson for this group." Her smile warms Tom a little and the tension in his shoulders shifts.

He focuses on a faded picture of the Virgin Mary on the far wall of the room while Amanda keeps talking, her voice becomes muffled background noise.

A few moments pass before Tom refocuses and realises the room is silent and all eyes are on him.

He straightens in his chair, "Um…" He looks at Amanda, "Sorry, I was…" He swallows.

"It's not a problem. I thought you may like to introduce yourself?"

Oh, fuck no.

Tom's eyes sweep around the circle, making him nauseous. Resting his gaze back on Amanda, she smiles again and clasps her hands in front of her.

"No bother, let's check in with Chris." She smiles at a middle aged, balding man.

Chris leans forward. "Ah, Yes. I'm Chris and I'm an alcoholic."

"Hello, Chris." Everyone except Tom answers.

Jesus.

"Ah, three years and seven months sober."

The group gives a polite clap.

Tom tunes Chris out and stares at the Virgin Mary again. Though the picture is faded, her eyes stare straight into his being. He leans forward and hides his face in his hands.

Isabella's voice echoes around his head. *"I've worried about you every day since you left."*

He runs his hands off his face and up through his hair before sitting up again. He feels Amanda's eyes on him. He looks at her and she raises her eyebrows.

Bringing his gaze back to the rest of the group, they're watching him.

Waiting. Tom lets out a slow breath and claws his hands on his knees. Adrenaline courses through his veins and sweat trickles down his back.

He cracks his neck side to side and holds his breath a moment before letting it out. His heart speeds up while his mouth goes dry.

"Ah, I'm..." He bites his lip. "Tom..."

I sabella lifts the kettle off the old stovetop and pours into a hot water bottle.

"*Malen'kaya kukla, ne zabyvay kur.*" Her father's crackly voice trickles in from the bedroom where he lies.

Isabella smiles to herself. *I won't forget the chickens, Papa.*

She screws the top on and walks into his bedroom. Her eyes widen and she drops the hot water bottle, scurrying across to his bedside.

"Papa!" She strokes his forehead and hair. He is covered in sweat and shivering violently.

"*YA zdes' papa,*" she whispers. *How do you break into a fever in literally three minutes?* She reaches across to his bedside and grabs a damp face washer, pressing it to his head.

He grasps her arm with both of his hands. "*Tam ne dolgo.*"

Isabella drops her head at her father's words.

I know there isn't long.

His hands move to either side of her face and she looks up at him, tears brimming her eyes.

"Papa…"

"*Ty pomnish' svoye obeshchaniye?*" His eyes, wide and alive with fever, search her face.

Isabella nods.

I remember my promise.

She drops her forehead against his and sobs. "*Pozhaluysta, ne ostavlyay menya,*" she whispers. *Please don't leave me.*

Her father pulls her head down under his chin and she lies against his heartbeat.

✻

ISABELLA'S EYES OPEN. THE EVENING SKY IS PURPLE WITH STORM clouds. She lifts her head from her father's chest and hears his breath rattle in his throat. She curses herself for falling asleep.

I can't miss a single moment with you.

She reaches to his head and feels his temperature. The chill from his skin shoots through her arm and into her heart.

"Papa?"

Even though he breathes, he is not responding to her. His skin has taken on a strange waxy appearance and he looks older than he did only an hour ago.

She holds both of his hands and lies alongside him on the bed, resting her head on his shoulder. "*YA tebya lyublyu,*" she whimpers. *I love you.*

I will be here with you until the end.

Australia
Lifeline Australia - 13 11 14 - Crisis Support. Suicide Prevention.
www.lifeline.org.au

National Suicide Prevention Lifeline
We can all help prevent suicide. The Lifeline provides 24/7, free and confidential support for people in distress, prevention and crisis resources for you or your loved ones, and best practices for professionals.
1-800-273-8255

United States
SAMHSA's National Helpline
1-800-662-HELP (4357)
SAMHSA's National Helpline is a free, confidential, 24/7, 365-day-a-year treatment referral and information service (in English and Spanish) for individuals and families facing mental and/or substance use disorders.

ABOUT THE AUTHOR

Samantha Adair lives on the Northern Beaches of Sydney Australia with her family and golden retriever.

When she isn't writing, she can be found in her favourite coffee nook reading a good book or nattering with friends.

Find out more about Samantha by visiting the following:
www.samanthaadairauthor.com.au

Join Adair's Assassins Here:
https://www.facebook.com/groups/356574645452483/

Become part of the street team here:
ARC offers - https://booksprout.co/author/19790/samantha-adair

facebook.com/samanthaadairauthor

instagram.com/samantha_adair_author

goodreads.com/samantha_adair

bookbub.com/authors/samantha-adair

.

www.ingramcontent.com/pod-product-compliance
Lightning Source LLC
Chambersburg PA
CBHW020546120726
47903CB00001B/149